The Trial

88.160.1

The first page of Kafka's manuscript of *The Trial*.

FRANZ KAFKA

The Trial

A NEW TRANSLATION, BASED ON THE RESTORED TEXT

Translated and with a preface by

BREON MITCHELL

SCHOCKEN BOOKS

NEW YORK

Library of Congress Cataloging-in-Publication Data

Kafka, Franz 1883–1924.
[Prozess. English]
The Trial / Franz Kafka; a new translation, based on the
restored text; translated and with a preface by Breon
Mitchell.
p.   cm.
ISBN 0-8052-4165-5
I. Mitchell, Breon.   II. Title
PT2621.A6P7613   1998
833'.912—dc21   98-3447

Random House Web Address: http://www.randomhouse.com/

Book design by Maura Fadden Rosenthal

Printed in the United States of America
First Edition

2   4   6   8   9   7   5   3

CONTENTS

PUBLISHER'S NOTE

"Dearest Max, my last request: Everything I leave behind me . . . in the way of diaries, manuscripts, letters (my own and others'), sketches, and so on, [is] to be burned unread. . . . Yours, Franz Kafka"

These famous words written to Kafka's friend Max Brod have puzzled Kafka's readers ever since they appeared in the postscript to the first edition of *The Trial,* published in 1925, a year after Kafka's death. We will never know if Kafka really meant for Brod to do what he asked; Brod believed that it was Kafka's high artistic standards and merciless self-criticism that lay behind the request, but he also believed that Kafka had deliberately asked the one person he knew would not honor his wishes (because Brod had explicitly told him so). We do know, however, that Brod disregarded his friend's request and devoted great energy to making sure that all of Kafka's works—his three unfinished novels, his unpublished stories, diaries, and letters—would appear in print. Brod explained his reasoning thus:

I would like to acknowledge the scholarly assistance given by Professor Mark Anderson and Dr. Anthony David Skinner in the preparation of this note.

My decision [rests] simply and solely on the fact that Kafka's unpublished work contains the most wonderful treasures, and, measured against his own work, the best things he has written. In all honesty I must confess that this one fact of the literary and ethical value of what I am publishing would have been enough to make me decide to do so, definitely, finally, and irresistibly, even if I had had no single objection to raise against the validity of Kafka's last wishes. (From the Postscript to the first edition of *The Trial*)

In 1925, Max Brod convinced the small avant-garde Berlin publisher Verlag die Schmiede to publish *The Trial,* which Brod prepared for publication from Kafka's unfinished manuscript. Next he persuaded the Munich publisher Kurt Wolff to publish his edited manuscript of *The Castle,* also left unfinished by Kafka, in 1926, and in 1927 to bring out Kafka's first novel, which Kafka had meant to entitle *Der Verschollene* (The Man Who Disappeared), but which Brod named *Amerika.* The first English translation of *The Trial,* by Edwin and Willa Muir (who had already translated *The Castle* in 1930), appeared in 1937 simultaneously in England and the United States, the latter edition published by Knopf with illustrations by Georg Salter. Neither the German nor the English-language editions sold well, although they were critically well received.

Undeterred, Max Brod enlisted the support of Martin Buber, André Gide, Hermann Hesse, Heinrich Mann, Thomas Mann, and Franz Werfel for a public statement urging the publication of Kafka's collected works as "a spiritual act of unusual dimensions, especially now, during times of chaos." Since Kafka's previous publishers had closed during

Germany's economic depression, he appealed to Gustav Kiepenheuer to undertake the project. Kiepenheuer agreed, but on condition that the first volume be financially successful. But the Nazi rise to power in 1933 forced Kiepenheuer to abandon his plans. Between 1933 and 1938 German Jews were barred from teaching or studying in "German" schools, from publishing or being published in "German" newspapers or publishing houses, or from speaking and performing in front of "German" audiences. Publishers that had been owned or managed by Jews, such as S. Fischer Verlag, were quickly "Aryanized" and ceased to publish books by Jews. Kafka's works were not well enough known to be banned by the government or burned by nationalist students, but they were "Jewish" enough to be off limits to "Aryan" publishers.

When the Nazis introduced their racial laws they exempted Schocken Verlag, a Jewish publisher, from the ban against publishing Jewish authors on condition that its books would be sold only to Jews. Founded in 1931 by the department store magnate Salman Schocken, this small publishing company had already published the works of Martin Buber and Franz Rosenzweig as well as those of the Hebrew writer S. Y. Agnon as part of its owner's interest in fostering a secular Jewish literary culture.

Max Brod offered Schocken the world publishing rights to all of Kafka's works. This offer was initially rejected by Lambert Schneider, Schocken Verlag's editor in chief, who regarded Kafka's work as outside his mandate to publish books that could reacquaint German Jewry with its distinguished heritage. He also doubted its public appeal. His employer also had his doubts about the marketability of six volumes of Kafka's novels, stories, diaries, and letters, although he recognized their universal literary quality as well as their potential to undermine the official campaign to denigrate German Jewish culture. But he was urged by one of his editors, Moritz Spitzer, to see in Kafka a quintessentially "Jewish" voice that could give meaning to the new reality that had befallen German Jewry and would demonstrate the central role of Jews in German culture. Accordingly, *Before the Law,* an anthology drawn from Kafka's diaries and short stories, appeared in 1934 in Schocken Verlag's Bucherei series, a collection of books aimed to appeal to a popular audience, and was followed a year later—the year of the infamous Nuremburg Laws—by Kafka's three novels. The Schocken editions were the first to give Kafka widespread distribution in Germany. Martin Buber, in a letter to Brod, praised these volumes as "a great possession" that could "show how one can live marginally with complete integrity and without loss of background." (From *The Letters of Martin Buber* [New York: Schocken Books, 1991], p. 431)

Inevitably, many of the books Schocken sold ended up in non-Jewish hands, giving German readers—at home and in exile—their only access to one of the century's greatest writers. Klaus Mann wrote in the exile journal *Sammlung* that "the collected works of Kafka, offered by the Schocken Verlag in Berlin, are the noblest and most significant publications that have come out of Germany." Praising Kafka's books as "The epoch's purest and most singular works of literature," he noted with astonishment that "this spiritual event has occurred within a splendid isolation, in a ghetto far from the German cultural ministry." Quite probably in response to Mann's article, on July 22, 1935, a functionary of the German cultural ministry wrote to Schocken complaining that the publisher was "still selling the complete works of Franz Kafka, edited by Max Brod," although the work of both Kafka and Brod had been placed by the Nazis on the "list of harmful and undesirable writings" three months earlier. Schocken moved his production to Prague, where he published Kafka's diaries and letters. Interestingly, despite the Nazi protest against the collected works, he was able to continue printing and distributing his earlier volume of Kafka's short stories in Germany itself until the government closed down Schocken Verlag in 1939. The German occupation of Prague that same year put an end to Schocken's operations in Europe.

In 1939, he re-established Schocken Books in Palestine, where he had lived intermittently since 1934, and editions of Kafka's works in the renewed Hebrew language were among its first publications. In 1940, he moved to New York, where five years later he opened Schocken Books with Hannah Arendt and Nahum Glatzer as his chief editors. While continuing to publish Kafka in German, Schocken reissued the existing Muir translations of the novels in 1946 and commissioned translations of the letters and diaries in the 1950s, thus placing Kafka again at the center of his publishing program. Despite a dissenting opinion from Edmund Wilson in *The New Yorker* (where he nonetheless compared Kafka to Nikolai Gogol and Edgar Allan Poe), a postwar Kafka craze began in the United States; translations of all of Kafka's works began to appear in many other languages; and in 1951 the German Jewish publisher S. Fischer of Frankfurt (also in exile during the Nazi period) obtained the rights to publish Kafka in Germany. As Hannah Arendt wrote to

Salman Schocken, Kafka had come to share Marx's fate: "Though during his lifetime he could not make a decent living, he will now keep generations of intellectuals both gainfully employed and well-fed." (Letter, August 9, 1946, Schocken Books Archive, New York)

Along with the growing international recognition of Franz Kafka as one of the great writers of our century, scholars began to raise doubts about the editorial decisions made by Max Brod. In editing *The Trial* for its original German publication in 1925, Brod's primary concern had been to provide an accessible, unified text that would establish Kafka—hitherto known only as a "master of the small form"—as a great novelist. As he explained in the postscript to that edition, he had sought to reduce the fragmentary nature of the manuscript by publishing only the finished chapters and by making minor additions to the virtually finished eighth chapter ("Block, the Merchant, Dismissal of the Lawyer"), expanding the numerous contractions ("Fräulein Bürstner" for "F.B.," "Titorelli" for "T."), and correcting "obvious" slips of the pen. Another, serious question was raised by the sequence of the chapters, which Kafka had entitled but not numbered, and which Brod ordered for the first edition according to internal narrative logic, some textual evidence, and his own memory of Kafka's reading of the chapters to him. In the 1946 postscript to the third edition of the novel, Brod admitted that further scrutiny of the manuscript made it appear possible that "Kafka intended the episode now designated as the fifth chapter to be in fact the second." He did not change the original chapter sequence, however, claiming that the order "must forever remain doubtful."

Salmon Schocken was among the most eager for new, critical editions of Kafka's works. "The Schocken editions are bad," he wrote in an internal memo. "Without any question, new editions that include the incomplete novels would require a completely different approach." (September 29, 1940, Schocken Archives, Jerusalem) However, Max Brod's refusal to give up the Kafka archive in his Tel Aviv apartment or to allow scholars access to it made such new editions impossible until 1956, when the threat of war in the Middle East prompted him to deposit the bulk of the archives, including the manuscript of *The Castle,* in a Swiss vault. When the young Oxford Germanist Malcolm Pasley learned of the archives' whereabouts, he received permission from Kafka's heirs in 1961 to deposit them in Oxford's Bodleian Library, where they were subsequently made available for scholarly inspection. The manuscript of *The Trial,* which Kafka had given to Brod in 1920, remained in Brod's personal possession, passing to his companion and heiress Ilse Ester Hoffe when he died in 1968. It was not until the late 1980s that Ms. Hoffe agreed to sell the manuscript, which was auctioned for a record sum by Sotheby's in November 1988 to the German national literary archives in Marbach, where it is now kept.

Since 1978 an international team of Kafka experts has been working on German critical editions of all of Kafka's writings, which are being published by S. Fischer Verlag with financial support from the German government. The first of these editions, *The Castle,* appeared in 1982, edited by Malcolm Pasley in two volumes, one for the restored text of the novel drawn from Kafka's handwritten manuscript, the second for textual variants and editorial notes. *The Man Who Disappeared,* edited by Jost Schillemeit, also in two volumes, was published the following year; *The Trial,* edited by Malcolm Pasley, appeared in 1990.

Our new English translation of *The Trial,* by Breon Mitchell, is based on the restored text in the first volume of the Fischer critical edition, which removed all previous editorial interventions, including numerous changes to adapt Kafka's Prague orthography and vocabulary to standard High German. The new translation reproduces the poetics of Kafka's prose with particular care, rendering with unusual fidelity the intricate texture of terms, images, and symbols that characterizes Kafka's style. Following Pasley's decision for the Fischer critical edition, this translation makes slight changes in the chapter divisions and sequence of chapter fragments: "B's Friend," which was the second chapter in Max Brod's edition, has been put with the fragments in the appendix. The first chapter has been broken into two separate chapters, "Arrest" and "Conversation with Frau Grubach, Then Fräulein Bürstner." Otherwise, Brod's original ordering of the chapters remains unchanged. Variants and deletions made by Kafka, which Pasley included in the second volume of the German critical edition, have not been included in this translation. The chief objective of this new edition, which is intended for the general public, is to present the text in a form that is as close as possible to the state in which the author left the manuscript.

ARTHUR H. SAMUELSON
Editorial Director,
Schocken Books, New York

TRANSLATOR'S PREFACE

Translating Kafka was once my dream. Now I only dream of how I might have done it better. From the moment I first read *The Trial,* as a teenager on the plains of Kansas in the late 1950s, I was drawn into Kafka's world so strongly that I have never quite escaped it. I had no idea then that scarcely five years later I would be studying with Malcolm Pasley in Oxford, hearing first hand the tale of how he had retrieved most of Kafka's manuscripts and arranged for their deposit in the Bodleian Library, nor that my next summer would be spent walking the streets of Prague on a pilgrimage that, in the mid-60s, still retained its spiritual excitement, and even a hint of danger, under a regime that had forbidden the publication and sale of Kafka's works.

Thirty years have passed, and Kafka now gazes from the shop windows of every bookstore in Prague. Nor did Kafka ever leave my life. Now, after almost three decades of reading, teaching, and writing about Kafka, I have undertaken the closest reading of all, faced with the challenge of doing him justice.

Historians of literary translation have often noted a strange phenomenon: although an original text still gives us pleasure even centuries after it was written, almost all translations age quickly. Why translations should be more time-bound than literary works of art remains a mystery, but the consequences are clear: each new age demands its own versions of the literary past. The appearance of the definitive Fischer edition of the works of Franz Kafka offers a fitting moment to see him through new eyes.

There are, or should be, as many philosophies of translation as there are works to be translated. Each text is unique and demands unique solutions. Any given philosophy of translation is invariably modified according to the work at hand, often in the course of the act of translation itself. We take for granted, however, that the translation should be accurate, complete, and faithful to the style of the original. But what do we mean by such terms? George Steiner has suggested that a translation that improves upon the original is the greatest betrayal of all. Yet most contemporary translations have precisely that in mind when they strive to produce flowing and readable versions for the public, even if that means smoothing over stylistic lapses and supposed errors on the part of the author. The Muirs clearly took this approach when they first translated Kafka's novels in the 1930s, and their versions have continued to wear well over the years. Yet it can be argued that Kafka presents a very special case, one that demands a quite different approach to translation.

For all its power, Kafka's *Trial* is clearly an unfinished novel with rough edges. At the same time, in place of a polished final version, it offers a revealing portrait of a writer at work. Malcolm Pasley has noted that as Kafka became more engrossed in the writing process his punctuation tended to loosen, periods turning into semicolons or commas, and commas themselves disappearing, as if a bird were lifting off in flight. I have attempted to reproduce the feel of his text as a work in progress by respecting that sense of fluidity. Yet even in works published during his lifetime, Kafka's style and world are often reflected most tellingly in passages marked by a sense of slight unease, perhaps even discomfort. A translation must attempt to match those moments closely, whether it be by means of an equally unexpected word choice, the exact repetition of a phrase where style would normally require some elegant variation, or the retention of a complex and even occasionally awkward syntactic structure. In offering this new version of *The Trial* to the American public, I have attempted to follow Kafka's text with unusual fidelity, in order to give the reader a true feel for both the flow of the unfinished manuscript and his unique style.

In the present translation the structure of the definitive text of *The Trial* is rendered precisely, paragraph by paragraph, and sentence by sentence. Punctuation generally follows established English usage, since Kafka's own punctuation, even where it loosens substantially, normally remains well within the range of accepted German usage, and I do not wish for it to appear falsely ungrammatical. It should be noted in particular that Kafka's prevalent use of what we call a comma splice has been perfectly acceptable in German prose since the eighteenth century, as are the long and complex sentences resulting from this practice. I have, however, attempted to reflect every truly unusual use of punctuation, including the occasional omission of commas in a series, or a period where one would expect a question mark.

The present version thus attempts to mirror the critical edition of the text quite closely. But rendering Kafka's prose involves far more than punctuation and paragraphing. The power of Kafka's text lies in the language, in a nuanced use of the discourses of law, religion, and the theater, and in particular in a closely woven web of linguistic motifs that must be rendered consistently to achieve their full impact. Here the Muirs, for all the virtues of their translation, fell far short, for in attempting to create a readable and stylistically refined version of Kafka's *Trial,* they consistently overlooked or deliberately varied the repetitions and interconnections that echo so meaningfully in the ear of every attentive reader of the German text. Which is not to say that there are any easy solutions to the challenges Kafka presents.

Jemand mußte Josef K. verleumdet haben, denn ohne daß er etwas Böses getan hätte, wurde er eines Morgens verhaftet.

The translator's trial begins with the first sentence, in part because the hint of uncertainty so subtly introduced by the subjunctive verb "hätte[n]" is inevitably lost in the standard translation, even with E. M. Butler's later revisions: "Someone must have been telling lies about Joseph K., for without having done anything wrong he was arrested one fine morning." Although in this version it is by no means clear why Josef K. has been arrested, there is no doubt about his innocence. The mere presence of the German subjunctive, however, tends to undermine this reading even as it asserts it. Of course nothing is ever that simple in Kafka, even in translation, and we might argue that since the information received is filtered through Josef K.'s own mind from the very beginning, it is constantly suspect in any case. On a strictly literal level, however, the standard English translation declares K.'s innocence too simply.

There are other questions as well. Why render the common phrase "eines Morgens" with the false irony of "one fine morning"? Why not end the sentence, as in German, with the surprise of his arrest? And why has the legal resonance of "verleumden" (to slander) been reduced to merely "telling lies"? A further problem is posed by "Böses," a word that, when applied to the actions of an adult, reverberates with moral and philosophical overtones ranging from the story of the Fall in the Garden of Eden to Nietzsche's discussion of the origins of morality in *Jenseits von Gut und Böse* (Beyond Good and Evil). To claim that K. has done nothing "Böses" is both more and less than to claim he has done nothing wrong. Josef K. has done nothing *truly* wrong, at least in his own eyes.

In wrestling with these problems I settled upon the following: "Someone must have slandered Josef K., for one morning, without having done anything truly wrong, he was arrested." My choice of "truly wrong" for "Böses" has a double purpose: to push the word "wrong" toward the province of the criminally malicious and to introduce, on a level corresponding to the almost subliminal use of the subjunctive in German, the question of truth.

There are no totally satisfying solutions to the difficulties presented by Kafka's opening sentence. But it is crucial to recognize and grapple with them. Such a struggle is not inappropriate in a novel that deals with Josef K.'s attempts throughout the course of a year to twist and turn his way through the process of his own trial. And indeed, having made it through the first sentence, the translator is im-

mediately confronted by problems of another sort in the
second.

> Die Köchin der Frau Grubach, seiner Zimmervermieterin, die
> ihm jeden Tag gegen acht Uhr früh das Frühstück brachte, kam
> diesmal nicht.

Here Kafka himself is partly to blame. He originally began
the sentence quite straightforwardly: "Die Köchin seiner
Zimmervermieterin, die ihm jeden Tag . . ."; but the manuscript reveals that he inserted the words "der Frau Grubach"
between the lines, introducing her immediately into the cast
of characters. Literal versions such as "The cook of Frau
Grubach, his landlady, who brought him breakfast . . ." or
"His landlady Frau Grubach's cook, who brought him breakfast . . ." are impossibly awkward and even grammatically
misleading. The Muirs solved this problem by simply omit-
ting her name: "His landlady's cook, who always brought
him his breakfast . . ." Here as so often, the Muirs smooth
away the difficulties at some cost, since when Frau Grubach's
name first comes up later in the scene, it is not clear in the
English version who she is. In order to reflect Kafka's obvious
intentions, I have retained her by name: "His landlady, Frau
Grubach, had a cook who brought him breakfast . . ."
Although this solution is less readable, it remains true to
Kafka's text, even in its slightly awkward construction.

Of course, Kafka may well have smoothed out such sentences, or even rewritten them entirely, had he completed the
novel and prepared it for publication. He would surely have
removed inconsistencies in the spelling of a character's name,
Kullich and Kullych, both versions of which are retained in

the critical edition; he would probably have straightened out the confusion with time in the cathedral chapter, where K. plans to meet the Italian at ten o'clock, then later refers to eleven instead; he might well have cleared up the matter of the maid's room where Block works and sleeps, which is at first windowless ("fensterlos"), although a few pages later it includes a window that looks out onto an air shaft. But we can hardly hold the author of *The Metamorphosis* to a strict standard of reality. Kafka constantly distorts time and space, and often underlines the frailty of human perception. The critical edition therefore retains such apparent anomalies, allowing the reader direct access to Kafka's text in progress, and here too I have followed the German version faithfully.

The Trial begins as farce and ends in tragedy. The opening chapter has a strong theatrical air, complete with an audience across the way. Later that evening, when Josef K. reenacts the scene for an amused Fräulein Bürstner, who has just returned from the theater herself, he takes on both his own role and that of his accuser, replaying the farce, shouting his own name aloud with comedic consequences. The final chapter of the novel offers a carefully balanced counterpart in which the men who are sent for him, like a pair of "old supporting actors," stage the final scene in the deserted quarry before yet another audience at a distant window. But this time no one is laughing.

Josef K.'s appearance before the examining magistrate at the initial inquiry is yet another farce, a staged gathering in which the supposed parties of the assembly are merely acting out their roles before the gallery under the direction of the magistrate. In the lawyer's apartment, Huld calls in the merchant Block and offers a performance intended solely to demonstrate his power to K. Even the priest's appearance in the cathedral has all the trappings of a private show for K.'s benefit.

Throughout the novel the line between farce and tragedy is blurred in such scenes. Although they are connected at the level of the plot, the relationships are made striking and forceful in the language itself. The Muirs' translation weakens these connections by failing time and again to render Kafka's language precisely. When K. accuses the inspector of staging "the most senseless performance imaginable" before the "audience" at the opposite window, the Muirs misread "führen . . . auf" as a reflexive verb and simply have him "carry on in the most senseless way imaginable," while the group opposite is turned into a "crowd of spectators." When K. reenacts that same scene for Fräulein Bürstner in the second chapter, moving the nightstand to the center of the room for his performance, he tells her she should "visualize the cast of characters" ("die Verteilung der Personen") including himself, "the most important character," before the action begins. The Muirs lessen the effect of this language by having her simply "picture where the various people are," including K., "the most important person," and undermine the sense of a rising curtain implied by "Und jetzt fängt es an," with a colorless: "And now we can really begin."

In the final chapter, the two "supporting actors" (the Muirs call them "tenth-rate," but "untergeordnet" is not pejorative in German) work hard to stage the execution properly. They seek out a loose block of stone lying by the rock face of the quarry and attempt to place Josef K. upon it in a posture that seems "plausible." Then the appalling action of the final scene begins. The Muirs, evidently unfammiliar with quarries, have the men approach a "spot near the cliffside where a loose boulder [is] lying," and prop K. up against the "boulder." This transformation from the manmade to a natural formation, however, creates a scene that is not only less theatrical, but impoverished in meaning, since it obscures any sense of the rectangular quarry stone as a sacrificial altar, and thus weakens the connection made throughout K.'s trial between religion and the Law. When, at the crucial moment, it becomes obvious that K. is expected to seize the butcher knife and plunge it into his own heart, it is clear in what sense the two men are "supporting actors." Josef K. is still the most important figure in the drama, even if he cannot perform the final act himself.

Over the course of the novel, such verbal echoes accumulate with great power. Kafka took special care to create links between important passages in his work, links the Muirs consistently missed or unintentionally weakened. One extended example must suffice here.

Fräulein Bürstner's apparent reappearance in the final chapter reminds the reader how crucially related she is to K.'s fate. Kafka has reinforced this in many ways, including in particular his use of the verb "überfallen" (to attack by surprise, assault). Although this verb has a range of meanings, including "mugging" if it occurs on the street, it is of crucial importance to render it consistently. In the opening chapter K. wonders: "wer wagte ihn in seiner Wohnung zu überfallen" ("who dared assault him in his own lodgings"). On two further occasions in that first chapter he refers specifically to this "assault," and when he appears before the examining magistrate at the initial inquiry he repeats the same word again. Thus when he hesitates to speak to Fräulein Bürstner because his sudden emergence from his own darkened room might have "den Anschein eines Überfalls" ("resemble an assault"), and even more strikingly, when he suggests to her "Wollen Sie verbreitet haben, daß ich Sie überfallen habe" ("If you want it spread around that I assaulted you"), and repeats the phrase a sentence later, the verbal link between his slander and arrest and his relationship to the young typist is made abundantly clear. A final link in the chain of associations is forged when K. worries that his lawyer is simply lulling him to sleep, "um ihn dann plötzlich mit der Entscheidung zu überfallen" ("so that they could assault him suddenly with the verdict"). The Muirs, however, render the five occurrences where K. is referring to his own arrest or the possible verdict as: "seize him," "grab me," "fall upon me," "seized," and "overwhelm him," while the three times Kafka uses the term in Josef K.'s conversation with Fräulein Bürstner are rendered as "waylaying her" and "assaulted" (twice). Thus no reader of the English version is in the position to recognize one of the central links in the novel, nor fully understand why her appearance in the final chapter is such a strong reminder of the futility of all resistance.

The dominant discourse in *The Trial* is of course legal. Some critics have gone so far as to suggest that the whole of the novel is written in legalese, reflecting Kafka's own training as a lawyer and his abiding interest in the law, effacing all distinctions of tone, so that "everybody in *The Trial,* high or low, uses the same language." But in fact the voices of the novel are clearly varied. They include not only the long legal disquisitions of the lawyer Huld, but also the voices of women, of K.'s uncle, of the merchant, the painter, and the priest. Moreover, the narrative itself is recounted in a voice we have long since come to recognize as distinctly Kafka's own. The translator's task includes rendering these voices individually, even if they are all entangled in the web of the law.

The German word "Prozeß," as has often been noted, refers not only to an actual trial, but also to the proceedings surrounding it, a process that, in this imaginary world, includes preliminary investigations, numerous hearings, and a wide range of legal and extra-legal maneuvering. "The Trial" is a reasonable translation of the German, combining as it does the literal and figurative associations surrounding Josef K.'s yearlong struggle. Yet the shadowy and seemingly infinite hierarchy of mysterious courts depicted in *The Trial* does not correspond to any actual legal system so far as we know, then or now. Nevertheless, Kafka employs a vocabulary of recognizable legal terms that have come down to us relatively intact from the period in which he practiced law. Somewhat surprisingly, the Muir translation misses several of these scattered throughout the novel, often with unfortunate consequences, as in the following two examples, chosen from among many.

The three possibilities the painter Titorelli presents to Josef K. as outcomes for his trial are "wirkliche Freisprechung," "scheinbare Freisprechung," and "Verschleppung." The first two of these, "actual acquittal" and "apparent acquittal," represent a distinction with no parallel in actual law, but the third, which seems on the surface least likely to be real, is in fact a common German legal term referring to drawing out a trial by delaying tactics, or "protraction." When the Muirs chose to translate this as "indefinite postponement," they misrepresented both the tactic itself (the trial is not in fact indefinitely postponed) and its basis in actual law.

Perhaps the most striking use of a legal term occurs in the

final lines of the novel, yet up to now a reader of the standard English version could have no idea it was there. When the two men thrust the knife into Josef K.'s heart, then draw near his face to observe the "Entscheidung," the Muirs tell us they are "watching the final act." Yet "Entscheidung" is not only the ordinary German word for "decision," but also the legal term for a judge's verdict. This is the verdict K. has been moving toward throughout his trial, the verdict he feared would be sprung upon him, like an assault, once he was lulled into sleep or a state of helplessness. The lessons of such a final verdict are lost, he has been told, even on the officials of the court. They can be learned only by the accused, for he alone follows the trial to its very end. Thus when the two men draw near his face and lean cheek-to-cheek "to observe the verdict," they seek it in Josef K.'s own eyes.

Over the course of a year, Josef K. gradually weakens in his struggle with the mysterious forces that surround him. His true trial begins with the first sentence and ends only with his death. The translator's trial is in its own way a similar ordeal. Faced with his own inadequacy, acutely aware each time he falls short, the translator too is impelled toward a final sentence in an imperfect world. No one is more aware of these imperfections than one who, like Josef K., has followed that process to its very end. It is always dangerous to translate an author one reveres as deeply as I do Kafka. The journey has not been an easy one, but it has brought me even closer to the most complex and intriguing writer of our century.

BREON MITCHELL

The Trial

ARREST

Someone must have slandered Josef K., for one morning, without having done anything truly wrong, he was arrested. His landlady, Frau Grubach, had a cook who brought him breakfast each day around eight, but this time she didn't appear. That had never happened before. K. waited a while longer, watching from his pillow the old woman who lived across the way, who was peering at him with a curiosity quite unusual for her; then, both put out and hungry, he rang. There was an immediate knock at the door and a man he'd never seen before in these lodgings entered. He was slender yet solidly built, and was wearing a fitted black jacket, which, like a traveler's outfit, was provided with a variety of pleats, pockets, buckles, buttons and a belt, and thus appeared eminently practical, although its purpose remained obscure. "Who are you?" asked K., and immediately sat halfway up in bed. But the man ignored the question, as if his presence would have to be accepted, and merely said in turn: "You rang?" "Anna's to bring me breakfast," K. said, scrutinizing him silently for a moment, trying to figure out who he might be. But the man didn't submit to his inspection for long, turning instead to the door and opening it a little in order to tell someone who was apparently standing just behind it: "He wants Anna to bring him breakfast." A short burst of laughter came from the adjoining room; it was hard to tell whether more than one person had joined in. Although the stranger could hardly have learned anything new from this, he nonetheless said to K., as if passing on a message: "It's impossible." "That's news to me," K. said, jumping out of bed and quickly pulling on his trousers. "I'm going to find out what sort of people those are next door, and how Frau Grubach can justify allowing this disturbance." Although he realized at once that he shouldn't have spoken aloud, and that by doing so he had, in a sense, acknowledged the stranger's right to oversee his actions, that didn't seem important at the moment. Still, the stranger took it that way, for he said: "Wouldn't you rather stay here?" "I have no wish to stay here, nor to be addressed by you, until you've introduced yourself." "I meant well," the stranger said, and now opened the door of his own accord. In the adjoining room, which K. entered more slowly than he had intended, everything looked at first glance almost exactly as it had on the previous evening. It was Frau Grubach's living room; perhaps there was slightly more space than usual amid the clutter of furniture coverlets china and photographs, but it wasn't immedi-

ately obvious, especially since the major change was the presence of a man sitting by the open window with a book, from
which he now looked up. "You should have stayed in your
room! Didn't Franz tell you that?" "What is it you want,
then?" K. said, glancing from the new man to the one called
Franz, who had stopped in the doorway, and then back
again. Through the open window the old woman was visible
again, having moved with truly senile curiosity to the window directly opposite, so she could keep an eye on everything. "I'd still like Frau Grubach—" K. said, and started to
walk out, making a gesture as if he were tearing himself loose
from the two men, who were, however, standing some distance from him. "No," said the man by the window, tossing
his book down on a small table and standing up. "You can't
leave, you're being held." "So it appears," said K. "But
why?" "We weren't sent to tell you that. Go to your room
and wait. Proceedings are under way and you'll learn everything in due course. I'm exceeding my instructions by talking
with you in such a friendly way. But I hope no one hears
except Franz, and he's being friendly with you too, although
it's against all regulations. If you're as fortunate from now on
as you've been with the choice of your guards, you can rest
easy." K. wanted to sit down, but he now saw that there was
nowhere to sit in the entire room except for the chair by the
window. "You'll come to realize how true that all is," said
Franz, walking toward him with the other man. The latter in
particular towered considerably over K. and patted him several times on the shoulder. Both of them examined K.'s nightshirt, saying that he would have to wear a much worse one
now, but that they would look after this one, as well as the
rest of his undergarments, and if his case turned out well,

they'd return them to him. "You're better off giving the things to us than leaving them in the depository," they said, "there's a lot of pilfering there, and besides, they sell everything after a time, whether the proceedings in question have ended or not. And trials like this last so long, particularly these days! Of course you'd get the proceeds from the depository in the end, but first of all they don't amount to much, since sales aren't based on the size of the offer but on the size of the bribe, and secondly, experience shows that they dwindle from year to year as they pass from hand to hand." K. scarcely listened to this speech; he attached little value to whatever right he might still possess over the disposal of his things, it was much more important to him to gain some clarity about his situation; but he couldn't even think in the presence of these men: the belly of the second guard—they surely must be guards—kept bumping against him in a positively friendly way, but when he looked up he saw a face completely at odds with that fat body: a dry, bony face, with a large nose set askew, consulting above his head with the other guard. What sort of men were they? What were they talking about? What office did they represent? After all, K. lived in a state governed by law, there was universal peace, all statutes were in force; who dared assault him in his own lodgings? He'd always tended to take things lightly, to believe the worst only when it arrived, making no provision for the future, even when things looked bad. But that didn't seem the right approach here; of course he could treat the whole thing as a joke, a crude joke his colleagues at the bank were playing on him for some unknown reason, perhaps because today was his thirtieth birthday, that was certainly possible, perhaps all he had to do was laugh in the guards' faces and they would laugh with him, perhaps they were porters off the street-corner, they looked a little like porters—nevertheless, from the moment he'd first seen the guard named Franz, he had decided firmly that this time he wouldn't let even the slightest advantage he might have over these people slip through his fingers. K. knew there was a slight risk someone might say later that he hadn't been able to take a joke, but he clearly recalled—although he generally didn't make it a practice to learn from experience—a few occasions, unimportant in themselves, when, unlike his friends, he had deliberately behaved quite recklessly, without the least regard for his future, and had suffered the consequences. That wasn't going to happen again, not this time at any rate: if this was a farce, he was going to play along.

He was still free. "Pardon me," he said, and walked quickly between the guards into his room. "He seems to be reasonable," he heard them say behind him. In his room he yanked open the drawers of his desk at once; everything lay there in perfect order, but at first, in his agitation, he couldn't find the one thing he was looking for: his identification papers. Finally he found his bicycle license and was about to take that to the guards, but then it seemed too insignificant a document and he kept on looking until his found his birth certificate. When he returned to the adjoining room, the door opposite opened and Frau Grubach started to enter. She was only visible for a moment, for no sooner had she noticed K. than she seemed seized by embarrassment, apologized, and disappeared, closing the door carefully behind her. "Come on in," K. barely had time to say. But now he remained standing in the middle of the room with his papers, still staring at the door, which did not reopen, until he was brought to himself by a call from the guards, who were sitting at the small table by the open window and, as K. now saw, eating his breakfast. "Why didn't she come in?" he asked. "She's not allowed to," said the tall guard, "after all, you're under arrest." "How can I be under arrest? And in this manner?" "Now there you go again," said the guard, dipping his buttered bread into the little honey pot. "We don't answer such questions." "You're going to have to answer them," said K. "Here are my papers, now show me yours, starting with the arrest warrant." "Good heavens!" said the guard, "you just can't accept your situation; you seem bent on annoying us unnecessarily, although we're probably the human beings closest to you now." "That's right, you'd better believe it," said Franz, not lifting the coffee cup in his hand to his mouth but staring at K. with a long and no doubt meaningful, but incomprehensible, look. K. allowed himself to become involved in an involuntary staring match with Franz, but at last thumped his papers and said: "Here are my identification papers." "So what?" the taller guard cried out, "you're behaving worse than a child. What is it you want? Do you think you can bring your whole damn trial to a quick conclusion by discussing your identity and arrest warrant with your guards? We're lowly employees who can barely make our way through such documents, and whose only role in your affair is to stand guard over you ten hours a day and get paid for it. That's all we are, but we're smart enough to realize that before ordering such an arrest the higher authorities who employ us inform themselves in great detail about the person they're arresting and the grounds for the arrest. There's been no mistake. After all, our department, as far as I know, and I know only the lowest level, doesn't seek out guilt among the

general population, but, as the Law states, is attracted by
guilt and has to send us guards out. That's the Law. What
mistake could there be?" "I don't know that law," said K.
"All the worse for you," said the guard. "It probably exists
only in your heads," said K.; he wanted to slip into his
guards' thoughts somehow and turn them to his own advantage or accustom himself to them. But the guard merely said
dismissively: "You'll feel it eventually." Franz broke in and
said: "You see, Willem, he admits that he doesn't know the
Law and yet he claims he's innocent." "You're right there,
but he can't seem to understand anything," said the other. K.
said nothing more; why should I let the idle talk of these
lowly agents—they admit themselves that's what they are—
confuse me even further? he thought. After all, they're discussing things they don't understand. Their confidence is
based solely on ignorance. A few words spoken with someone of my own sort will make everything incomparably
clearer than the longest conversations with these two. He
paced back and forth a few times through the cleared space
of the room; across the way he saw the old woman, who had
pulled an ancient man far older than herself to the window
and had her arms wrapped about him; K. had to bring this
show to an end: "Take me to your supervisor," he said.
"When he wishes it; not before," said the guard called
Willem. "And now I advise you," he added, "to go to your
room, remain there quietly, and wait to find out what's to be
done with you. We advise you not to waste your time in useless thought, but to pull yourself together; great demands will
be placed upon you. You haven't treated us as we deserve,
given how accommodating we've been; you've forgotten that
whatever else we may be, we are at least free men with

respect to you, and that's no small advantage. Nevertheless we're prepared, if you have any money, to bring you a small breakfast from the coffeehouse across the way."

K. stood quietly for a moment without responding to this offer. Perhaps if he were to open the door to the next room, or even the door to the hall, the two would not dare stop him, perhaps the best solution would be to bring the whole matter to a head. But then they might indeed grab him, and once subdued he would lose any degree of superiority he might still hold over them. Therefore he preferred the safety of whatever solution would surely arise in the natural course of things and returned to his room without a further word having passed on either side.

He threw himself onto his bed and took from the nightstand a nice apple that he had set out the previous evening to have with breakfast. Now it was his entire breakfast, and in any case, as he verified with the first large bite, a much better breakfast than he could have had from the filthy all-night café through the grace of his guards. He felt confident and at ease; he was missing work at the bank this morning of course, but in light of the relatively high position he held there, that would be easily excused. Should he give the real excuse? He considered doing so. If they didn't believe him, which would be understandable given the circumstances, he could offer Frau Grubach as a witness, or even the two old people across the way, who were probably even now on the march to the window opposite him. K. was surprised, at least from the guards' perspective, that they had driven him into his room and left him alone there, where it would be ten times easier to kill himself. At the same time he asked himself from his own perspective what possible reason he could have

for doing so. Because those two were sitting next door and
had taken away his breakfast? Committing suicide would be
so irrational that even had he wished to, the irrationality of
the act would have prevented him. Had the intellectual limi-
tations of the guards not been so obvious, he might have
assumed this same conviction led them to believe there was
no danger in leaving him alone. Let them watch if they liked
as he went to the little wall cupboard in which he kept good
schnapps and downed a small glass in place of breakfast,
then a second one as well, to give himself courage, a mere
precaution, in the unlikely event it might be needed.

Then a shout from the adjoining room startled him so that
he rattled his teeth on the glass. "The inspector wants you!"
It was the cry alone that startled him: a short clipped military
cry that he would never have expected from the guard Franz.
The order itself he gladly welcomed: "It's about time," he
called back, locked the cupboard, and hurried into the
adjoining room. The two guards were standing there and, as
if it were a matter of course, chased him back into his room.
"What are you thinking of?" they cried. "Do you want to see
the inspector in your nightshirt? He'll have you soundly
flogged and us along with you!" "Let go of me, damn you,"
cried K., who was already pushed back against his wardrobe,
"if you assault me in bed, you can hardly expect to find me in
an evening jacket." "It's no use," said the guards, who,
whenever K. shouted at them, fell into a calm, almost sad
state that either put him at a loss or restored him somewhat
to his senses. "Ridiculous formalities!" he grumbled, but he
was already lifting a coat from the chair and holding it up for
a moment in both hands, as if submitting it to the judgment
of the guards. They shook their heads. "It has to be a black

coat," they said. K. threw the coat to the floor in response
and said—without knowing himself in what sense he meant
it—: "But this isn't the main hearing yet." The guards smiled,
but stuck to their words: "It has to be a black coat." "If that
will speed things up, it's fine with me," said K., opened the
wardrobe himself, took his time going through his many
clothes, selected his best black suit, an evening jacket that
had caused a small sensation among his friends because it
was so stylish, then changed his shirt as well and began dressing with care. He secretly believed he'd managed to speed up
the whole process after all, for the guards had forgotten to
make him bathe. He watched to see if they might recall it
now, but of course it didn't occur to them, although Willem
did remember to send Franz to the inspector with the message that K. was getting dressed.

When he was fully dressed, he had to walk just ahead of
Willem through the empty room next door into the following
room, the double doors to which were already thrown open.
As K. well knew, this room had been newly occupied not long
ago by a certain Fräulein Bürstner, a typist, who usually left
for work quite early and came home late, and with whom K.
had exchanged no more than a few words of greeting. Now
the nightstand by her bed had been shoved to the middle of
the room as a desk for the hearing and the inspector was sitting behind it. He had crossed his legs and placed one arm on
the back of the chair. In a corner of the room three young
men stood looking at Fräulein Bürstner's photographs, which
were mounted on a mat on the wall. A white blouse hung on
the latch of the open window. Across the way, the old couple
were again at the opposite window, but their party had
increased in number, for towering behind them stood a man

with his shirt open at the chest, pinching and twisting his red-dish goatee.

"Josef K.?" the inspector asked, perhaps simply to attract K.'s wandering gaze back to himself. K. nodded. "You're no doubt greatly surprised by this morning's events?" asked the inspector, arranging with both hands the few objects lying on the nightstand—a candle with matches, a book, and a pin-cushion—as if they were tools he required for the hearing. "Of course," said K., overcome by a feeling of relief at finally standing before a reasonable man with whom he could dis-cuss his situation, "of course I'm surprised, but by no means greatly surprised." "Not greatly surprised?" asked the inspector, placing the candle in the middle of the table and grouping the other objects around it. "Perhaps you misun-derstand me," K. hastened to add. "I mean—" Here K. inter-rupted himself and looked around for a chair. "I can sit down, can't I?" he asked. "It's not customary," answered the inspector. "I mean," K. continued without further pause, "I'm of course greatly surprised, but when you've been in this world for thirty years and had to make your way on your own, as has been my lot, you get hardened to surprises and don't take them too seriously. Particularly not today's." "Why particularly not today's?" "I'm not saying I think the whole thing's a joke, the preparations involved seem far too extensive for that. All the lodgers at the boardinghouse would have to be in on it, and all of you, which would go far beyond a joke. So I'm not saying it's a joke." "That's right," said the inspector, checking the number of matches in the matchbox. "But on the other hand," K. continued, as he turned to all of them, and would have gladly turned even to the three by the photographs, "on the other hand, it can't be too important a matter. I conclude that from the fact that I've been accused of something but can't think of the slightest offense of which I might be accused. But that's also beside the point, the main question is: Who's accusing me? What authorities are in charge of the proceedings? Are you officials? No one's wearing a uniform, unless you want to call your suit"—he turned to Franz—"a uniform, but it's more like a traveler's outfit. I demand clarification on these matters, and I'm convinced that once they've been clarified we can part on the friendliest of terms." The inspector flung the matchbox down on the table. "You're quite mistaken," he said. "These gentlemen and I are merely marginal figures in your affair, and in fact know almost nothing about it. We could be wearing the most proper of uniforms and your case would not be a whit more serious. I can't report that you've been accused of anything, or more accurately, I don't know if you have. You've been arrested, that's true, but that's all I know. Perhaps the guards have talked about other things, if so it was just that, idle talk. If, as a result, I can't answer your questions either, I can at least give you some advice: think less about us and what's going to happen to you, and instead think more about yourself. And don't make such a fuss about how innocent you feel; it disturbs the otherwise not unfavorable impression you make. And you should talk less in general; almost everything you've said up to now could have been inferred from your behavior, even if you'd said only a few words, and it wasn't terribly favorable to you in any case."

K. stared at the inspector. Was he to be lectured like a schoolboy by what might well be a younger man? To be reprimanded for his openness? And to learn nothing about why

he had been arrested and on whose orders? He grew increasingly agitated, paced up and down, freely and without hin-
drance, pushed his cuffs back, felt his chest, brushed his hair
into place, went past the three men, muttering, "It's completely senseless," at which they turned and looked at him
in a friendly but serious way, and finally came to a stop before the inspector's table. "Hasterer, the public prosecutor,
is a good friend of mine," he said, "can I telephone him?"
"Certainly," said the inspector, "but I don't see what sense
it makes, unless you have some private matter to discuss
with him." "What sense?" K. cried out, more startled than
annoyed. "Who do you think you are? You ask what sense it
makes, while you stage the most senseless performance imaginable? Wouldn't it break a heart of stone? First these gentlemen assault me, and now they sit around or stand about and
put me through my paces before you. What sense is there in
telephoning a lawyer when I've supposedly been arrested?
Fine, I won't telephone." "But do," said the inspector, and
waved toward the hall, where the telephone was, "please do
telephone." "No, I no longer wish to," K. said, and went to
the window. Across the way the group was still at the window, their peaceful observation now slightly disturbed as K.
stepped to the window. The old couple started to rise, but the
man behind them calmed them down. "There's more of the
audience over there," K. cried out to the inspector and
pointed outside. "Get away from there," he yelled at them.
The three immediately retreated a few steps, the old couple
even withdrawing behind the man, who shielded them
with his broad body and, judging by the movement of his
lips, apparently said something that couldn't be understood
at that distance. They didn't disappear entirely, however,

but instead seemed to wait for the moment when they could approach the window again unnoticed. "Obnoxious, thoughtless people!" said K., turning back to the room. The inspector may have agreed with him, as he thought he noticed with a sideways glance. But it was equally possible he hadn't been listening at all, for he had pressed his hand firmly down on the table and seemed to be comparing the length of his fingers. The two guards were sitting on a chest draped with an embroidered coverlet, rubbing their knees. The three young men had placed their hands on their hips and were gazing around aimlessly. Everything was silent, as in some deserted office. "Now, gentlemen," K. said firmly, and for a moment it seemed to him as if he bore them all upon his shoulders, "judging by your expressions, this affair of mine must be closed. In my view, it would be best to stop worrying whether or not your actions were justified and end the matter on a note of reconciliation, by shaking hands. If you share my view, then please—" and he stepped up to the inspector's table and held out his hand. The inspector looked up, chewed his lip, and regarded K.'s outstretched hand; K. still believed that the inspector would grasp it. But instead he rose, lifted a hard bowler from Fräulein Bürstner's bed, and donned it carefully with both hands, like someone trying on a new hat. "How simple everything seems to you!" he said to K. as he did so. "So you think we should end this matter on a note of reconciliation? No, I'm afraid we really can't. Although that's not at all to say you should despair. Why should you? You're under arrest, that's all. I was to inform you of that, I've done so, and I've noted your reaction. That's enough for today, and we can take our leave, temporarily of course. No doubt you wish to go to the bank now?" "To the bank?" K. asked.

"I thought I was under arrest." K. said this with a certain insistence, for although no one had shaken his hand, he was beginning to feel increasingly independent of these people, particularly once the inspector had stood up. He was toying with them. If they did leave, he intended to follow them to the door of the building and offer to let them arrest him. And so he said again: "How can I go to the bank if I'm under arrest?" "Oh, I see," said the inspector, who was already at the door, "you've misunderstood me; you're under arrest, certainly, but that's not meant to keep you from carrying on your profession. Nor are you to be hindered in the course of your ordinary life." "Then being under arrest isn't so bad," said K., approaching the inspector. "I never said it was," he replied. "But in that case even the notification of arrest scarcely seems necessary," said K., stepping closer still. The others had approached as well. Everyone was now gathered in a small area by the door. "It was my duty," said the inspector. "A stupid duty," said K. relentlessly. "Perhaps so," replied the inspector, "but let's not waste our time with such talk. I assumed you wished to go to the bank. Since you weigh every word so carefully, let me add that I'm not forcing you to go to the bank, I simply assumed you would want to. And to facilitate that, and to render your arrival at the bank as inconspicuous as possible, I've arranged for three of your colleagues here to be placed at your disposal." "What?" K. cried out, and stared at the three in amazement. These so uncharacteristically anemic young men, whom he recalled only as a group by the photographs, were indeed clerks from his bank, not colleagues, that would be an overstatement, and indicated a gap in the inspector's omniscience, but they were certainly lower-level clerks from the bank. How could

K. have failed to notice that? How preoccupied he must have been by the inspector and the guards not to recognize these three. Wooden, arm-swinging Rabensteiner, blond Kullich with his deep-set eyes, and Kaminer with his annoying smile, produced by a chronic muscular twitch. "Good morning!" K. said after a moment, and held out his hand to the men, who bowed courteously. "I completely failed to recognize you. So now we can go to work, right?" The men nodded, laughing and eager, as if that was what they'd been waiting for all along, but when K. missed his hat, which he'd left in his room, all three tripped over each other's heels to get it, which indicated a certain embarrassment on their part after all. K. stood still and watched them pass through the two open doors, the lethargic Rabensteiner bringing up the rear, of course, having broken into no more than an elegant trot. Kaminer handed over the hat and K. had to remind himself, as he often did at the bank, that Kaminer's smile was not deliberate and that in fact he couldn't smile deliberately at all. In the hall, Frau Grubach, not looking as if she felt any particular sense of guilt, opened the outer door for the whole company and K. looked down, as so often, at her apron strings, which cut so unnecessarily deeply into her robust body. Downstairs, watch in hand, K. decided to go by car so as not to extend unnecessarily what was already a half-hour delay. Kaminer ran to the corner to get a cab; the other two apparently felt they should entertain K. somehow, since Kullich suddenly pointed to the door of the building across the way, in which the man with the blond goatee had just appeared, and, at first embarrassed by now showing himself full-length, had retreated to the wall and leaned against it. The old couple were probably still on the stairs. K. was

annoyed at Kullich for having pointed out the man, since he
had already seen him himself, and in fact had been expecting
him. "Don't look over there," he said quickly, without realizing how strange it must sound to speak that way to grown
men. But no explanation was necessary, for at that moment
the cab arrived, they got in, and it pulled away. Then K.
remembered that he hadn't seen the inspector and the guards
leave: the inspector had diverted his attention from the three
clerks, and now the clerks had done the same for the inspector. That didn't show much presence of mind, and K. resolved
to pay greater attention to such things. Even now he turned
around involuntarily and leaned across the rear panel of the
car to see if the inspector and guards might still be in sight.
But he turned around again immediately, without having
made the slightest effort to locate anyone, and leaned back
comfortably into the corner of the cab. Despite appearances,
he could have used some conversation, but now the men
seemed tired: Rabensteiner gazed out of the car to the right,
and Kullych to the left, leaving only Kaminer and his grin,
which common decency unfortunately forbade as a topic of
humor.

CONVERSATION WITH FRAU GRUBACH
THEN FRÄULEIN BÜRSTNER

That spring K. generally spent his evenings as follows: after work, if there was still time—he usually stayed at the office until nine—he would take a short walk, alone or with acquaintances, then go to a tavern, where he would sit with a group of regulars, mostly older men, until eleven o'clock. But there were also exceptions to this routine; for example, when K. was invited by the bank president, who valued his diligence and reliability highly, for a drive in his car or for supper at his villa. In addition K. paid a weekly visit to a young woman named Elsa, who worked at night and late into the morning as a waitress in a wine house, and by day received visitors only in bed.

But on this particular evening—the day had passed

quickly, filled with hard work and a number of friendly and deferential birthday greetings—K. wanted to go straight home. He had thought about it during all the small breaks throughout the workday: without knowing exactly how, it seemed to him as if the morning's events had thrown the whole of Frau Grubach's boardinghouse into disarray, and that he was the one needed to restore order. Once that order had been restored, all trace of what had happened would be wiped away, and the old routine would resume. There was nothing in particular to fear from the three clerks; they had faded back into the larger realm of the bank's bureaucracy without any noticeable change. K. had called them to his office several times, both individually and as a group, for no other purpose than to observe them; he had always been able to dismiss them totally satisfied.

When, at nine-thirty that evening, he arrived at the building where he lived, he met a young fellow standing spread-legged at the entrance, smoking a pipe. "Who are you," K. asked straightaway and brought his face close to that of the fellow; the semidarkness of the entranceway made it hard to see. "I'm the caretaker's son, sir," the fellow answered, removing the pipe from his mouth and stepping aside. "The caretaker's son?" K. asked, tapping the floor impatiently with his cane. "Is there anything I can do for you, sir? Shall I get my father?" "No, no," said K. with a note of forgiveness, as if the fellow had done something truly wrong, but he was willing to forgive him. "That's all right," he said, and passed on; but before he went up the stairs, he turned around once more.

He could have gone straight to his room, but since he wanted to speak with Frau Grubach, he knocked first at her door. She sat darning a stocking at a table piled with other old stockings. K. excused himself absentmindedly for calling so late, but Frau Grubach was very friendly and would hear of no apology: he could visit her anytime, he was her best and dearest boarder, as he well knew. K. looked around the room: it had been fully restored to its former state; the breakfast dishes that had stood on the table by the window that morning had been removed as well. A woman's hand indeed works quiet wonders, he thought; he might have smashed the dishes on the spot, but he certainly couldn't have carried them out. He looked at Frau Grubach with a touch of gratitude. "Why are you working so late?" he asked. Now they were both sitting at the table, and from time to time K. buried his hand in the stockings. "There's a lot of work to do," she said, "during the day I belong to my boarders, evenings are the only time I have to put my own affairs in order." "I probably caused you a lot of extra work today." "How is that?" she asked, becoming more animated, her work resting in her lap. "I mean the men who were here this morning." "Oh, that," she said, returning to her state of calm, "that was no particular work." K. watched in silence as she again took up the stocking she was darning. "She seems surprised I'm talking about it," he thought, "she doesn't seem to think I should. All the more reason to do so. The only person I can discuss it with is an old woman." "Oh, it surely caused some work," he continued, "but it won't happen again." "No, it can't happen again," she said reassuringly and smiled at K. in an almost melancholy way. "Do you really think so?" asked K. "Yes," she said softly, "but above all you mustn't take it too seriously. All sorts of things go on in this world! Since you're talking so openly with me, Herr K., I'll confess that I listened a little behind the door, and the guards told me a few things too. It involves your happiness after all, and I really take that to heart, more than I should perhaps, since after all, I'm only your landlady. Well anyway, I heard a few things, but I can't say that it was anything very bad. No. You're under arrest all right, but not the way a thief would be. If you're arrested like a thief, that's bad, but this arrest—. It seems like something scholarly, I'm sorry if that sounds stupid, but it seems like something scholarly that I don't understand, but that I don't need to understand either."

"What you've said is not at all stupid, Frau Grubach, at any rate I agree with you in part, except that I judge the whole matter even more harshly; I don't even regard it as something scholarly, but simply as nothing at all. I was caught by surprise, that's all. If I'd just gotten up the moment I awoke, without letting myself be thrown by the fact that Anna didn't appear, and come to you without worrying about anyone's standing in my way; if I'd eaten breakfast in the kitchen for once, and had you bring my clothes from my room; in short, if I'd behaved sensibly, nothing more would have happened, everything else would have been nipped in the bud. At the bank, for instance, I'm always prepared, nothing like this could ever happen to me there; I have my own assistant, the office phone and my outside line stand before me on the desk, people are constantly coming in, clients and officers; but even more importantly, I'm always involved in my work, and so I have my wits about me; it would be a positive pleasure to confront a situation like this at my office. Well, it's all over now and I really didn't want to talk about it any more, I just wanted to hear your judgment on the matter, the judgment of a sensible woman, and I'm glad we agree about it. But now you must give me your hand; an agreement like this has to be confirmed by shaking hands."

Will she shake my hand? The inspector didn't, he thought, and he looked at the woman in a new way, scrutinizing her. She stood up because he had already done so; she was a little embarrassed because she hadn't understood everything that K. was saying. In her embarrassment, however, she said something she didn't mean to, something totally inappropriate: "Don't take it so hard, Herr K.," she said with tears in her voice, forgetting of course to shake his hand. "I didn't think I was taking it hard," K. said, suddenly weary, and realizing how worthless this woman's assent was.

At the door he asked: "Is Fräulein Bürstner home?" "No," said Frau Grubach, and as she delivered this dry piece of information she smiled with belated, shared understanding. "She's at the theater. Did you want something from her? Do you want me to give her a message?" "Oh, I just wanted to say a few words to her." "I'm sorry, I don't know when she'll be back; when she's at the theater she usually comes home late." "It doesn't matter," said K., and was already turning to the door to leave, his head bowed, "I just wanted to beg her pardon for using her room today." "That's not necessary, Herr K., you're too considerate; she doesn't know anything about it, she hasn't been home since early this morning, and everything's already been straightened up, see for yourself." And she opened the door to Fräulein Bürstner's room. "Thanks, I believe you," said K., but nevertheless walked to the open door. The moon shone softly into the dark room. As far as one could tell, everything was really back in its place, and the blouse no longer hung from the window handle. The bolsters seemed strikingly plump on the bed, lying partially in moonlight. "She often returns home quite late," K. said, and stared at Frau Grubach as if she were responsible. "Like all young people," said Frau Grubach by way of pardon. "Of course, of course," said K., "but it can go too far." "It can indeed," said Frau Grubach, "you're certainly right there, Herr K. And perhaps it has in this case. I certainly have no wish to slander Fräulein Bürstner, she's a fine and dear young woman, friendly, neat, punctual, and industrious, I appreciate all that, but it's true she should show more pride, and more reserve. I've already seen her twice this month in other neighborhoods and each time with a different man. I find it very embarrassing; I swear to the dear Lord I've mentioned it to no one but you, Herr K., but there's no getting around it, I'll have to speak to the young woman about it. And that's not the only thing I find suspicious about her." "You're totally off track," said K., scarcely able to conceal his fury, "it seems you've misunderstood my remarks about the young woman; that's not at all what I meant. In fact I warn you frankly not to say anything to her; you're completely mistaken, I know the young woman quite well, and there's no truth at all in what you've said. But perhaps I'm going too far; I don't wish to stand in your way, say whatever you want to her. Good night." "Herr K.," said Frau Grubach imploringly and rushed after K. to his door, which he had already opened, "I really don't want to speak to her; of course I'll first keep an eye on her a while longer, you're the only one I've told what I know. After all, it's surely in the boarders' best interest to try to run a clean house, and that's all I'm trying to do." "Clean!" K. cried through the crack in the door; "if you want to run a clean house, you'll have to start by giving me notice." Then he slammed the door shut, paying no attention to the timid knocks that followed.

However, since he didn't feel like sleeping, he decided to stay up, and use the opportunity to find out when Fräulein Bürstner would arrive. It might even be possible, though hardly proper, to exchange a few words with her. As he lay in the window, rubbing his weary eyes, he even thought for a moment of punishing Frau Grubach by talking Fräulein Bürstner into joining him in giving notice. But he saw at once that this would be a gross overreaction and even suspected himself of wishing to change lodgings because of the morning's events. Nothing would be more irrational, and above all more pointless and contemptible.

When he grew tired of looking out onto the empty street, he lay down on the divan, having opened the door to the hall slightly so that he could see anyone entering the lodgings directly from where he was lying. He lay on the divan smoking a cigar until around eleven. After that he couldn't hold out there any longer, and went instead out into the hall for a little while, as if he could speed up Fräulein Bürstner's arrival that way. He had no particular desire to see her, he couldn't even quite remember what she looked like, but now he wanted to talk to her, and he was annoyed that by coming home so late she was bringing disturbance and disarray to this day's end as well. And it was her fault he hadn't eaten anything that evening, and that he'd skipped his intended visit to Elsa that day. Of course, he could make up for both now by going to the wine bar where Elsa worked. He'd do that later, after he had spoken with Fräulein Bürstner.

It was past eleven-thirty when he heard someone on the stairs. K., who had been pacing up and down the hall noisily, lost in thought, as if he were in his own room, fled behind his door. It was Fräulein Bürstner, returning. Shivering, she pulled a silk shawl around her slim shoulders as she locked the door. In another moment she would be entering her room, which K. certainly wouldn't be permitted to invade this close to midnight; he had to speak to her now, but unfortunately he'd forgotten to switch on the light in his room, so that when he stepped out of the darkened room it would resemble an assault, and at the very least would give her a real shock. At a loss, and since there was no time to lose, he whispered through the crack in the door: "Fräulein Bürstner." It sounded like a plea, not a call. "Is someone there?" asked Fräulein Bürstner and looked around wide-eyed. "It's me," said K., and stepped forward. "Oh, Herr K.!" said Fräulein Bürstner with a smile; "Good evening," and she held out her hand. "I wanted to have a few words with you, may I do so now?" "Now?" asked Fräulein Bürstner; "does it have to be now? Isn't that a little unusual?" "I've been waiting for you since nine o'clock." "Well, I was at the theater, I had no idea you were waiting." "What I wanted to talk to you about was occasioned by something that occurred just today." "Well, I really don't mind, except that I'm so tired I'm about to drop. Come into my room for a few minutes then. We certainly can't talk here, we'll wake everyone up, and that would be even more unpleasant for us than for the others. Wait here until I've lit the lamp in my room and then turn this light off." K. did so but then remained waiting until Fräulein Bürstner softly invited him in again from her room. "Sit down," she said, and pointed toward the ottoman, while she herself remained standing by the bedpost, in spite of her talk of fatigue; she didn't even take off her small hat, which overflowed with flowers. "So what is it you want? I'm really curious." She crossed her legs lightly. "Perhaps you'll say," K. began, "that the matter wasn't so pressing that we had to talk about it now, but—" "I never listen to long preliminaries," said Fräulein Bürstner. "That makes my task easier," said K. "Your room was slightly disturbed today, and in a sense it was my fault; it was done by strangers and against my will, and yet, as I say, it was my fault; that's what I wanted to ask your pardon for." "My room?" asked Fräulein Brüstner, scrutinizing K. instead of the room. "That's right," said K. and now they both looked each other in the eyes for the first time, "exactly how it happened isn't worth talking about." "But that's what's really interesting," said Fräulein Bürstner. "No," said K. "Well," said Fräulein Bürstner, "I don't want to pry into secrets; if you claim it's of no interest, I won't bother to argue. I gladly grant the pardon you seek, particularly since I see no trace of any disorder." She made a tour of the room, her hands flat and low on her hips. She stopped in front of the mat with the photographs. "Yes, look," she cried out, "my photos have been all mixed up. That's really annoying. Someone's been in my room without permission." K. nodded and silently cursed the clerk Kaminer, who could never control his stupid, senseless fidgeting. "I find it odd," said Fräulein Bürstner, "to be forced to forbid you to do something your own conscience should forbid, namely, to enter my room when I'm away." "But I explained to you, Fräulein," said K., going over to the photographs as well, "I'm not the one who took liberties with your photographs; but since you don't believe me, I must confess that the commission of inquiry brought along three bank clerks, and that one of them, whom I'll have dismissed from the bank at the first opportunity, probably handled your photographs." "Yes, there was a commission of inquiry here," K. added, since the young woman was staring at him with a questioning look. "Because of you?" the young woman asked. "Yes," K. replied. "No," the young woman cried with a laugh. "Oh, yes," said K. "Do you think I'm guiltless then?" "Well, guiltless . . . ," said the young woman, "I don't want to make a hasty judgment that might possibly have serious consequences, and I don't really know you, but it does seem that you'd have to be a serious criminal to have a commission of inquiry come down on you right from the start. But since you're free—at least I gather from your calm state that you haven't escaped from prison—you can't have committed any serious crime." "Yes," said K., "but it may have been that the commission of inquiry realized I'm guiltless or at least not quite as guilty as they thought." "Yes, that could be," said Fräulein Bürstner, paying close attention. "You see," said K., "you don't have much experience in court matters." "No, I don't," said Fräulein Bürstner, "and I've often regretted that, because I would like to know everything, and I'm fascinated with court matters. The court has a strange attraction, doesn't it? But I'll certainly be able to increase my knowledge in that area, because I start next month as a secretary in a law firm." "That's very good," said K., "then you'll be able to help me a little with my trial." "Perhaps," said Fräulein Bürstner, "why not? I enjoy using my knowledge." "I'm serious too," said K., "or at least half serious, like you. It's too minor an affair to bring in a lawyer, but I could use someone to advise me." "Yes, but if I'm to advise you, I have to know what it's all about," said Fräulein Bürstner. "That's just the problem," said K., "I don't know myself." "Then you've just been teasing me," said Fräulein Bürstner, exceedingly disappointed, "you hardly needed to pick such a late hour to do it." And she walked away from the photographs, where they had been standing together for so long. "But Fräulein," K. said, "I'm not teasing. Why won't you believe me? I've already told you everything I know. More than I know in fact, because it wasn't a commission of inquiry. I just called it that because I don't know any other name for it. There was no inquiry, I was simply arrested, but by a commission." Fräulein Bürstner sat down on her ottoman and laughed again: "What was it like?" she asked. "Terrible," said K., although now he wasn't thinking about it at all, but was instead totally engrossed by the sight of Fräulein Bürstner, who was resting her head on one hand—her elbow propped on the cushion of the ottoman—while she slowly stroked her hip with the other. "That's too general," said Fräulein Bürstner. "What's too general?" K. asked. Then he came to himself and asked: "Do you want me to show you how it was?" He wanted to move about and yet not leave. "I'm already tired," said Fräulein Bürstner. "You got in so late," said K. "And now it ends with reproaches; I deserve it, I should never have let you in. And it wasn't really necessary, as it turned out." "It was necessary, you'll see that now," said K. "May I move the nightstand away from your bed?" "What an idea!" said Fräulein Bürstner; "of course you can't!" "Then I can't show you," K. said, all upset, as if this would cause him immense harm. "Well, if you need it for your performance, then go ahead and move the stand," said Fräulein Bürstner, adding in a faint voice, after a pause: "I'm so tired that I'm letting you take more liberties than I should." K. placed the little table in the middle of the room and sat down behind it. "You have to visualize the cast of characters, it's very interesting. I'm the inspector, two guards are sitting over there on the chest, three young men are standing by the photographs. From the window handle, I'm just noting it in passing, hangs a white blouse. And now the action begins. Oh, I'm forgetting myself, the most important character: I'm standing here, in front of the table. The inspector is sitting totally at ease, his legs crossed, his arm hanging down like this from the back of the chair, an unbelievable boor. And now the action really begins. The inspector cries out as if he has to wake me up, practically shouting; unfortunately I'll have to shout too, to show you how it was; all he shouts is my name, by the way." Fräulein Bürstner, laughing as she listened, held her finger to her lips to keep K. from yelling, but it was too late, K. had entered too deeply into his role: "Josef K.!" he cried, drawing it out slowly, not, after all, as loudly as he had threatened, yet in such a way that the cry, having suddenly burst forth, seemed to spread only gradually throughout the room.

There was a knock at the door to the adjoining room, a brief, loud series of blows. Fräulein Bürstner turned pale and put her hand to her heart. The shock was even greater for K., since for a short while he could think of nothing but that morning's events and the young woman he was reenacting them for. As soon as he came to himself he sprang to Fräulein Bürstner and took her hand. "Don't worry," he whispered, "I'll straighten everything out. But who can it be? That's just the living room next door, and no one's sleeping there." "Oh, yes," Fräulein Bürstner whispered in K.'s ear,

"Frau Grubach's nephew has been staying there since yesterday, a captain. There's no other room free at the moment. I'd forgotten about it too. You had to shout so! That makes me very unhappy." "There's no reason to be," said K. and kissed her on the forehead as she sank back upon the cushion. "Go, go," she said, and quickly straightened up again, "go on, go away. What do you want, he's listening at the door, he can hear everything. You're tormenting me!" "I'm not going," said K., "until you've calmed down a bit. Come over to the other corner of the room; he can't hear us there." She let him lead her there. "Just remember," he said, "this may be unpleasant for you, but you're in no danger. You know how Frau Grubach, whose voice will count most, particularly since the captain is her nephew, practically worships me, and believes anything I say. She's beholden to me in another way too, since she's borrowed a large sum from me. I'll accept any suggestion you offer as to why we were together, as long as it's halfway reasonable, and I guarantee I'll get Frau Grubach not only to accept it in public, but to truly and honestly believe it. You needn't spare me in any way. If you want it spread around that I assaulted you, that's what Frau Grubach will be told and what she will believe, without losing confidence in me, that's how devoted she is to me." Fräulein Bürstner stared silently at the floor in front of her, slumping slightly. "Why shouldn't Frau Grubach believe that I assaulted you," K. added. He saw before him her hair, parted, tightly drawn reddish hair, gathered together lightly on her neck. He thought she would look up at him, but she spoke without changing her posture: "Pardon me, it was the sudden knocking that frightened me, not so much the possible consequences of the captain's presence. It was so quiet

after you cried out, and then the knocking came, that's why I
was so frightened, and I was sitting so close to the door, the
knocking was right beside me. I appreciate your suggestions,
but I can't accept them. I can take full responsibility for what
happens in my room and face anyone. I'm surprised you
don't realize the insult to me implicit in your suggestions,
along, of course, with your good intentions, which I certainly
recognize. But go now, leave me to myself, I need that more
than ever now. The few minutes you requested have turned
into more than half an hour." K. seized her by the hand and
then by the wrist: "You're not mad at me, are you?" he said.
She pushed his hand away and answered: "No, no, I never
get angry at anyone." He reached for her wrist again, she
allowed it now and led him to the door. He firmly intended to
leave. But at the door, as if he hadn't expected to find one
there, he hesitated; Fräulein Bürstner used this moment to
free herself, open the door, slip into the hall, and implore
K. softly from there: "Now come on, please. Look"—
she pointed at the captain's door, beneath which a strip of
light emerged—"his light is on and he's amusing himself over
us." "I'm coming," said K., rushed out, seized her, kissed her
on the mouth, then all over her face, like a thirsty animal
lapping greedily at a spring it has found at last. Then he
kissed her on the neck, right at her throat, and left his
lips there for a long time. A noise from the captain's room
caused him to look up. "I'll go now," he said; he wanted
to call Fräulein Bürstner by her given name, but he didn't
know it. She nodded wearily, allowed him to take her hand
for a kiss as she was already half turned away, as if she
were unaware of it, and entered her room with bowed
head. Shortly thereafter K. lay in his bed. He fell asleep

very quickly; before falling asleep he reflected briefly on his conduct: he was pleased with it, but was surprised that he didn't feel even more pleased; he was seriously concerned on Fräulein Bürstner's behalf because of the captain.

INITIAL INQUIRY

K. was informed by telephone that a brief inquiry into his affair would take place the following Sunday. He was notified that such inquiries would now be held on a regular basis, perhaps not every week, but with increasing frequency. On the one hand, it was in the general interest to bring his trial to a rapid conclusion; on the other, the inquiries must be thorough in every respect, yet never last too long, due to the strain involved. Therefore they had selected the expedient of this succession of closely spaced but brief inquiries. Sundays had been chosen for the inquiries to avoid disturbing K.'s professional life. It was assumed he would find this acceptable; if he preferred some other fixed time, they would try their best to accommodate him. For example the inquiries could be held at night, but K. probably wouldn't be fresh enough then. At any rate, as long as K. had no objection, they would stay with Sundays. Of course he was required to appear; it was probably not really necessary to point that out. He was given the number of the building in which he was to appear: it was a building on a street in a distant suburb K. had never been to before.

Having received this message, K. hung up the phone without replying; he had resolved at once to go on Sunday; it was clearly necessary, the trial was getting under way and he had to put up a fight; this initial inquiry must also be the last. He was still standing lost in thought by the phone when he heard the voice of the executive vice president behind him, who wanted to make a phone call, but found K. blocking the way. "Bad news?" the vice president asked lightly, not because he wanted to know, but to get K. away from the phone. "No, no," said K., stepping aside but not walking off. The vice president picked up the phone and, while waiting to be put through, spoke across the receiver: "May I ask you something, Herr K.? Will you do me the pleasure of coming to a party on my sailboat Sunday morning? There'll be quite a few people, I'm sure you'll know some of them. Among others Hasterer, the public prosecutor. Would you like to come? Please do!" K. tried to concentrate on what the vice president was saying. It was not without importance for him, since this invitation from the vice president, with whom he had never got along particularly well, indicated an attempt at reconciliation on the other's part, and showed how important K. had become to the bank, and how valuable his friendship, or at least his neutrality, must seem to the bank's second-highest officer. The invitation humbled the vice president, even if it had merely been delivered across the receiver while waiting for a call to go through. But K. was forced to humble him a second time by replying: "Thank you very much! But unfortunately I'm busy on Sunday, I have a previous engagement." "Too bad," the vice president said, and returned to his call, which had just been put through. It was no brief conversation, but in his preoccupied state K. remained standing by the phone the whole time. It wasn't until the vice president hung up that he came to himself with a start and said, to excuse himself somewhat for having simply stood around, "I just received a call asking me to go somewhere, but they forgot to tell me the time." "Call them back and ask," said the vice president. "It's not that important," said K., although in doing so his previous excuse, which was already weak enough, crumbled even further. As they walked away the vice president talked of other things, and K. forced himself to answer, but he was really thinking that it would be best to arrive Sunday morning at nine, since that was when courts opened session on workdays.

The weather was dull on Sunday, and K. was very tired, having stayed at the tavern celebrating with the regulars late into the night, so that he almost overslept. He dressed hastily, without having time to think things over or review the various plans he'd worked out during the week, and skipping breakfast, hurried to the suburb they had indicated. Strangely enough, although he had little time to look about, he ran across the three clerks who were involved in his affair: Rabensteiner, Kullych, and Kaminer. The first two were riding in a tram that crossed K.'s path, but Kaminer was sitting on the terrace of a coffeehouse and, just as K. was walking by, leaned inquisitively over the railing. They probably all gazed after him, wondering why their supervisor was in such a rush; some sort of stubbornness had prevented K. from taking a cab; he had an aversion to even the slightest outside help in this affair of his; he didn't want to enlist anyone's aid and thus initiate them in the matter even distantly; nor, finally, did he have the least desire to humble himself before the commission of inquiry by being overly punctual. Of course he was now running to get there by nine if at all possible, although he had not even been given a specific hour at which to appear.

He had thought he would recognize the building, even at a distance, by some sign he hadn't visualized precisely, or by some unusual activity at the entrance. But Juliusstrasse, where it was supposedly located and at the top of which K. paused for a moment, was flanked on both sides by almost completely identical buildings, tall gray apartment houses inhabited by the poor. On this Sunday morning most of the windows were occupied; men in shirtsleeves leaned there smoking, or held small children with tender care at the windowsill. Other windows were piled high with bedding, above which the disheveled head of a woman briefly appeared. People called across the street to each other; one such exchange directly over K.'s head aroused loud laughter. At regular intervals along the long street, small shops offering various foodstuffs lay below street level, reached by a few steps. Women went in and out of them, or stood on the steps chatting. A fruit vendor who was offering his wares to the windows above, paying as little attention as K., almost knocked him to the ground with his pushcart. Just then a gramophone that had served its time in better sections of the city began to murder a tune.

K. continued down the street, slowly, as if he had plenty of time now, or as if the examining magistrate had seen him from some window and knew he had arrived. It was shortly after nine. The building stretched some distance; it was almost unusually extensive, the entrance gate in particular was high and broad. It was evidently intended for heavy wagons belonging to the various warehouses, now locked shut, which lined the inner courtyard, with signs bearing the names of firms, some of which K. knew from the bank. Contrary to his normal habit, he was taking close note of all these surface details, and he paused a while at the entrance to the courtyard. On a crate nearby sat a barefoot man reading a newspaper. Two boys rocked back and forth on a handcart. A frail young girl in her night jacket stood at a pump and gazed at K. as the water poured into her jug. In one corner of the courtyard a line with wash to be dried already dangling from it was being stretched between two windows. A man stood below and directed the task with a few shouts.

K. turned to the stairs to find the room for the inquiry, but then paused as he saw three different staircases in the courtyard in addition to the first one; moreover, a small passage at the other end of the courtyard seemed to lead to a second courtyard. He was annoyed that they hadn't described the location of the room more precisely; he was certainly being treated with strange carelessness or indifference, a point he intended to make loudly and clearly. Then he went up the first set of stairs after all, his mind playing with the memory of the remark the guard Willem had made that the court was attracted by guilt, from which it actually followed that the room for the inquiry would have to be located off whatever stairway K. chanced to choose.

On his way up he disturbed several children who were playing on the steps and who looked angrily at him as he passed through their midst. "The next time I'm to come," he said to himself, "I'll either have to bring candy to win them over or my cane to flog them." Shortly before reaching the first floor he even had to pause for a moment until a marble had completed its journey, while two little boys with the pinched faces of grown tramps held him by the trouser legs; if he had wanted to shake them off he would have had to hurt them, and he feared their cries.

On the first floor the real search began. Since he couldn't simply ask for the commission of inquiry he invented a carpenter named Lanz—the name occurred to him because Frau Grubach's nephew, the captain, was called that—intending to ask at each apartment if a carpenter named Lanz lived there, hoping to get a chance to look into the rooms. That proved to be easy enough in general, however, since almost all the doors were standing open, with children running in and out. As a rule they were small, one-window rooms, where people cooked as well. A few women held babies in one arm as they worked at the stove with their free hand. Half-grown girls, apparently clad only in smocks, ran busily back and forth. In every room the beds were still in use, with someone sick or still asleep in them, or people stretched out in their clothes. K. knocked at the apartments with closed doors and asked if a carpenter named Lanz lived there. Generally a woman would open the door, listen to the question, and turn to someone in the room who rose up from the bed. "The gentleman wants to know if a carpenter named Lanz lives here." "A carpenter named Lanz?" asked the one in bed. "Yes," K. said, despite the fact that the commission of inquiry clearly wasn't here and therefore his task was ended. Several people believed K. badly needed to find the carpenter Lanz, thought long and hard, recalled a carpenter, but not one named Lanz, remembered a name that bore some faint similarity to Lanz, asked their neighbors, or accompanied K. to some far distant door, where they fancied such a man might possibly be subletting an apartment, or where there was someone who could provide him with better information than they could. In the end K. scarcely needed even to ask, but was instead pulled along in this manner from floor to floor. He regretted his plan, which had at first seemed so practical. As he was approaching the fifth floor he decided to give up the search, took his leave from a friendly young worker who wanted to lead him further upward, and started back down. But then, annoyed once more by the futility of the whole enterprise, he returned and knocked at the first door on the fifth floor. The first thing he saw in the little room was a large wall clock that already showed ten o'clock. "Does a carpenter named Lanz live here?" he asked. "This way, please," said a young woman with shining black eyes, who was washing diapers in a tub, and pointed with her wet hand toward the open door of the adjoining room.

K. thought he had walked into a meeting. A crowd of the most varied sort—no one paid any attention to the newcomer—filled a medium-size room with two windows, surrounded by an elevated gallery just below the ceiling that was likewise fully occupied, and where people were forced to crouch with their backs and heads pushing against the ceiling. K., who found the air too stuffy, stepped out again and said to the young woman, who had probably misunderstood him: "I was looking for a carpenter, a man named Lanz?"

"Yes," said the woman, "please go on in." K. might not have obeyed if the woman hadn't walked over to him, grasped the door handle and said: "I have to lock it after you, no one else is permitted in." "Very sensible," said K., "but it's already too crowded." But he went back in anyway.

Between two men who were conversing near the door— one of them was going through the motions of counting out money with outstretched hands, the other was looking him sharply in the eye—a hand reached out for K. It was a little red-cheeked boy. "Come on, come on," he said. K. let him lead the way; it turned out that there was indeed a narrow path free through the swirling crowd, one that possibly divided two parties; this possibility was further supported by the fact that K. saw scarcely a face turned toward him in the closest rows on his left and right, but merely the backs of people addressing their words and gestures solely to those in their own party. Most were dressed in black, in old, long, loosely hanging formal coats. This was the only thing K. found confusing; otherwise he would have taken it all for a local precinct meeting.

K. was led to the other end of the hall, where a small table had been placed at an angle on a low and equally over-crowded platform, and behind the table, near the platform's edge, sat a fat little man, wheezing and chatting with some-one standing behind him—the latter was leaning with his elbow on the back of the chair and had crossed his legs— laughing heartily all the while. Now and then he would fling his arms in the air, as if he were caricaturing someone. The boy who was leading K. found it difficult to deliver his mes-sage. Twice already he'd tried to say something, standing on tiptoe, without being noticed by the man above. It was only

when one of the people up on the platform drew attention to
the boy that the man turned and bent down to listen to his
faint report. Then he pulled out his watch and glanced over
at K. "You should have been here an hour and five minutes
ago," he said. K. was about to reply, but he didn't have time,
for the man had scarcely spoken when a general muttering
arose from the right half of the hall. "You should have been
here an hour and five minutes ago," the man repeated more
loudly, and glanced down into the hall as well. The muttering
immediately grew louder still and, since the man said nothing
more, died out only gradually. It was now much quieter in the
hall than it had been when K. entered. Only the people in the
gallery continued making comments. They seemed, as far as
one could tell in the semidarkness, haze, and dust overhead,
to be dressed more shabbily than those below. Some of them
had brought along cushions that they placed between their
heads and the roof of the hall so as not to rub themselves raw.

K. had decided to observe more than speak, and therefore
waived any defense of his supposedly late arrival, merely saying: "I may have arrived late, but I'm here now." A burst of
applause followed, once again from the right half of the hall.
"These people are easily won over," thought K. and was only
disturbed by the silence in the left half of the hall, which lay
immediately behind him and from which only thinly scattered applause had arisen. He considered what he might say
to win all of them over at once, or if that was not possible, at
least to win the others for the time being.

"Yes," said the man, "but now I'm no longer required
to examine you"—again the muttering, but this time mistakenly, for the man waved the people off and continued—
"however, I'll make an exception for today. But such

tardiness must not be repeated. And now step forward!" Someone jumped down from the platform to free a space for K., and he stepped up into it. He was standing right up against the table; the pressure of the crowd behind him was so great that he had to actively resist if he didn't want to push the examining magistrate's table, and perhaps even the magistrate himself, right off the platform.

The examining magistrate wasn't worried about that, however, but sat comfortably enough in his chair and, after a closing remark to the man behind him, reached for a little notebook, the only object on his table. It resembled a school exercise book, old and totally misshapen from constant thumbing. "So," said the examining magistrate, leafing through the notebook and turning to K. as if simply establishing a fact: "You're a house painter?" "No," said K., "I'm the chief financial officer of a large bank." This reply was followed by such hearty laughter from the right-hand party below that K. had to join in. The people propped their hands on their knees, shaken as if by fits of coughing. There were even a few laughing up in the gallery. The examining magistrate, who had become quite angry and was probably powerless to do anything about the people below, tried to compensate for this by jumping up and threatening the gallery, while his ordinarily inconspicuous eyebrows contracted bushy black and large above his eyes.

The left half of the hall, however, was still silent, the people standing there in rows, their faces turned toward the platform, listening to the words exchanged above as quietly as to the clamor of the other party, now and then even allowing a few members within their own ranks to go along with the other side. The people in the party on the left, who were in fact less numerous, may have been no more important than those in the party on the right, but their calm demeanor made them appear more so. As K. now started to speak, he was convinced that he was expressing their thoughts.

"Your question, Your Honor, about my being a house painter—and you weren't really asking at all, you were telling me outright—is characteristic of the way these entire proceedings against me are being conducted. You may object that these aren't proceedings at all, and you're certainly right there, they are only proceedings if I recognize them as such. But I do recognize them, for the moment, out of compassion, so to speak. One can only view them compassionately, if one chooses to pay any attention to them at all. I'm not saying these proceedings are sloppy, but I would like to propose that description for your own personal consideration."

K. interrupted himself and looked down into the hall. What he had said was harsh, harsher than he had intended, but nonetheless accurate. It should have earned applause here and there, but all was still; they were evidently waiting tensely for what was to come; perhaps in that silence an outburst was building that would put an end to everything. It was disturbing that the door at the end of the hall now opened, and the young washerwoman, who had probably finished her work, entered, drawing a few glances in spite of her painstaking caution. Only the examining magistrate gave K. direct cause for joy, for he appeared to have been struck at once by his words. Up to that point he had been standing as he listened, for K.'s speech had caught him by surprise as he rose to admonish the gallery. As K. now paused, he slowly lowered himself back into his chair, as if hoping to keep anyone from noticing. In an attempt to regain his composure, no doubt, he took out his little notebook again.

"It's no use, Your Honor," K. continued, "even your little notebook confirms what I'm saying." Pleased that his own calm words alone were to be heard in that strange assembly, K. even dared to snatch the notebook from the magistrate's hands and lift it in his fingertips by a single center page, as if he were repelled by it, so that the foxed and spotted leaves filled with closely spaced script hung down on both sides. "These are the records of the examining magistrate," he said, letting the notebook drop to the table. "Just keep reading through them, Your Honor, I really have nothing to fear from this account book, although it's closed to me, since I can barely stand to touch it with the tips of two fingers." It could only be a sign of deep humiliation, or at least so it seemed, that the examining magistrate took the notebook from where it had fallen on the table, tried to put it to rights somewhat, and lifted it to read again.

The faces of the people in the front row were turned toward K. so intently that he gazed down at them for a short time. They were all older men, a few with white beards. Perhaps they were the decisive ones, capable of influencing the whole assembly, men whom even the examining magistrate's humiliation could not stir from the quiescent state they'd fallen into since K.'s speech.

"What has happened to me," K. continued, somewhat more quietly than before, and constantly searching the faces of those in the front row, which made his speech seem slightly disjointed, "what has happened to me is merely a single case and as such of no particular consequence, since I don't take it very seriously, but it is typical of the proceedings being brought against many people. I speak for them, not for myself."

He had instinctively raised his voice. Someone clapped somewhere with raised hands and cried out: "Bravo! Why not? Bravo! And encore bravo!" Those in the front row pulled at their beards now and then; no one turned around at the cry. Nor did K. grant it any importance, yet it cheered him; he no longer considered it necessary for everyone to applaud, it was enough that the audience in general was beginning to think the matter over and that someone was occasionally won over by his words.

"I don't seek success as an orator," K. said with this in mind, "nor could I necessarily achieve it. The examining magistrate is no doubt a much better speaker; after all, it goes with his profession. What I seek is simply a public discussion of a public disgrace. Listen: Around ten days ago I was arrested; the arrest itself makes me laugh, but that's another matter. I was assaulted in the morning in bed; perhaps they'd been ordered to arrest some house painter—that can't be ruled out after what the examining magistrate has said—someone as innocent as I am, but they chose me. The room next door had been taken over by two coarse guards. If I had been a dangerous thief, they couldn't have taken better precautions. These guards were corrupt ruffians as well; they talked my ear off, they wanted bribes, they tried to talk me out of my undergarments and clothes under false pretenses, they wanted money, supposedly to bring me breakfast, after they'd shamelessly eaten my own breakfast before my very eyes. And that wasn't all. I was led into a third room to see the inspector. It was the room of a young woman for whom I have the highest respect, yet I was forced to look on while this room was defiled, so to speak, by the presence of the guards and the inspector, on my account, but through no fault of my own. It wasn't easy to stay calm. However, I managed to, and I asked the inspector quite calmly—if he were here he'd have to confirm that—why I had been arrested. And what was the reply of this inspector, whom I still see before me, sitting on the chair of the young woman I mentioned, the very image of mindless arrogance? Gentlemen, he really had no reply at all, perhaps he actually knew nothing, he had arrested me and that was enough for him. He had taken the additional step of bringing to the young lady's room three minor employees from my bank, who spent their time fingering photographs, the property of the lady, and mixing them all up. The presence of these employees served another purpose, of course: they were meant, like my landlady and her maid, to spread the news of my arrest, damage my public reputation, and in particular to undermine my position at the bank. Well, none of this met with the slightest success; even my landlady, a very simple person—I pronounce her name in all honor, she's called Frau Grubach—even Frau Grubach was sensible enough to realize that an arrest like that means as little as a mugging on the street by teenage hoodlums. I repeat, the whole affair has merely caused me some unpleasantness and temporary annoyance, but might it not have had more serious consequences as well?"

As K. interrupted himself at this point and glanced at the silent magistrate, he thought he noticed him looking at someone in the crowd and giving him a signal. K. smiled and said: "The examining magistrate here beside me has just given one of you a secret signal. So there are those among you who are being directed from up here. I don't know if the signal is meant to elicit hisses or applause, and I deliberately waive my opportunity to learn what the signal means by having revealed the matter prematurely. It's a matter of complete indifference to me, and I publicly authorize His Honor the examining magistrate to command his paid employees below out loud, rather than by secret signals, and to say something like: 'Now hiss' and the next time: 'Now clap.'"

The examining magistrate shifted about in his chair in embarrassment or impatience. The man behind him, with whom he had been talking earlier, bent down to him again, either to give him some general words of encouragement or to pass on special advice. The people below conversed quietly but animatedly. The two parties, which had appeared to hold such contrasting opinions before, mingled with one another, some people pointing their fingers at K., others at the examining magistrate. The foglike haze in the room was extremely annoying, even preventing any closer observation of those standing further away. It must have been particularly disturbing for the visitors in the gallery, who were forced, with timid side glances at the examining magistrate of course, to address questions under their breath to the members of the assembly in order find out what was happening. The answers were returned equally softly, shielded behind cupped hands.

"I'm almost finished," said K. striking his fist on the table, since no bell was available, at which the heads of the examining magistrate and his advisor immediately drew apart, startled: "I'm completely detached from this whole affair, so I can judge it calmly, and it will be to your distinct advantage to pay attention, always assuming you care about this so-called court. I suggest that you postpone your mutual discussion of what I'm saying until later, because I don't have much time, and will be leaving soon."

There was an immediate silence, so completely did K. now control the assembly. People weren't shouting back and forth as they had at the beginning; they no longer even applauded but seemed by now convinced, or on the verge of being so.

"There can be no doubt," K. said very quietly, for he was pleased by the keen attention with which the whole assembly was listening, a murmuring arising in that stillness that was more exciting than the most delighted applause, "there can be no doubt that behind all the pronouncements of this court, and in my case, behind the arrest and today's inquiry, there exists an extensive organization. An organization that not only engages corrupt guards, inane inspectors, and examining magistrates who are at best mediocre, but that supports as well a system of judges of all ranks, including the highest, with their inevitable innumerable entourage of assistants, scribes, gendarmes, and other aides, perhaps even hangmen, I won't shy away from the word. And the purpose of this extensive organization, gentlemen? It consists of arresting innocent people and introducing senseless proceedings against them, which for the most part, as in my case, go nowhere. Given the senselessness of the whole affair, how could the bureaucracy avoid becoming entirely corrupt? It's impossible, even the highest judge couldn't manage it, even with himself. So guards try to steal the shirts off the backs of arrested men, inspectors break into strange apartments, and innocent people, instead of being examined, are humiliated before entire assemblies. The guards told me about depositories to which an arrested man's property is taken; I'd like to see these depository places sometime, where the hard-earned goods of arrested men are rotting away, if they haven't already been stolen by pilfering officials."

K. was interrupted by a shriek from the other end of the hall; he shaded his eyes so that he could see, for the dull daylight had turned the haze into a blinding white glare. It was the washerwoman, whom K. had sensed as a major disturbance from the moment she entered. Whether or not she was at fault now was not apparent. K. saw only that a man had pulled her into a corner by the door and pressed her to himself. But she wasn't shrieking, it was the man; he had opened his mouth wide and was staring up toward the ceiling. A small circle had gathered around the two of them, and the nearby visitors in the gallery seemed delighted that the serious mood K. had introduced into the assembly had been interrupted in this fashion. K.'s initial reaction was to run toward them, in fact he thought everyone would want to restore order and at least banish the couple from the hall, but the first rows in front of him stood fast; not a person stirred and no one let K. through. On the contrary they hindered him: old men held out their arms and someone's hand—he didn't have time to turn around—grabbed him by the collar from behind; K. wasn't really thinking about the couple anymore, for now it seemed to him as if his freedom were being threatened, as if he were being arrested in earnest, and he sprang from the platform recklessly. Now he stood eye-to-eye with the crowd. Had he misjudged these people? Had he overestimated the effect of his speech? Had they been pretending all the time he was speaking, and now that he had reached his conclusions, were they fed up with pretending? The faces that surrounded him! Tiny black eyes darted about, cheeks drooped like those of drunken men, the long beards were stiff and scraggly, and when they pulled on them, it seemed as if they were merely forming claws, not pulling beards. Beneath the beards, however—and this was the true discovery K. made—badges of various sizes and colors shimmered on the collars of their jackets. They all had badges, as far as he could see. They were all one group, the apparent parties on the left and right, and as he suddenly turned, he saw the same badges on the collar of the examining magistrate, who was looking on calmly with his hands in his lap. "So!" K. cried and flung his arms in the air, this sudden insight demanding space; "I see you're all officials, you're the corrupt band I was speaking about; you've crowded in here to listen and snoop, you've formed apparent parties and had one side applaud to test me, you wanted to learn how to lead innocent men astray. Well I hope you haven't come in vain; either you found it entertaining that someone thought you would defend the innocent or else— back off or I'll hit you," cried K. to a trembling old man who had shoved his way quite near to him"—or else you've actually learned something. And with that I wish you luck in your trade." He quickly picked up his hat, which was lying at the edge of the table, and made his way through the general silence, one of total surprise at least, toward the exit. The examining magistrate, however, seemed to have been even quicker than K., for he was waiting for him at the door. "One moment," he said. K. stopped, looking not at the examining magistrate but at the door, the handle of which he had already seized. "I just wanted to draw your attention to the fact," said the examining magistrate, "that you have today deprived yourself—although you can't yet have realized it— of the advantage that an interrogation offers to the arrested man in each case." K. laughed at the door. "You scoundrels," he cried, "you can have all your interrogations"; then he opened the door and hurried down the stairs. Behind him rose the sounds of the assembly, which had come to life again, no doubt beginning to discuss what had occurred, as students might.

IN THE EMPTY COURTROOM

THE STUDENT

THE OFFICES

K. waited from day to day throughout the following week for further notification; he couldn't believe they had taken his waiver of interrogations literally, and when the expected notification had not arrived by Saturday evening, he took it as an implicit summons to appear again in the same building at the same time. So he returned on Sunday, but this time he went straight up the stairs and along the passageways; a few people who remembered him greeted him from their doors, but he no longer needed to ask the way and soon reached the right door. It opened at once at his knock, and without even glancing at the familiar face of the woman, who remained standing by the door, he headed directly for the adjoining room. "There's no session today," the woman said. "Why wouldn't there be a session?" he asked, not really believing it. But the woman convinced him by opening the door to the next room. It was indeed empty and in its emptiness looked even more sordid than it had last Sunday. On the table, which stood unchanged on the platform, lay several books. "Can I look at the books?" K. asked, not out of any particular curiosity, but simply so that his presence was not entirely pointless. "No," said the woman and shut the door again, "that's not allowed. Those books belong to the examining magistrate." "Oh, I see," said K. and nodded, "they're probably law books, and it's in the nature of this judicial system that one is condemned not only in innocence but also in ignorance." "It must be," said the woman, who hadn't really understood him. "Well, then I'll leave," said K. "Shall I give the examining magistrate any message?" asked the woman. "You know him?" K. asked. "Of course," said the woman, "after all, my husband is a court usher." Only then did K. see that the room, which had contained only a washtub last time, was now a fully furnished living room. The woman noticed his astonishment and said: "Yes, we live here rent free, but we have to move our furniture out on days when the court is in session. My husband's job has a few disadvantages." "It's not so much the room that astonishes me," said K., giving her an angry look, "as the fact that you're married." "Are you referring perhaps to the incident last session, when I interrupted your speech?" asked the woman. "Of course," said K., "today that's all over and practically forgotten, but it really angered me at the time. And now you yourself say you're a married woman." "It wasn't to your disadvantage to have your speech interrupted. You were judged quite unfavorably afterwards." "That may be," said K. brushing the remark aside, "but that doesn't excuse you." "I'm excused in the eyes of those who know me," said the woman, "the man who was embracing me has been persecuting me for a long time. I may not be tempting in general, but I am to him. There's no way to protect myself, even my husband has finally come to terms with it; he has to put up with it if he wants to keep his job, because the man involved is a student and will presumably become even more powerful. He's always after me; he left just before you arrived." "It fits in with all the rest," said K., "I'm not surprised." "You'd probably like to improve a few things around here?" the woman asked slowly and tentatively, as if she were saying something dangerous for her as well as for K. "I gathered that from your speech, which personally I liked a lot. Of course I heard only part of it, since I missed the beginning and at the end I was on the floor with the student." "It's so disgusting here," she said after a pause, and took K.'s hand. "Do you think you'll be able to improve things?" K. smiled and turned his hand slightly in her soft hands. "Actually," he said, "it's not my job to improve things here, as you put it, and if you said that to someone like the examining magistrate you'd be laughed at or punished. I certainly wouldn't have become involved in these matters of my own free will, and I would never have lost any sleep over the shortcomings of this judicial system. But because I was supposedly placed under arrest—I've been arrested, you see— I've been forced to take action in my own behalf. But if I can be of any help to you in the process, I'll of course be happy to do so. Not simply out of compassion, but because you can help me in turn." "How could I do that?" asked the woman. "By showing me those books on the table now, for example." "But of course," cried the woman, dragging him quickly after her. They were old dog-eared books; one of the bindings was almost split in two at the spine, the covers barely hanging by the cords. "How dirty everything is," said K., shaking his head, and before K. could reach for the books, the woman wiped at least some of the dust off with her apron. K. opened the book on top, and an indecent picture was revealed. A man and a woman were sitting naked on a divan; the obscene intention of the artist was obvious, but his ineptitude was so great that in the end there was nothing to be seen but a man and woman, emerging far too corporeally from the picture, sitting rigidly upright, and due to the poor perspective, turn-ing toward each other quite awkwardly. K. didn't leaf through any further, but simply opened to the frontispiece of the second book, a novel entitled *The Torments Grete Suf-fered at the Hands of Her Husband Hans.* "So these are the law books they study," said K. "I'm to be judged by such men." "I'll help you," said the woman. "Do you want me to?" "Could you really do so without endangering yourself, after all, you said before that your husband was highly dependent on his superiors." "Even so, I'll help you," said the woman. "Come on, we have to discuss it. Forget about my danger; I only fear danger when I want to. Come on." She pointed to the platform and asked him to sit with her on the step. "You have beautiful dark eyes," she said, after they were seated, looking up into K.'s face, "they say I have beau-tiful eyes as well, but yours are much more beautiful. By the way, I was struck by them right away, the first time you came here. They were the reason I came into the assembly room later, which I never do otherwise; in fact, it's more or less for-bidden." "So that's all it is," thought K., "she's offering her-self to me; she's depraved, like everyone else around here, she's had her fill of court officials, which is understandable, so she accosts any stranger who comes along with a compliment about his eyes." And K. stood up without saying anything, as if he had spoken his thoughts aloud and thus explained his conduct to the woman. "I don't think you can help me," he said, "to be of real help a person would have to have connections with higher officials. But I'm sure you know only the low-level employees who hang around here in such great numbers. Of course those you know quite well, and you might be able to get somewhere with them, I don't doubt that, but the best you could hope to achieve through them would have no effect whatsoever on the final outcome of the trial. And you would have lost a few friends in the process. I don't want that. Keep your present relationship with these people, it seems to me you really can't do without it. I say that with some regret, because, to return your compliment at least in part, I like you, too, especially when you look at me as sadly as you do right now, although you really have no reason to. You're part of the group I have to fight, but you're quite comfortable among them; you even love the student, or if you don't love him, you at least prefer him to your husband. That was easy to tell from what you said." "No," she cried, remaining seated and simply reaching for K.'s hand, which he failed to withdraw quickly enough, "you can't leave now, you mustn't go away having judged me falsely. Could you really bring yourself to leave now? Am I really so worthless that you won't even do me the kindness of staying here a tiny bit longer?" "You misunderstand me," said K, sitting down, "if it means so much to you for me to stay, I'll do so gladly; after all, I have plenty of time, since I came here today thinking there would be a hearing. All I meant by what I said earlier was that you shouldn't try to do anything about my trial for me. But there's no reason to feel hurt by that either, knowing that I'm not at all concerned about the outcome of the trial, and would only laugh at a conviction. Assuming the trial ever comes to an actual conclusion, which I greatly doubt. I think it much more likely that the proceedings have already been dropped through laziness or forgetfulness or perhaps even fear on the part of the officials, or that they will be dropped in the near future. Of course it's always possible that they'll seem to continue the trial in hopes of some sort of sizable bribe, totally in vain, I can tell you right now, for I won't bribe anyone. You would be doing me a favor, however, if you would tell the examining magistrate, or some other person who enjoys spreading important information, that I will never bribe anyone, nor be brought to do so by any of the rich store of tricks these gentlemen no doubt possess. There's no chance of success, you can tell them that quite frankly. But they may well have realized that already, and even if they haven't, it makes no real difference to me for them to find out now. Afer all, it would only spare these gentlemen work, and me a few annoyances as well of course, ones I'll happily accept, if I know that each is a blow against them in turn. And I'll make sure that that's the case. Do you really know the examining magistrate?" "Of course," said the woman, "in fact he's the first person I thought of when I offered to help. I didn't know he was only a low-level official, but since you say so, that's probably right. Even so, I think that the report he sends to his superiors still has some influence. And he writes so many reports. You say the officials are lazy, but surely not all, and particularly not this examining magistrate, he writes a lot. Last Sunday, for example, the session went on almost into the evening. Everyone left, but the examining magistrate remained behind in the hall, and had me bring him a lamp; all I had was a little kitchen lamp, but he was satisfied with it and immediately started writing. In the meantime my husband, who had been off duty that particular Sunday, returned, we carried in our furniture, arranged our room once more, then some neighbors arrived, we talked a while longer by candlelight, in short, we forgot the examining magistrate and went to bed. Suddenly, that night, it must have been late at night by then, I awake and find the examining magistrate standing by my bed, shielding the lamp with his hand so that no light falls upon my husband, a needless precaution, since the way my husband sleeps the light wouldn't have awakened him anyway. I was so startled I almost screamed, but the examining magistrate was very friendly, cautioned me against crying out, whispered that he had been writing till then, that he was bringing the lamp back now, and that he would never forget the picture I made when he found me sleeping. I'm telling you all this simply to show that the examining magistrate really does write a lot of reports, especially about you: for your hearing was certainly one of the major events of the Sunday session. Such long reports surely can't be totally meaningless. But you can also see from this incident that the examining magistrate is interested in me, and it's precisely at this early stage, for he must have just noticed me, that I can have a major influence on him. And I now have other indications that he sets great store by me. Yesterday he sent me silk stockings through the student, whom he trusts, and who is his colleague, supposedly because I tidy up the courtroom, but that's only an excuse, because after all that's my duty and my husband gets paid for it. They're pretty stockings, see"—she stretched out her legs, pulled her dress up to her knees, and viewed her legs herself as well—"they're pretty stockings, but really they're too nice, and not suitable for me."

Suddenly she interrupted herself, placed her hand on K.'s as if to calm him, and whispered: "Hush, Bertold is watching us!" K. slowly lifted his gaze. In the doorway to the courtroom stood a young man; he was short, with slightly crooked legs, and attempted to lend himself an air of dignity by means of a short, scraggly reddish beard he kept fingering. K. looked at him with curiosity; he was the first student of the unknown system of jurisprudence he'd met on more or less human terms, a man who would presumably advance at some stage to higher official positions. The student, on the other hand, seemed to pay no attention at all to K., but simply gestured to the woman with one finger, which he removed for a moment from his beard, and walked over to the window; the woman bent down to K. and whispered: "Don't be angry with me, please, please don't, and don't think badly of me; I have to go to him now, to this horrible man, just look at his bandy legs. But I'll come right back, and then I'll go with you; if you'll take me along, I'll go anywhere you wish, you can do with me what you like, I'll be happy to get out of here for as long as I can, the best of course would be forever." She stroked K.'s hand once more, sprang up, and ran to the window. Instinctively, K. grabbed for her hand in the empty air. The woman did tempt him, and no matter how hard he thought about it, he could see no good reason not to give in to that temptation. The fleeting objection that the woman was ensnaring him on the court's behalf he easily brushed aside. How could she ensnare him? Wouldn't he still be free enough to simply smash the entire court, at least insofar as it touched him? Couldn't he grant himself that small degree of self-confidence? And her offer of help sounded sincere, and was perhaps not without value. And there was perhaps no better way to revenge himself upon the examining magistrate and his retinue than taking this woman away from them for himself. Then the time might come when, late one night, after long hours of exhausting labor on his false reports about K., the examining magistrate would find the bed of the woman empty. And empty because she belonged to K., because this woman at the window, this voluptuous, supple, warm body in a dark dress of heavy, coarse material, belonged to K., and K. alone.

Once he had overcome his doubts about the woman in this way, the low conversation at the window grew too long for him, and he rapped on the platform with his knuckle, then with his fist. The student glanced briefly at K. over the woman's shoulder, but continued undisturbed; in fact he drew even closer to the woman and put his arms around her. She lowered her head as if she were listening closely to him, and he kissed her loudly on the neck as she leaned over, not even really interrupting what he was saying. Seeing in this a confirmation of the tyranny the student exercised over the woman, as she had complained, K. rose and paced up and down the room. Glancing sideways toward the student, he contemplated the quickest way to get rid of him, and so he was happy enough when the student, apparently disturbed by K.'s pacing, which had meanwhile degenerated into full-blown tromping, remarked: "If you're impatient, why don't you leave? You could have left even earlier, no one would have missed you. In fact you should have left the moment I arrived, and as quickly as possible." This remark may have been an outburst of utmost anger, but it contained as well the arrogance of a future court official speaking to an unpopular defendant. K. paused quite close to him and said with a smile: "I'm impatient, that's true, but the easiest way to alleviate my impatience is for you to leave. But if by chance you came here to study—I hear you're a student—I'll gladly leave you to yourself and go off with this woman. By the way, you have a lot more studying to do before you can become a judge. I don't really know much about your judicial system yet, but I take it that crass language alone, of the sort you're certainly shamelessly good at already, is hardly sufficient." "They shouldn't have allowed him to run around so freely," said the student, as if offering the woman an explanation for K.'s insulting remarks, "it was a mistake. I told the examining magistrate so. He should at least have been confined to his room between interrogations. Sometimes I just don't understand the examining magistrate." "You're wasting your breath," said K., stretching out his hand toward the woman. "Come on." "Aha," said the student, "no, no, you're not going to get her," and with a strength one wouldn't have expected, he lifted her in one arm and ran to the door, his back bent, gazing up at her tenderly. A certain fear of K. was unmistakable in his action, yet he dared to provoke K. even further by stroking and squeezing the woman's arm with his free hand. K. ran along beside him a few steps, ready to grab him, and if necessary to throttle him, when the woman said: "It's no use, the examining magistrate has sent for me, I can't go with you, this little monster," she said, stroking the student's face, "this little monster won't let me go." "And you don't want to be freed," yelled K., placing his hand on the shoulder of the student, who snapped at it with his teeth. "No," the woman cried out, and pushed K. away with both hands, "no, no, don't do that, what do you think you're doing! I'll be ruined. Let go of him, oh please, let go of him. He's just following the examining magistrate's orders and carrying me to him." "Then let him go, and I hope I never see you again," said K. in enraged disappointment, and shoved the student in the back so sharply that he stumbled for a moment, only to leap higher into the air with his burden in joy at not having fallen. K. followed them slowly; he realized that this was the first clear defeat he had suffered at the hands of these people. Of course there was no reason to let that worry him, he had suffered defeat only because he had sought to do battle. If he stayed home and led his normal life he was infinitely superior to any of these people, and could kick any one of them out of his path. And he pictured how funny it would be, for example, to see this miserable student, this puffed-up child, this bandy-legged, bearded fellow, kneeling at Elsa's bedside, clutching his hands and begging for mercy. This vision pleased K. so greatly that he decided, if the opportunity ever arose, to take the student along to Elsa one day.

Out of curiosity, K. hurried to the door, wanting to see where the woman was being taken; the student surely wouldn't carry her through the streets in his arms. It turned out the path was much shorter. Directly across from the apartment door a narrow flight of wooden stairs led upward, probably to an attic area; they made a turn, so you couldn't see where they ended. The student was carrying the woman up these stairs, very slowly now, and groaning, for he was weakened by his previous efforts. The woman waved down at K., and tried to show by a shrug of her shoulders that the abduction wasn't her fault, but there wasn't a great deal of regret in the gesture. K. looked at her without expression, like a stranger, wishing to show neither his disappointment, nor that he could easily overcome it.

The two had already disappeared, but K. was still standing in the doorway. He could only assume that the woman had not only deceived him, but lied to him as well by saying she was being carried to the examining magistrate. The examining magistrate surely wasn't sitting around waiting for her in the attic. The wooden steps explained nothing, no matter how long one stared at them. Then K. noticed a small sign beside the stairs, walked over, and read in a childish, awkward script: "Law Court Offices Upstairs." So the law court offices were in the attic of this apartment building? That was an arrangement scarcely calculated to inspire much respect, and for a defendant it was reassuring to imagine what limited funds this court must have at its disposal if its offices were located where tenants who were themselves among the poorest of the poor tossed their useless trash. Of course the possibility could not be ruled out that there was enough money, but that the officials grabbed it before it could be used for the court's purposes. Based on K.'s prior experience that even seemed likely, and although such a dissolute court was humiliating for a defendant, in the end it was even more reassuring than a poverty-stricken court would have been. Now K. could see why they'd been ashamed to invite the defendant to these garrets for the initial interrogation, and chose instead to pester him in his lodgings. What a position K. was in, after all, compared to the judge who sat in a garret, while he himself had a large office in the bank, with a waiting room, and could look down upon the busy city square through a huge plate-glass window. Of course he received no supplementary income from bribes or embezzlement, and he couldn't have an assistant carry a woman in his arms to his office for him. But K. would gladly waive that right, at least in this life.

K. was still standing in front of the sign when a man came up the stairs, peered through the open door into the living room, from which the hall of inquiry could be seen as well, and finally asked K. if he had seen a woman there a short while ago. "You're the court usher, aren't you?" K. asked. "Yes," said the man, "oh, you're the defendant K., now I recognize you too, welcome." And he held out his hand to K., who hadn't expected that at all. "But there's no session scheduled today," the court usher said, as K. remained silent. "I know," K. said, and observed the court usher's civilian jacket, which, in addition to the normal buttons, bore as sole emblem of his office two gold buttons, which seemed to have been taken off an old officer's uniform. "I spoke with your wife a short while ago. She's not here anymore. The student carried her off to the examining magistrate." "You see," said the court usher, "they're always taking her away from me. Today is Sunday, and I have no official duties, but just to get me out of the way, they send me off with a message that's meaningless anyway. And in fact I'm not sent far, so that the hope remains that if I really hurry, I might get back in time. I run as fast as I can to the office they've sent me to, shout my message so breathlessly through the half-open door that they probably don't understand it, and race back again, but the student has moved even faster than I have, and of course he doesn't have as far to go, he has only to run down the attic stairs. If I weren't so dependent on them, I would have long

since crushed the student against this wall. Right here next to
the sign. I keep dreaming about it. He's squashed flat a little
above floor level here, his arms stretched out, his fingers
spread, his crooked legs curved in a circle with blood spat-
tered all about. But it's just been a dream up to now."
"There's nothing else you can do?" K. asked with a smile.
"I don't know of anything," said the court usher. "And now
it's getting worse: up to this point he's just carried her off for
himself, but now, as I've been expecting for some time of
course, he's carrying her to the examining magistrate as
well." "Does your wife bear no blame at all in the matter?"
asked K.; he had to control himself as he asked this question,
so strong was the jealousy he too now felt. "Of course," said
the court usher, "she bears the greatest blame of all. She
threw herself at him. As for him, he chases all the women. In
this building alone, he's already been thrown out of five
apartments he wormed his way into. Of course my wife is the
most beautiful woman in the building, and I'm the only one
who doesn't dare protect himself." "If that's the way it is,
then obviously nothing can be done," said K. "Why not?"
asked the court usher. "Someone needs to give the student,
who's a coward, a thorough flogging the next time he tries to
touch my wife, so he'll never try it again. But I can't do it
myself, and no one will do me the favor, because they all fear
his power. Only a man like you could do it." "Why me?"
asked K. in astonishment. "You are a defendant, after all,"
said the court usher. "Yes," said K., "but I should fear his
influence all the more, not on the outcome of the trial perhaps, but at least on the preliminary investigation." "Yes, of
course," said the court usher, as if K.'s opinion were equally
valid. "But as a rule we don't conduct pointless trials." "I

don't share your opinion," said K., "but that needn't keep me from dealing with the student when the occasion arises." "I would be very grateful to you," said the court usher somewhat formally, not really seeming to believe that his greatest wish could ever be fulfilled. "There may be other officials," K. went on, "perhaps all of them, who deserve the same treatment." "Oh, yes," said the court usher, as if that were self-evident. Then he gazed at K. with a look of trust he hadn't shown before, in spite of all his friendliness, and added: "People are always rebelling." But the conversation appeared to have taken a slightly uncomfortable turn in his opinion, for he broke it off by saying: "Now I have to report to the law court offices. Do you want to come along?" "I don't have any business there," said K. "You could look around the offices. No one will bother you." "Are they worth seeing?" asked K. hesitantly, but feeling a strong urge to go along. "Well," said the court usher, "I just thought you'd be interested." "Fine," said K. at last, "I'll come along," and he ran up the stairs more quickly than the court usher.

As he entered he almost stumbled, for there was an extra step beyond the door. "They don't show much consideration for the public," he said. "They show no consideration of any kind," said the court usher, "just look at this waiting room." It was a long hallway, with ill-fitting doors leading to the individual offices of the attic. Although there was no direct source of light, it was not completely dark, since some of the offices had been constructed with open wooden grillwork instead of solid wooden boards facing the hall, reaching to the ceiling to be sure, through which some light penetrated, and beyond which a few officials were visible writing at desks, or standing for the moment near the grille, looking out through the gaps at the people in the hallway. There were very few people in the hallway, probably because it was Sunday. They made a very modest impression. Spaced out at nearly regular intervals, they sat in two rows on long wooden benches situated on both sides of the hallway. All of them were carelessly dressed, in spite of the fact that most, to judge by their expression, their posture, the style of their beards, and numerous other small details difficult to pin down, belonged to the upper classes. Since no coathooks were available, they had placed their hats beneath the bench, probably following each other's lead. As those sitting closest to the door caught sight of K. and the court usher, they rose in greeting; when those behind them noticed, they thought they had to do so as well, so that all of them rose as the two men passed by. They never straightened entirely; backs bowed and knees bent, they stood like beggars in the street. K. waited for the court usher, who was a few steps behind him, and said: "How humbled they must be." "Yes," said the court usher, "they're defendants, everyone you see is a defendant." "Really?" said K. "Then they're my colleagues." And he turned to the closest one, a tall slim man whose hair was already turning gray. "What is it you're waiting for?" K. asked politely. The unexpected question, however, confused the man, which was even more embarrassing since he was obviously a man of the world, who would certainly have retained his self-confidence elsewhere and did not easily relinquish the superiority he had attained over so many others. But here he couldn't even answer such a simple question and looked at the others as if it were their duty to come to his aid, and as if no one could expect an answer from him if such aid were not forthcoming. Then the court usher stepped forward and said, trying to calm the man and lend him encouragement: "The gentleman is only asking what you're waiting for. Go ahead and answer." The no doubt familiar voice of the court usher was more effective: "I'm waiting—" he began, and hesitated. He had apparently chosen this opening in order to answer the question exactly as it was posed, but could not think how to go on now. A few among those waiting had drawn near and gathered about them; the court usher said to them: "Get back, get back, keep the hallway clear." They retreated somewhat, but did not return to their original places. In the meantime the man who had been questioned had pulled himself together and even managed a faint smile as he answered: "A month ago I submitted several petitions to hear evidence in my case, and I'm waiting for them to be acted upon." "You seem to be taking great pains," said K. "Yes," said the man, "after all, it's my case." "Not everyone shares your view," said K., "for example I'm a defendant too, but I'll be blessed if I've submitted a petition to hear evidence or done anything at all of that sort. Do you really think it's necessary?" "I'm not certain," said the man, once more completely unsure of himself; he apparently thought K. was making fun of him, and would have evidently preferred to repeat his earlier answer in full, for fear of making some new mistake, but in the face of K.'s impatient gaze he simply said: "For my part, I've submitted petitions to hear evidence." "You probably don't think I'm really a defendant," K. said. "Oh, yes, certainly," said the man, and stepped aside slightly, but anxiety, not belief, lay in his reply. "So you don't believe me?" asked K., seizing the man by the arm, unconsciously provoked by his humbleness, as if he wished to compel him to believe. He had no intention of hurting him, however, and squeezed quite gently, but even so the man screamed as if K. had applied a pair of red-hot pincers, and not merely two fingers. With this ridiculous outcry K. finally had enough of the man; if he didn't believe he was a defendant, so much the better; perhaps he even took him for a judge. And now, in parting, he indeed squeezed him harder, pushed him back down onto the bench, and walked on. "Most defendants are so sensitive," said the court usher. Behind them almost all those who were waiting gathered around the man, who had already stopped screaming, apparently quizzing him closely about the incident. K. was now approached by a guard, who could be recognized chiefly by a saber whose scabbard, to judge by its color, was made of aluminum. K. was amazed by this and even reached out toward it. The guard, who had been drawn by the screams, asked what had happened. The court usher attempted to pacify him with a few words, but the guard said he'd have to look into it himself, saluted and hurried on, taking extremely rapid but quite short steps, probably hindered by gout.

K. soon ceased worrying about him and the people in the hallway, particularly since he saw, about halfway down the hall, a turn to the right through an opening with no door. He checked with the court usher whether it was the right way, the court usher nodded, and K. took the turn. It annoyed him that he always had to walk a pace or two ahead of the court usher, since, given the location, it might appear that he was an arrested man under escort. So he slowed up several times for the court usher, who, however, kept hanging back. Finally, to put an end to his discomfort, K. said: "Well, I've seen what things look like here, and I'm ready to leave." "You haven't seen everything yet," said the court usher, completely without guile. "I don't want to see everything," said K., who was in fact feeling quite tired, "I want to leave, where's the exit?" "Surely you're not lost already," asked the court usher in amazement, "you go to the corner there, turn right and go straight down the hall to the door." "Come with me," said K. "Show me the way; I'll miss it, there are so many ways here." "It's the only way," said the court usher, reproachfully now, "I can't go back with you; I have to deliver my report, and I've already lost a good deal of time because of you." "Come with me," K. repeated more sharply, as if he had finally caught the court usher in a lie. "Don't shout so," whispered the court usher, "there are offices all around here. If you don't want to go back by yourself, then come along with me a ways, or wait here until I've delivered my report, then I'll gladly go back with you." "No, no," said K., "I won't wait and you have to go with me now." K. hadn't even looked around the room he was in; not until one of the many wooden doors surrounding him opened did he glance over. A young woman, no doubt drawn by K.'s loud voice, stepped in and asked: "May I help you, sir?" Behind her in the distance a man could be seen approaching in the semidarkness. K. looked at the court usher. After all, he'd said that no one would pay any attention to K., and now here came two people already; it wouldn't take much and the official bureaucracy would notice him and demand an explanation for his presence. The only reasonable and acceptable one was that he was a defendant trying to discover the date of his next hearing, but that was precisely the explanation he didn't wish to give, particularly since it wasn't true, for he had come out of pure curiosity or, even less acceptable as an explanation, out of a desire to confirm that the interior of this judicial system was just as repugnant as its exterior. And it seemed that he had been right in that assumption; he had no wish to intrude any further, he was inhibited enough by what he had already seen, and he was certainly in no mood now to confront some high official who might appear from behind any door; he wanted to leave, with the court usher or alone if need be.

But the way he was silently standing there must have been striking, and the young woman and the court usher were actually looking at him as if they thought he was about to undergo some profound metamorphosis at any moment, one they didn't want to miss. And in the doorway stood the man K. had noticed in the background earlier, holding on tightly to the lintel of the low door and rocking back and forth slightly on the tips of his toes, like an impatient spectator. It was the young woman, however, who first realized that K.'s behavior was the result of a slight indisposition; she brought him a chair and asked: "Wouldn't you like to sit down?" K. sat down immediately and propped his elbows on the arms of the chair for better support. "You're a little dizzy, aren't you?" she asked him. Her face was now quite near; it bore the severe expression some young women have precisely in the bloom of youth. "Don't worry," she said, "there's nothing unusual about that here, almost everyone has an attack like this the first time. You are here for the first time? Well, you see then, it's nothing at all unusual. The sun beats down on the attic beams and the hot wood makes the air terribly thick and stifling. That's why this isn't such a good location for the offices, in spite of the many other advantages it offers. But as far as the air is concerned, on days when the traffic of involved parties is heavy you can hardly breathe, and that's

almost daily. Then if you take into consideration that a great
deal of wash is hung out here to dry as well—the tenants
can't be entirely forbidden from doing so—it will come as no
surprise that you feel a little sick. But in the end people get
quite used to the air. When you come here the second or third
time, you'll hardly notice the stuffiness at all. Do you feel better yet?" K. didn't reply; he was too embarrassed that this
sudden weakness had placed him at these people's mercy;
moreover, now that he knew the cause of his nausea he didn't
feel better, but instead a little worse. The young woman
noticed this right away, picked up a hooked pole leaning
against the wall and, to give K. a little fresh air, pushed open
a small hatch directly above K. that led outside. But so much
soot fell in that the young woman had to close the hatch
again immediately and wipe the soot from K.'s hands with
her handkerchief, since K. was too tired to do it himself. He
would gladly have remained sitting there quietly until he had
gathered the strength to leave, and the less attention they
paid to him, the sooner that would happen. But now the
young woman added: "You can't stay here, we're interrupting the flow of traffic"—K. looked around to see what traffic
he could possibly be interrupting—"if you want, I'll take you
to the infirmary." "Help me please," she said to the man in
the doorway, who approached at once. But K. didn't want to
go to the infirmary; that was precisely what he wanted to
avoid, being led farther on, for the farther he went, the worse
things would get. So he said, "I can walk now," and stood up
shakily, spoiled by the comfort of sitting. But then he couldn't
hold himself upright. "I can't do it," he said, shaking his
head, and sat down again with a sigh. He remembered the
court usher, who could easily lead him out in spite of every-

thing, but he appeared to be long gone; K. peered between
the young woman and the man, who were standing in front
of him, but couldn't find the court usher.

"I believe," said the man, who was elegantly dressed, with
a striking gray waistcoat that ended in two sharply tailored
points, "the gentleman's illness can be traced to the air in
here, so it would be best, and please him most, if we simply
skipped the infirmary and led him out of the law offices."
"That's it," K. cried out, so overjoyed he barely let the man
finish his sentence, "I'm sure I'll feel better soon, I'm not that
weak, I just need a little support under the arms, I won't be
much trouble, it's not very far, just take me to the door, I'll sit
on the steps a bit and be fine soon, I never have attacks like
this, it surprised me too. After all, I'm an official myself and
I'm used to office air, but it does seem really bad here, you say
so yourself. Would you be so kind as to help me a little, I'm
dizzy, and I feel sick when I stand on my own." And he lifted
his shoulders to make it easier for the others to grab him
under the arms.

But the man didn't follow his suggestion; instead he kept
his hands calmly in his pockets and laughed aloud. "You
see," he said to the young woman, "I hit the nail on the head.
It's only here that the gentleman feels unwell, not in general."
The young woman smiled too, but she tapped the man lightly
on the arm with her fingertips, as if he'd carried a joke with
K. too far. "Oh, don't worry," the man said, still laughing,
"of course I'll show the gentleman out." "All right then,"
said the young woman, inclining her charming head for a
moment. "Don't attach too much meaning to his laughter,"
the young woman said to K., who had lapsed into dejection
again, staring vacantly, and didn't seem in need of any expla-

nation, "this gentleman—may I introduce you?" (the man gave his permission with a wave of his hand) "—this gentleman is our information officer. He provides waiting parties with any information they may need, and since our judicial system is not very well known among the general population, a great deal of information is requested. He has an answer for every question; you can try him out if you feel like it. But that's not his only asset, a second is his elegant dress. We— the staff that is—decided that the information officer, who's always the first person the parties meet and the one they deal with most often, should be dressed elegantly, to create a respectable first impression. The rest of us, sadly enough, are, as you can see in my own case, poorly dressed, in old-fashioned clothes; it doesn't make much sense to spend anything on clothing, since we're almost always in the offices, and even sleep here. But as I said, in the information officer's case we thought fancy clothes were necessary. But since we couldn't get them from the administration, which is funny about that sort of thing, we took up a collection—the parties pitched in too—and we bought him this handsome suit and a few others as well. So everything was set to make a good impression, but he ruins it by the way he laughs, which startles people." "So it does," the man said with an annoyed air, "but I don't understand, Fräulein, why you're telling this gentleman all our intimate secrets, or more accurately, forcing them upon him, since he has no interest in knowing them. Just look at him sitting there, obviously immersed in his own affairs." K. didn't even feel like objecting; the young woman probably meant well; perhaps she was trying to take his mind off things, or give him a chance to pull himself together, but she'd chosen the wrong method. "I had to explain why you

laughed," the young woman said. "After all, it was insulting." "I think he'd forgive much worse insults if I would just
show him the way out." K. said nothing, he didn't even look
up; he put up with the fact that the two were discussing him
like a case, indeed, he preferred it that way. But suddenly he
felt the hand of the information officer on one arm and the
hand of the young woman on the other. "Up with you now,
you feeble fellow," said the information officer. "Thank you
both very much," said K. pleasantly surprised, rose slowly,
and guided the others' hands to the places where he most
needed their support. "It seems like I'm overly concerned to
place the information officer in a good light," the young
woman said softly in K.'s ear, as they approached the hallway, "but believe me, what I say is true. He's not hard-
hearted. It's not his duty to accompany sick parties out and
yet he does, as you can see. Perhaps none of us is hard-
hearted, perhaps we'd all like to help, but as court officials it
can easily appear that we're hard-hearted and don't want to
help anyone. That really bothers me." "Wouldn't you like to
sit here for a bit?" asked the information officer; they were
already in the hallway, directly in front of the defendant K.
had spoken to earlier. K. was almost ashamed to face him:
earlier he had stood so erect before him, while now two people had to hold him up, the information officer balanced his
hat on his outspread fingers, and his tousled hair fell across
his sweat-covered brow. But the defendant seemed to notice
none of this; he stood humbly before the information officer,
who stared right past him, and merely attempted to excuse
his presence. "I realize there can't be any response to my petitions today," he said. "But I came anyway; I thought I could
at least wait here, since it's Sunday, and I have plenty of time

and won't disturb anyone." "You don't have to be so apologetic about it," said the information officer, "your concern is quite praiseworthy; of course you're taking up space unnecessarily, but as long as it doesn't begin to annoy me, I certainly won't hinder you from following the course of your affair in detail. Having seen others who scandalously neglect their duty, one learns to be patient with people like you. You may be seated." "He really knows how to talk to the parties," whispered the young woman. K. nodded, but immediately flared up as the information officer asked him again: "Wouldn't you like to sit down here?" "No," said K., "I don't want to rest." He had said it as firmly as he could, but in reality it would have done him a great deal of good to sit down; he felt seasick. He thought he was on a ship, rolling in heavy seas. It seemed to him that the waters were pounding against the wooden walls, there was a roar from the depths of the hallway like the sound of breaking waves, the hallway seemed to pitch and roll, lifting and lowering the waiting clients on both sides. That made the calm demeanor of the young woman and man who led him even more incomprehensible. He was at their mercy; if they let go of him, he would fall like a plank. Sharp glances shot back and forth from their small eyes; K. felt their steady tread without matching it, for he was practically carried along from step to step. He realized at last that they were speaking to him, but he couldn't understand them; he heard only the noise that filled everything, through which a steady, high-pitched sound like a siren seemed to emerge. "Louder," he whispered with bowed head, and was ashamed, for he knew that they had spoken loudly enough, even though he hadn't understood. Then finally, as if the wall had split open before him, a draft of fresh air reached him, and he heard beside him: "First he wants to leave, then you can tell him a hundred times that this is the exit and he doesn't move." K. saw that he was standing at the outer door, which the young woman had opened. Instantly, all his strength seemed to return; to get a foretaste of freedom he stepped down immediately onto the first step and from there took leave of his escorts, who bowed to him. "Thank you very much," he said again, shaking hands with both of them repeatedly, stopping only when he thought he noticed that they were unable to bear the comparatively fresh air from the stairway, accustomed as they were to the air in the offices of the court. They could hardly reply, and the young woman might have fallen had K. not shut the door as quickly as possible. K. stood quietly for a moment, smoothed his hair into place with the help of a pocket mirror, picked up his hat, which was lying on the landing below—the information officer must have tossed it there—and then raced down the steps with such long, energetic leaps that he was almost frightened by the sudden change. His normally sound constitution had never provided him with such surprises before. Was his body going to rebel and offer him a new trial, since he was handling the old one so easily? He didn't entirely rule out the thought of consulting a doctor at the first opportunity; in any case—and here he could advise himself—he would spend his Sunday mornings more profitably than this from now on.

THE FLOGGER

A few evenings later, as K. passed through the corridor that led from his office to the main staircase—he was almost the last to leave that night, only two assistants in shipping were still at work in the small circle of light from a single bulb—he heard the sound of groans behind a door that he had always assumed led to a mere junk room, though he had never seen it himself. He stopped in amazement and listened again to see if he might not be mistaken—it was quiet for a little while, but then the groans came again. —At first, feeling he might need a witness, he was about to call one of the assistants, but then he was seized by such uncontrollable curiosity that he practically tore the door open. It was, as he had suspected, a junk room. Old obsolete printed forms and overturned empty ceramic ink bottles lay beyond the threshold. In the little room itself, however, stood three men, stooping beneath the low ceiling. A candle stuck on a shelf provided light. "What's going on here?" K. blurted out in his excitement, but not loudly. One man, who was apparently in charge of the others and drew K.'s attention first, was got up in some sort of dark leather garment that left his neck and upper chest, as well as his entire arms, bare. He didn't reply. But the other two cried out: "Sir! We're to be flogged because you complained about us to the examining magistrate." And only then did K. recognize that it was indeed the guards Franz and Willem, and that the third man held a rod in his hand to flog them with. "Well now," said K. staring at them, "I didn't complain, I just told them what went on in my lodgings. And your behavior wasn't exactly impeccable." "Sir," said Willem, while Franz apparently tried to seek safety behind him from the third man, "if you knew how poorly we're paid, you'd judge us more kindly. I have a family to feed and Franz here wants to get married, you try to make money however you can, just working isn't enough, no matter how hard you try, I was tempted by your fine undergarments, guards are forbidden to act that way of course, it was wrong, but it's a tradition that the undergarments belong to the guards, it's always been that way, believe me; and you can see why, what difference do such things make to a person unlucky enough to be arrested. If he makes it public, of course, then punishment must follow." "I didn't know any of that, and I certainly didn't demand your punishment, it was a matter of principle." "Franz," Willem turned to the other guard, "didn't I tell you the gentleman didn't demand our punishment? Now, as you hear, he didn't even realize we'd have to be punished."

"Don't be swayed by that sort of talk," the third man said to K., "their punishment is as just as it is inevitable." "Don't listen to him," said Willem, interrupting himself only to lift a hand, across which he had received a blow of the rod, quickly to his mouth, "we're only being punished because you reported us. Otherwise nothing would have happened, even if they had found out what we had done. Do you call that justice? Both of us have proved ourselves as guards over a long period of time, especially me—you have to admit we did a good job from the authorities' point of view—we had prospects for advancement and would soon have been floggers ourselves, like him, who was simply fortunate enough never to be reported by anyone, for such reports are really quite rare. And now everything is lost, sir, our careers are finished, we'll have to work at a much lower level than a guard, and undergo this terribly painful flogging as well." "Can a rod cause that much pain?" K. asked, and examined the rod, which the flogger swung before him. "We have to strip completely," said Willem. "Oh, I see," said K., looking more closely at the flogger, who had a sailor's tan and a savage, ruddy face. "Is there any possibility of sparing these two a flogging?" he asked him. "No," said the flogger, and shook his head with a smile. "Strip," he ordered the guards. And to K. he said: "You mustn't believe everything they say. They're already a bit weak in the head because they're so afraid of the flogging. What this one was saying, for example"—he pointed at Willem—"about his prospective career is totally ridiculous. Look how overweight he is—the first blows of the rod will be lost in fat. —Do you know how he got so fat? He's in the habit of eating the breakfast of anyone who's arrested. Didn't he eat yours as well? Well, what did I tell

you? But a man with a belly like that can never become a
flogger, it's totally out of the question." "There are floggers
like me," insisted Willem, who was just undoing his belt.
"No!" said the flogger, stroking him across the neck with the
rod in a way that made him twitch, "you shouldn't be listening, you should be stripping." "I'll reward you well if you'll
let them go," said K., taking out his wallet without looking at
the flogger again, such matters being best conducted by both
parties with lowered eyes. "Then you'll probably report me
too," said the flogger, "and earn me a flogging as well. No
thanks!" "Be reasonable," said K., "if I'd wanted to have
these two punished, I wouldn't be trying to buy them off. I
could simply shut the door, close my eyes and ears, and head
home. But I'm not doing that, instead I'm serious about getting them off; if I'd suspected they'd be punished, or even
known they faced possible punishment, I would never have
mentioned their names. Because I don't even consider them
guilty; it's the organization that's guilty, it's the high officials
who are guilty." "That's right," cried the guards, and immediately received a blow across their now bare backs. "If you
had a high judge here beneath your rod," said K., pressing
down the rod, which was about to rise again as he spoke, "I
really wouldn't stop you from flailing away; on the contrary,
I'd pay you extra, to strengthen you in your good work." "I
believe what you say," said the flogger, "but I can't be bribed.
I've been hired to flog, and flog I will." The guard Franz, who
had kept somewhat in the background up to that point, perhaps in hope of a favorable outcome based on K.'s interven-
tion, now stepped to the door dressed only in his trousers, fell
to his knees, and clinging to K.'s arm whispered: "If you can't
manage to get us both off, please try to at least save me.

Willem is older than me, less sensitive in every way, and he already received a minor flogging once a few years ago, but I've never been disgraced that way, and was only following the lead of Willem, who is my mentor in all things good and bad. My poor bride is waiting for me below in front of the bank; I'm so terribly ashamed." He dried his tearstained face on K.'s jacket. "I'm not waiting any longer," said the flogger, seized the rod with both hands, and laid into Franz, while Willem cowered in a corner and peeked over without daring to turn his head. The scream that Franz expelled rose steady and unchanging, scarcely human, as if it came from some tortured instrument; the whole corridor rang with it, the entire building would hear. "Don't scream," cried K., unable to stop himself, and as he looked intently in the direction from which the assistants would be coming, he pushed Franz, not hard, but hard enough that the witless man fell to the floor and clawed convulsively about with his hands; he didn't escape the blows, however, the rod found him on the floor as well, as he writhed beneath it, its tip swung up and down steadily. And in the distance an assistant had already appeared, and a few steps behind him a second one. K. slammed the door quickly, stepped up to a nearby courtyard window, and opened it. The screams had ceased completely. To keep the assistants from coming nearer, he called out: "It's me." "Good evening, sir," the call came back. "Has anything happened?" "No, no," K. replied, "it's just a dog howling in the courtyard." When the assistants still didn't stir, he added: "You can go on with your work." And to avoid getting involved in a conversation with them, he leaned out the window. When he looked down the corridor again a while later, they were gone. But now K. remained at the window; he didn't dare go into the junk room, and he didn't want to go home either. The small, rectangular courtyard he looked down upon was lined with offices; all the windows were dark by now, only the highest ones catching a reflection of the moon. K. peered down intently, trying to penetrate the darkness of a corner of the courtyard where several pushcarts had been shoved together. It tormented him that he had been unable to prevent the flogging, but it wasn't his fault; if Franz hadn't screamed—of course it must have hurt terribly, but at critical moments you have to control yourself—if he hadn't screamed, K. could very probably have still found some way to convince the flogger. If the entire lowest level of the bureaucracy was made up of riff-raff, why should the flogger, who had the most inhuman job of all, be an exception; K. had also taken close note of the way his eyes gleamed at the sight of the bank note; he had obviously taken the flogging so seriously solely to raise the amount of the bribe. And K. wouldn't have been stingy, he really wanted to get the guards off; having already begun to fight corruption in the judicial system, it was only natural to take this approach as well. But the moment Franz started screaming, it was all over of course. K. couldn't permit the assistants, and perhaps all sorts of other people, to arrive and catch him negotiating with this bunch in the junk room. No one could really demand such a sacrifice of him. If he had intended one, it would almost have been simpler for K. to strip and offer himself to the flogger in place of the guards. The flogger would hardly have accepted this substitution, however, since it would have been a grave dereliction of duty with nothing to gain, and no doubt a double dereliction, since surely no employee of the court had the right to harm him while his case was still in progress. Of course there might be special instructions in this respect as well. In any case, K. could not have done otherwise than slam the door, even though he had by no means escaped all danger by doing so even now. That he had shoved Franz at the end was unfortunate, and could only be excused by his state of agitation.

In the distance he heard the steps of the assistants; in order not to attract their attention, he closed the window and walked toward the main staircase. He stopped for a moment at the door of the junk room and listened. Silence reigned. The man might have beaten the guards to death; after all, they were completely in his power. K. reached toward the door handle, but then pulled back his hand. He couldn't help anyone now, and the assistants would be coming at any moment; he vowed to bring the subject up again, however, and insofar as it was within his power, to punish appropriately those who were truly guilty, the high officials, not one of whom had yet dared to show himself to him. As he descended the front steps of the bank, he took careful note of all the passersby, but there was no young woman in sight, even in the distance, who might have been waiting for someone. Franz's claim that his bride was waiting for him thus proved to be a lie, understandable of course, intended solely to awaken greater pity.

The next day K. still couldn't get the guards off his mind; he had difficulty concentrating on his work, and in order to finish up he had to stay at the office slightly longer than he had the day before. As he passed by the junk room again on his way home, he opened the door as if by habit. What he saw, in place of the expected darkness, bewildered him completely. Everything was unchanged, just as he had found it the previous evening when he opened the door. The printed forms and ink bottles just beyond the threshold, the flogger with the rod, the guards, still completely clothed, the candle on the shelf, and the guards began to wail, crying out: "Sir!" K. slammed the door shut at once and pounded his fists against it, as if to close it more tightly. Almost in tears, he ran to the assistants, who were working quietly at the copying press and paused in their work with astonishment. "Clear out that junk room once and for all," he cried. "We're drowning in filth." The assistants said they would be happy to do it the next day, and K. nodded; he couldn't force them to do it this late in the evening, as he had at first intended. He sat down for a moment to keep the assistants around a while longer, shuffled through a few copies, trying to give the impression that he was checking them over, and then, since he realized the assistants wouldn't dare leave with him, he headed for home, tired and with his mind a blank.

THE UNCLE

LENI

One afternoon—it was just before the final mail pickup and K. was very busy—K.'s Uncle Karl, a small landowner from the country, shoved his way between two assistants bringing in documents and entered the room. K. felt less alarm at seeing him than he had some time ago imagining his arrival. His uncle was bound to come, K. had been sure of that for over a month. Even back then he could picture him, slightly stooped, his Panama hat crushed in his left hand, his right hand already stretched out toward him from afar, thrusting it across the desk in reckless haste, knocking over everything in his way. His uncle was always in a hurry, for he was constantly driven by the unfortunate notion that he had to accomplish everything he'd set out to do within the single day to which his visits to the capital were always limited, nor did he dare let slip any opportunity for conversation, business, or pleasure that might happen to arise. K., who was particularly indebted to him because he was his former guardian, had to assist him in every way and put him up for the night as well. He called him "the Specter from the Countryside."

As soon as he'd said hello—he didn't have time to sit down in the armchair K. offered him—he asked K. for a brief private conference. "It's necessary," he said, swallowing with difficulty, "it's necessary for my peace of mind." K. sent the assistants from the room at once, with instructions to admit no one. "What's this I hear, Josef?" cried his uncle, once they were alone, seating himself on the desk and stuffing various papers under him without looking at them, to make himself more comfortable. K. said nothing. He knew what was coming, but released suddenly from the strain of work as he was, he gave himself up first to a pleasant languor and gazed out the window toward the opposite side of the street, of which only a small triangular section could be seen from his chair, a stretch of empty wall between two window displays. "Stop staring out the window," his uncle cried with uplifted arms, "for heaven's sake, Josef, answer me. Is it true, can it be true then?" "Dear Uncle," said K., tearing himself out of his reverie, "I have no idea what you're talking about." "Josef," said his uncle warningly, "to the best of my knowledge you've always told the truth. Should I take your last words as a bad sign." "I can guess what you want," said K. submissively, "you've probably heard about my trial." "That's right," said his uncle, nodding slowly, "I've heard about your trial." "From whom?" K. asked. "Erna wrote to me about it," said his uncle, "she doesn't see anything of you of course, you don't take any real interest in her, sadly enough, but she found out about it anyway. I received her letter today and of course came here immediately. For no other reason, since this seemed reason enough. I can read you the passage that concerns you." He pulled the letter from his wallet. "Here it is. She writes: 'It's been a long time since I've seen Josef, I was in the bank once last week, but Josef was so busy I couldn't see him; I waited for over an hour, but then I had to return home for my piano lesson. I would have liked to have talked to him, maybe I'll get a chance to before long. He sent me a big box of chocolates on my name day, it was very sweet and thoughtful. I forgot to write you about it earlier, and only remembered when you asked me. As I'm sure you know, chocolate disappears instantly at the boarding-house, you hardly realize you've been given chocolates and they're gone. But regarding Josef, there's something else I wanted to tell you: As I mentioned, I couldn't get in to see him because he was busy with a gentleman. After I'd waited patiently for a while, I asked an assistant whether the appointment would last much longer. He said that it might, since it probably had something to do with the trial the chief financial officer was involved in. I asked what sort of a trial it was, whether he might be mistaken, but he said it was no mistake, it was a trial and a serious one at that, but that's all he knew. He said he'd like to help the chief financial officer himself, because he was a good and honest man, but he didn't know how to go about it, and he could only hope that influential people would intervene in his behalf. He thought that would surely happen and that things would turn out well, but for the moment, as he gathered from the chief

financial officer's mood, things didn't look at all good. I
didn't attach much importance to his words of course, and
tried to calm the simple-minded fellow, telling him not to
mention it to anyone else, and I'm sure the whole thing is
just idle talk. Nevertheless, it might be a good idea if you,
dear Father, looked into the matter the next time you're here;
you could easily find out more about it and, if truly necessary, intervene through your wide circle of influential friends.
If, as is most likely, that doesn't prove necessary, it will at
least give your daughter an opportunity to embrace you
soon, which would give her great joy.' A good child," his
uncle said as he finished reading the letter, wiping a few tears
from his eyes. K. nodded; he had completely forgotten Erna
due to the various recent disturbances, had even forgotten
her birthday, and the story of the chocolates had obviously
been invented merely to cover for him with his aunt and
uncle. It was very touching, and the theater tickets he now
meant to send her on a regular basis would hardly make up
for it, but right now he didn't feel up to visits at her boardinghouse and chats with a seventeen-year-old high school girl.
"And now what do you have to say?" asked his uncle, who
because of the letter had temporarily forgotten his haste and
agitation, and was apparently reading it through once again.
"Yes, Uncle," said K., "it's true." "True?" his uncle cried out.
"What's true? How can it be true? What kind of a trial?
Surely not a criminal trial?" "A criminal trial," K. replied.
"And you sit there calmly with a criminal trial hanging over
your head?" cried his uncle, who kept getting louder. "The
calmer I am, the better, as far as the outcome is concerned,"
K. said wearily. "Don't worry." "That scarcely sets my mind
at rest," cried his uncle, "Josef, dear Josef, think of yourself,

think of your relatives, of our good name. You've always been our pride and joy, you mustn't disgrace us now. Your attitude," he looked at K. with his head sharply cocked, "doesn't please me at all, that's not how an innocent man acts who still has his strength. Just tell me quickly what it's all about, so I can help you. It's something with the bank of course?" "No," said K., standing up, "but you're talking too loudly, dear Uncle, the assistant's proba-bly eavesdropping at the door. I don't like that. We should go somewhere else. Then I'll answer all your questions as best I can. I'm well aware that I owe the family an explanation." "Right," his uncle burst out, "quite right, but hurry, Josef, hurry." "I still have a few instructions to give," said K. and summoned his administrative deputy by phone, who entered a few moments later. His uncle, still agitated, gestured toward K. to show that he was the one who had called, which was clear enough anyway. K., standing before his desk, went through various papers, explaining quietly to the young man, who listened calmly but attentively, what still needed to be done that day in his absence. His uncle disturbed him by standing there bit-ing his lips and staring wide-eyed, without listening of course, but just his presence was disturbing enough. Then he started pacing back and forth in the room, pausing now and then by the window or at a picture, and breaking out with: "I just don't understand it," or "What in the world's to come of all this?" The young man acted as if he didn't notice a thing, listened calmly until K. had finished his instructions, took a few notes, and departed, after bowing to both K. and his uncle, who however had turned his back to him to stare out the window, clutching the curtains in his outstretched hands. The door had barely closed when his uncle burst out: "At last

that jumping jack is gone, now we can leave too. Finally!"
Out in the lobby, unfortunately, there was no way he could
get his uncle to stop asking questions about the trial,
although several assistants and officers were standing about,
and the vice president himself was just passing by. "Now,
Josef," his uncle began, responding to the bows of the people
standing about with a brief salute, "now tell me frankly what
sort of trial this is." K. made a few noncommittal remarks,
gave a laugh or two, and only when he was on the steps did
he explain to his uncle that he hadn't wanted to speak openly
in front of other people. "Right," said his uncle, "but now
talk." He listened with bowed head, taking short, hasty puffs
on his cigar. "First of all, Uncle," said K., "it's not a trial
before the normal court." "That's bad," his uncle said. "I beg
your pardon?" said K. and looked at his uncle. "I said, that's
bad," his uncle repeated. They were standing on the front
steps, leading to the street; since the doorman seemed to be
listening, K. drew his uncle down the stairs; the busy traffic
on the street enveloped them. The uncle, who had taken K.'s
arm, no longer inquired about the trial so insistently, and
they even walked along for a while in silence. "But how did it
happen?" his uncle finally asked, stopping so suddenly that
the people walking behind him were startled and had to step
to the side. "These things don't happen all at once, they
build up over a long period of time; there must have been
some indications, why didn't you write to me? You know I'll
do anything for you; I'm still your guardian in a sense, and
until today I've been proud of it. Of course I'll still help you,
but it's going to be very difficult now that the trial is already
under way. In any case it would be best for you to take a brief
vacation and visit us in the countryside. You've lost some

weight too, I can see it now. You'll regain your strength in the country, which is a good thing, since this is obviously going to require a good deal of effort. And you'll be placed beyond the reach of the court somewhat. Here they have all sorts of instruments of power and they will necessarily, automatically use them against you; but in the country they would first have to delegate agents, or try to get at you entirely by letter or by telegraph or by telephone. Naturally that weakens the effect; it doesn't free you of course, but it gives you some breathing room." "They might forbid me to leave," said K., who was starting to be drawn in by his uncle's line of thought. "I don't think that they'll do that," his uncle said pensively, "they wouldn't lose that much power if you left town." "I thought," said K., taking his uncle by the arm to keep him from stopping again, "that you would attach even less importance to the whole matter than I did, and now you're taking it so hard." "Josef," his uncle cried, trying to twist away from him so he could pause, which K. prevented, "you've undergone a total metamorphosis; you've always had such a keen grasp of things, has it deserted you now, of all times? Do you want to lose this trial? Do you know what that means? It means you'll simply be crossed off. And that all your relatives will be drawn in, or at least dragged through the mud. Pull yourself together, Josef. Your indifference is driving me crazy. Looking at you almost makes me believe the old saying: 'Trials like that are lost from the start.'" "Dear Uncle," said K., "there's no use getting excited, it won't help either of us. Trials aren't won by getting excited, let my practical experience count for something, just as I've always valued yours and still do, even when I'm surprised by it. Since you say that the family will suffer too because of the trial—which for my part I really can't understand, but that's beside the point—I'll gladly do as you say in all things. Except that I don't think a stay in the country would be to my advantage, even in the sense you intend, because it would imply flight and a guilty conscience. And although they certainly follow me more closely here, I can also take a more active role in the case." "Right," said his uncle as if they were at last on the same track, "I only made that suggestion because I was afraid if you remained here your case would be damaged by your own indifference, and I thought it better to act in your behalf. But if you intend to pursue it as strongly as possible yourself, that's obviously far better." "So we seem to be in agreement on that," said K. "And now do you have a suggestion as to what I should do next?" "I still have to think the matter over of course," his uncle said, "you've got to remember that I've spent the past twenty years almost exclusively in the country-side, where one tends to lose the flair for this sort of thing. Various important connections with well-placed persons who might know more about such matters have weakened over time. I've been somewhat isolated in the countryside, as you well know. That's something you don't really realize yourself until something like this comes up. And your case has caught me partly by surprise, although in a strange way I suspected something like this after Erna's letter, and knew almost for certain the moment I saw you today. But that's beside the point, the important thing now is not to lose any time." Even as he was speaking he rose up on tiptoe and waved for a cab, and now he pulled K. after him into the car as he called out an address to the driver. "Now we're going to see Huld, the lawyer," he said, "he was my classmate in school. You know the name of course? No? That's odd. He has a considerable reputation as a defense counsel and poor man's lawyer. But it's his human qualities I place my trust in." "Anything you want to do is fine with me," K. said, in spite of the fact that the hasty and aggressive manner with which his uncle was handling the matter made him uncomfortable. As a defendant, it wasn't very pleasant to be heading for a poor man's lawyer. "I didn't know," he said, "that a person could engage a lawyer in this sort of case too." "But of course," his uncle said, "that goes without saying. Why not? And now tell me everything that's happened up to now, so I'm fully informed about the matter." K. began telling him immediately, without concealing anything; his total frankness was the only protest he could allow himself against his uncle's opinion that the trial was a terrible disgrace. He mentioned Fräulein Bürstner's name only once in passing, but that didn't detract from his frankness, since Fräulein Bürstner wasn't connected with the trial in any way. As he spoke he looked out the window and noticed that they were approaching the very suburb where the law court offices were located; he pointed this out to his uncle, who, however, did not find the coincidence particularly striking. The cab stopped in front of a dark building. His uncle rang the bell at the first door on the ground floor; while they waited he bared his large teeth in a smile and whispered: "Eight o'clock, an unusual hour for a client to visit. But Huld won't hold it against me." At a peephole in the door appeared two large dark eyes, stared at the two visitors for a moment, then disappeared; the door, however, did not open. K. and his uncle mutually confirmed the fact that they had seen two eyes. "A new maid who's afraid of strangers," his uncle said, and knocked again. Once more the eyes appeared; they could almost be considered sad now, but that might well have been a mere illusion produced by the open gas flame that burned with a hiss directly over their heads but shed little light. "Open up," his uncle called out, and pounded his fist against the door, "we're friends of Herr Huld." "Herr Huld is ill," came a whisper from behind them. In a doorway at the other end of the narrow hall stood a man in a dressing gown who delivered this message in the softest voice possible. His uncle, who was already furious at the long wait, turned around abruptly and cried out: "Ill? You say he's ill?" and walked over to him almost menacingly, as if the man were the illness. "The door's open now," the man said, pointed to the lawyer's door, gathered up his dressing gown, and disappeared. The door had indeed opened, and a young girl—K. recognized the dark, slightly protruding eyes—was standing in a long white apron in the entranceway, holding a candle in her hand. "Next time open more quickly," his uncle said instead of a greeting, while the girl made a small curtsy. "Come on, Josef," he said to K., who made his way slowly past the girl. "Herr Huld is ill," said the girl, since K.'s uncle was hurrying toward the door without pausing. K. was still staring at the girl as she turned around to relock the apartment door; she had a round, doll-like face, her pale cheeks and chin forming a circle completed by her temples and forehead. "Josef," his uncle cried again, and asked the girl: "Is it his heart condition?" "I think so," said the girl, who had found time to precede them with the candle and open the door. In a corner of the room the candlelight did not yet reach, a face with a long beard rose in the bed. "Leni, who is it?" asked the lawyer, who, blinded by the candle, did not yet recognize the guests. "It's your old friend Albert," his uncle said. "Oh, Albert," said the lawyer and fell back upon the pillows, as if he didn't have to pretend for this visit. "Are things really so bad?" asked his uncle, and sat down on the edge of the bed. "I don't believe it. It's just your heart acting up again; it will pass as it has before." "Possibly," the lawyer said softly, "but it's worse than it's ever been. I have a hard time breathing, I can't sleep at all, and I'm getting weaker every day." "I see," said K.'s uncle, and pressed his Panama hat firmly down on his knee with his large hand. "That's bad news. Are you sure you're receiving proper care? It's so dark and gloomy here, too. It's been a long time since I was here, but it seemed more cheerful in the past. And this little maid of yours doesn't seem very jolly, or else she's hiding it." The girl was still standing by the door, holding the candle; as far as one could judge from her vague gaze she was looking at K. rather than his uncle, even now that the latter was talking about her. K. was leaning against a chair he had placed near the girl. "When you're as sick as I am," said the lawyer, "you need peace and quiet. I don't find it gloomy." After a brief pause he added: "And Leni takes good care of me, she's a good girl." But that didn't convince K.'s uncle; he was obviously prejudiced against the nurse, and although he didn't contradict the sick man, he eyed her sternly as she now approached the bed, placed the candle on the nightstand, bent over the sick man, and whispered to him as she straightened his pillows. Almost forgetting his consideration for the sick man, he stood up and paced back and forth behind the nurse, and K. would not have been surprised to see him seize her from behind by the skirts and pull her away from the bed. K. himself watched all this calmly; in fact the lawyer's illness was not wholly unwelcome, for he had not been able to stem his uncle's zeal with regard to his case, and now he was glad to see that zeal deflected through no fault of his own. Then, perhaps merely intending to wound the nurse, his uncle said: "Young lady, please leave us alone for a while, I have a personal matter I wish to discuss with my friend." The nurse, who was still leaning across the sick man and was just smoothing the covers next to the wall, merely turned her head and said calmly, in striking contrast to his uncle, who had first choked with rage before bursting out in speech: "You can see he's too ill to discuss any personal matter." She'd probably repeated his uncle's words for simplicity's sake; nevertheless, even a neutral observer could have taken it for mockery, and his uncle naturally reacted as if he'd been stabbed. "You damned—" he said somewhat indistinctly in his first gurgle of agitation; K. was startled even though he'd expected something of the sort, and ran over to his uncle, firmly intending to cover his mouth with both hands. Fortunately, however, the sick man rose up behind the girl; K.'s uncle made a bitter face, as if he were swallowing something particularly nasty, and then said more calmly: "We haven't taken leave of our senses of course; if what I'm requesting weren't reasonable, I wouldn't request it. Now please leave." The nurse stood beside the bed, facing K.'s uncle fully, one hand, as K. thought he noticed, stroking the lawyer's hand. "You can say anything in front of Leni," the sick man said, in a clearly imploring tone. "But this doesn't concern me," said K.'s uncle, "it is not my secret." And he turned around as if he had no intention of discussing the matter further but would give him a little more time to think it over. "Whom does it concern then?" the lawyer asked, his voice fading, and lay back down. "My nephew," said the uncle, "and I've brought him along." Then he introduced him: "Chief Financial Officer Josef K." "Oh," said the sick man much more energetically, and put out his hand toward K., "please excuse me, I didn't see you at all." "Go on, Leni," he then said to his nurse, who put up no further resistance, and gave her his hand as if they were parting for some time. "So," he said at last to K.'s uncle, who had also drawn nearer, appeased, "you didn't come to pay a sick call, you came on business." It was as if this image of a sick call had paralyzed the lawyer up till then, so rejuvenated did he now appear, propping himself up on one elbow, which must have been something of a strain in itself, and repeatedly tugging at a strand in the middle of his beard. "You look much better already," K.'s uncle said, "now that that witch is gone." He broke off, whispered: "I'll bet she's eavesdropping," and sprang to the door. But there was no one behind the door; his uncle returned, not in disappointment, for her not listening struck him as an even greater act of malice, but no doubt embittered. "You misjudge her," said the lawyer, without defending her further; perhaps he wished to show by this that she needed no defense. But he continued in a much more engaged tone: "As far as the matter with your nephew is concerned, I would of course count myself fortunate if my strength were equal to this most difficult of tasks; I greatly fear it won't be, but I'll certainly try everything I possibly can; if I'm not equal to the task someone else can be brought in as well. To be honest, the affair interests me far too much for me to give up being involved in some way. If my heart can't take it, it will at least offer a worthy occasion for it to fail entirely." K. felt he hadn't understood a word of this entire speech; he looked at his uncle, seeking some explanation

there, but he was sitting with the candle in his hand on the little nightstand, from which a medicine bottle had already
rolled onto the carpet, nodding at everything the lawyer said,
agreeing with everything, and glancing at K. now and then,
urging the same assent from him. Had his uncle perhaps
already informed the lawyer about his trial, but that was
impossible, everything up to now spoke against it. So he said:
"I don't understand—" "Oh, have I perhaps misunderstood
you?" asked the lawyer, as surprised and embarrassed as K.
"Perhaps I spoke too soon. What was it you wanted to talk to
me about then? I thought it concerned your trial." "Of
course," said K.'s uncle, and then asked K.: "What's bothering you?" "Yes, but how do you know about me and my
trial?" asked K. "Oh, I see," said the lawyer with a smile,
"I'm a lawyer after all, I move in legal circles, various trials
are discussed, and the more striking ones stick in one's memory, particularly when they concern the nephew of a friend.
There's nothing unusual in that." "What's bothering you?"
the uncle asked K. again. "You're so agitated." "You move in
those legal circles," K. asked. "Yes," said the lawyer. "You're
asking questions like a child," said his uncle. "With whom
should I associate, if not my professional colleagues?" the
lawyer added. It sounded so irrefutable that K. didn't even
answer. "But you work at the court in the Palace of Justice,
not at the one in the attic," was what he wanted to say, but he
couldn't bring himself to actually do so. "You must consider
the fact," the lawyer continued in a perfunctory tone, as if
explaining something self-evident, superfluously and merely
in passing, "you must consider the fact that such associations
offer major advantages for my clients, in many respects, one
can't always even discuss them. Of course I'm a bit hampered

now by my illness, but I'm still visited by good friends from court and learn a few things. More perhaps than some people in perfect health who spend all day at court. For example I have a special visitor this very moment." And he pointed into a dark corner of the room. "Where?" K. demanded almost rudely, in his initial surprise. He looked around uncertainly; the light of the little candle fell far short of the opposite wall. And indeed something began to stir there in the corner. In the light of the candle his uncle now held high, an older gentleman could be seen sitting by a little table. He must not have even been breathing, to have remained unnoticed for so long. Now he arose laboriously, apparently displeased that he had been brought to their attention. It seemed as if he wanted to wave off all greetings and introductions with his hands, which he flapped like small wings, as if he wished under no circumstances to disturb the others by his presence, imploring them to return him once more to darkness, to forget his presence. But that could no longer be granted. "You caught us by surprise, you see," the lawyer said by way of explanation, waving encouragingly to the gentleman to draw nearer, which he did, slowly, looking about hesitantly, and yet with a certain dignity, "here's the Chief Clerk of the Court—oh, I beg your pardon, I haven't introduced you—this is my friend Albert K., his nephew, Chief Financial Officer Josef K., and this is the Chief Clerk of the Court—the Chief Clerk was kind enough to pay me a visit. Only an insider, who knows how overburdened the Chief Clerk is with work, can fully appreciate the value of such a visit. Yet even so he came, and we were conversing quietly, as far as my weakened state allows; we hadn't forbidden Leni to admit visitors, for none were expected, but we certainly thought we'd be left to ourselves; but then came the blows of your fist on the door, Albert, and the Chief Clerk moved into the corner with his table and chair, although it now turns out that we may have a common matter to discuss, that is, if you want to, and we may just as well sit back down together. Please, my dear sir," he said with bowed head and a subservient smile, pointing to an armchair near the bed. "Unfortunately I can only stay a few minutes longer," the chief clerk of the court said amiably, settling comfortably into the armchair and looking at the clock, "duty calls. In any case I don't want to miss the opportunity to meet a friend of my friend." He bowed slightly toward K.'s uncle, who seemed quite pleased by this new acquaintance, but being by nature incapable of expressions of humble respect, responded to the chief clerk's words with a loud and embarrassed laugh. An ugly sight! K. could observe everything at his leisure, for no one paid any attention to him; the chief clerk, now that he had been drawn forth, took the lead in the conversation, as seemed to be his custom; the lawyer, whose initial weakness may have been intended simply to cut short the new visit, listened attentively, his hand at his ear; K.'s uncle, the candle bearer—he balanced the candle on one thigh, the lawyer kept looking over anxiously—had soon overcome his embarrassment and was now simply delighted, both by the chief clerk's words and by the gentle, undulating gestures with which he accompanied them. K., who was leaning against the bedpost, was totally ignored by the chief clerk, perhaps even intentionally, and functioned merely as an auditor for the old men. Moreover he scarcely knew what they were talking about, and was thinking instead one moment about the nurse and how his uncle had mistreated her, and the next whether he hadn't seen the chief clerk somewhere before, perhaps even among the crowd during his initial hearing. Even if he was mistaken, the chief clerk of the court would certainly have fit perfectly into the front row of the assembly, those old men with their scraggly beards.

Then a sound like breaking china came from the hall, causing them all to prick up their ears. "I'll go see what's happened," said K., and walked out slowly, as if he was giving the others a chance to stop him. He had barely stepped into the hall and was trying to find his way about in the dark when a small hand, much smaller than K.'s, placed itself upon the hand he still held against the door and closed it softly. It was the nurse, who had been waiting there. "It was nothing," she whispered, "I just threw a plate against the wall to get you to come out." In his embarrassment, K. said: "I was thinking about you too." "All the better," said the nurse. "Come on." After a few steps they came to a door with frosted glass, which the nurse opened before K. "Go on in," she said. It must have been the lawyer's study; as far as could be seen in the moonlight, which now brightly illuminated only a small rectangle of the floor by each of the two large windows, it was furnished with old, heavy furniture. "This way," said the nurse, and pointed toward a dark bench chest with a carved wooden back. Even as he was sitting down, K. looked around the room: it was a large and lofty room; the clients of the poor man's lawyer must have felt lost in it. K. felt he could picture the tiny steps with which the visitors approached the massive desk. But then he forgot about that and had eyes only for the nurse, who was sitting right beside him, almost pressing him against the arm of the bench. "I thought you would come to me on your own," she said, "without my having to call you first. It was strange. First you stared at me from the moment you entered and then you kept me waiting." "By the way, call me Leni," she added abruptly, as if not a moment of their talk should be wasted. "Gladly," said K. "But it's easy enough to explain what you found so strange, Leni. First, I had to listen to the idle talk of those old men and couldn't walk out without a reason; second, I'm not very forward, I'm more on the shy side, and you, Leni, didn't really look like you could be had for the asking." "That's not it," said Leni, laying her arm along the back of the bench and looking at K., "I didn't please you and probably still don't." "Please isn't the half of it," said K. evasively. "Oh!" she said with a smile, and through K.'s remark and her little cry gained a certain advantage. So K. remained silent for a while. Since he had already grown accustomed to the darkness of the room, he could make out various details of the furnishings. He noticed in particular a large painting hanging to the right of the door and leaned forward to see it better. It showed a man in a judge's robe; he was sitting on a throne, its golden highlights gleaming forth from the painting in several places. The strange thing was that this judge wasn't sitting in calm dignity, but instead had his left arm braced against the back and arm of the chair, while his right arm was completely free, his hand alone clutching the arm of the chair, as if he were about to spring up any moment in a violent and perhaps wrathful outburst to say something decisive or even pass judgment. The defendant was probably to be thought of as at the foot of the stairs, the upper steps of which, covered with a yellow carpet, could be seen in the picture. "Perhaps that's my judge," said K. and pointed to the picture. "I know him," said Leni, looking up at the picture as well, "he comes here often. That's a portrait of him when he was young, but he surely never looked like that, he's so small he's almost tiny. Even so, he had himself stretched out that way in the painting, since he's ridiculously vain, like everyone here. But I'm vain too, and very unhappy that I don't please you." K. responded to this last remark simply by putting his arm around Leni and drawing her to him; she leaned her head quietly against his shoulder. But to the rest he said only: "What's his rank?" "He's an examining magistrate," she said, taking the hand K. had around her and playing with his fingers. "Just another examining magistrate," K. said in disappointment, "the higher judges stay in hiding. But yet he's sitting on a throne." "That's all an invention," said Leni, her head bent over K.'s hand, "he's actually sitting on a kitchen stool with an old horse blanket folded over it. But is your trial all you think about?" she added slowly. "No, not at all," said K. "I probably think too little about it." "That's not the mistake you make," said Leni, "you're too stubborn, the way I hear it." "Who said that?" asked K.; he felt her body against his chest and looked down at her thick, dark, tightly rolled hair. "I'd reveal too much if I told you," Leni responded. "Please don't ask for names, but stop making that mistake, don't be so stubborn; you can't defend yourself against this court, all you can do is confess. Confess the first chance you get. That's the only chance you have to escape, the only one. However, even that is impossible without help from others, but you needn't worry about that, I'll help you myself." "You know a lot about this court and the deceit it makes necessary," said K., lifting her up onto his lap since she was pressing against him all too insistently. "This is nice," she said, and arranged herself in his lap, smoothing her skirt and straightening her blouse. Then she put both her arms around his neck, leaned back, and took a long look at him. "And if I don't confess, you can't help me?" K. asked tentatively. I recruit women helpers, he thought, almost amazed: first Fräulein Bürstner, then the court usher's wife, and now this little nurse, who seems to have an inexplicable desire for me. The way she's sitting on my lap, as if it were the only proper place for her! "No," Leni replied, shaking her head slowly, "then I can't help you. But you don't want my help, you don't care about it, you're stubborn and refuse to be convinced." "Do you have a sweetheart?" she asked after a moment. "No," said K. "Oh, surely you must," she said. "In fact I do," said K., "just think, I denied her existence and yet I even carry her picture with me." At her request, he showed her a photograph of Elsa; curled in his lap, she studied the picture. It was a snapshot: Elsa was caught at the end of a whirling dance of the sort she enjoyed performing at the tavern, her dress still swirling about her, her hands on her hips, looking off to the side and laughing, her throat taut; the person at whom her laughter was directed couldn't be seen in the picture. "She's very tightly laced," said Leni, and pointed to the spot where, in her opinion, this was evident. "I don't like her, she's clumsy and rough. But perhaps she's kind and gentle with you, you could gather that from looking at the picture. Big strong girls like that often don't know how to be anything but kind and gentle. But would she sacrifice herself for you?" "No," K. said, "she's neither kind and gentle, nor would she sacrifice herself for me. But so far I haven't demanded either of her. I've never even examined the picture as closely as you have." "So you don't care that much about her," said Leni, "she's not really your sweetheart." "Oh yes," said K., "I won't take back what I said." "Well she may be your sweetheart now," said Leni, "but you wouldn't miss her much if you lost her, or traded her for someone else—me, for example." "Of course," said K. with a smile, "that's conceivable, but she has one major advantage over you: she doesn't know anything about my trial, and even if she did, she wouldn't think about it. She wouldn't try to talk me into giving in." "That's no advantage," said Leni. "If that's her only advantage, I won't lose heart. Does she have a physical defect of any sort?" "A physical defect?" asked K. "Yes," said Leni, "I have a slight defect of that sort, look." She spread apart the middle and ring fingers of her right hand, between which the connecting skin extended almost to the top knuckle of her short fingers. In the darkness, K. couldn't see at first what it was she wanted to show him, so she guided his hand to feel it. "What a whim of nature," K. said, and added, when he had examined her whole hand: "What a pretty claw!" Leni watched with a kind of pride as K. opened and closed her two fingers repeatedly in astonishment, until he finally kissed them lightly and released them. "Oh!" she cried out at once, "you've kissed me!" Hastily, with open mouth, she climbed up his lap on her knees; K. looked up at her in near dismay; now that she was so close to him an exciting, almost bitter odor, like pepper, rose from her; she pulled his head to her and bent over it, biting and kissing his neck, even biting his hair. "You've traded her for me," she cried from time to time, "you see, now you've traded her for me after all!" Then her knees slid from under her, and with a small cry she almost slipped to the carpet; K. put his arms around her to catch her and was drawn down with her. "Now you belong to me," she said.

"Here's the key to the building, come whenever you like," were her last words, and an aimless kiss struck him on the back while he was still on his way out. As he stepped out the door, a light rain was falling; he was about to walk out into the middle of the street on the chance he might still see Leni at the window, when, from a car K. hadn't noticed waiting in front of the building, his uncle suddenly emerged, grabbed him by the arms, and shoved him against the door of the building, as if to nail him fast to it. "My boy," he cried, "how could you do it! You've damaged your case terribly, when it was starting out so well. You crawl off to hide with a dirty little creature who obviously happens to be the lawyer's mistress, and stay away for hours. You don't even look for an excuse, make no effort to cover it up, no, you're totally open about it, run to her and stay with her. And meanwhile we're sitting there, the uncle who's working hard on your behalf, the lawyer who's to be won over for you, and most important of all the chief clerk of the court, this noteworthy gentleman, who is practically in charge of your case in its present stage. We're trying to figure out the best way to help you, I have to handle the lawyer carefully, he has to handle the chief clerk the same way, and you have every reason to at least offer me support. Instead you stay away. In the end there's no way to conceal it; now these are polite, sophisticated men, they don't say anything, they try to spare me, but in the end even they can't bring themselves to go on, and since they can't talk about the case, they fall silent. We sat there for several minutes without saying anything, listening to see if you might be returning at last after all. All in vain. Finally the chief clerk, who has remained much longer than he originally intended to, stands up, takes his leave, obviously sorry for me but unable to help, waits with incredible kindness a bit longer at the door, then leaves. Of course I was happy he was gone, I'd reached the point where I was having trouble even breathing. All this had an even stronger effect on the ailing lawyer; the good man couldn't even speak as I took my leave. You've probably contributed to his total collapse, thus hastening the death of a man you're dependent upon. And you leave me, your uncle, waiting here in the rain for hours: just feel, I'm soaked clear through."

LAWYER

MANUFACTURER

PAINTER

On a winter morning—outside, snow was falling in the dull light—K. was sitting in his office, already thoroughly fatigued in spite of the early hour. To shield himself from at least minor staff members, he had given instructions to his assistant not to let any of them in, since he was working on an important project. But instead of working he swung about in his chair, moved a few items around slowly on his desk, and then, without being aware of it, left his arm outstretched on the desktop and remained sitting motionless with bowed head.

The thought of his trial never left him now. He had often considered whether it might not be advisable to prepare a written defense and submit it to the court. In it he would offer a brief overview of his life, and for each event of any particular importance, explain why he had acted as he did, whether in his present judgment this course of action deserved approval or censure, and what reasons he could advance for the one or the other. The advantages of such a written defense over simply leaving things in the hands of his lawyer, who was far from perfect anyway, were obvious. After all, K. had no idea what action his lawyer was taking; in any case it wasn't much, it had been over a month now since he'd summoned him, nor had any of these earlier consultations given K. the impression the man would be able to do much for him. In the first place, he scarcely asked any questions. And yet there was so much to ask. Questions were the main thing. K. had the feeling he could ask all the necessary questions on his own. His lawyer on the other hand, instead of asking questions, did all the talking, or sat across from him in silence, leaning slightly forward over the desk, probably because of his poor hearing, tugging at a strand in the middle of his beard and looking down at the carpet, perhaps at the very spot where K. had lain with Leni. Now and then he gave K. a few empty admonitions, as if talking to a child. Speeches as useless as they were boring, for which K. had no intention of paying one red cent in the final billing. When the lawyer seemed to feel he had humbled him adequately, he usually began to cheer him up a little again. He would tell him how he had already won or come close to winning many similar trials, trials which, if not quite so difficult in reality as his, appeared even more hopeless on the surface. He had a list of those trials right there in his drawer—with this he tapped some compartment or other in his desk—unfortunately he couldn't show him the documents, since

they were officially secret. Nevertheless the extensive experience he had gained in all these trials would naturally be used
to K.'s benefit. He had of course set to work immediately, and
the first petition was already nearly finished. It was very
important, for the first impression made by the defense often
influenced the whole course of the proceedings. Unfortunately, and he felt he must point this out to K., on some occasions initial petitions were not even read by the court. They
were simply put in the file with a note that for the time being
the hearings and surveillance of the accused were much more
important than anything put in writing. If the petitioner
pressed the issue, it was added that once all the evidence had
been collected, and prior to the verdict, this first petition
would be considered as well, together with all other documents of course. Unfortunately that wasn't true either in
most cases; the first petition was generally misplaced or completely lost, and even if it was retained to the very end, the
lawyer had only heard this by way of rumor of course, it was
scarcely even glanced at. All that was regrettable, but not
entirely without justification; K. must not overlook the fact
that the proceedings are not public, they can be made public
if the court considers it necessary, but the Law does not insist
upon it. As a result, the court records, and above all the writ
of indictment, are not available to the accused and his
defense lawyers, so that in general it's not known, or not
known precisely, what the first petition should be directed
against, and for that reason it can only be by chance that it
contains something of importance to the case. Truly pertinent
and reasoned petitions can only be devised later, when, in the
course of the defendant's interrogations, the individual points
of the indictment and its basis emerge more clearly, or may be

surmised. Under these conditions the defense is naturally placed in a very unfavorable and difficult position. But that too is intentional. For the defense is not actually countenanced by the Law, but only tolerated, and there is even some controversy as to whether the relevant passages of the Law can truly be construed to include even such tolerance. In the strict sense, therefore, there are no court-recognized lawyers; all those who appear before the court as lawyers are basically shysters. Of course that has an extremely degrading effect upon the entire profession, and the next time K. went to the law court offices, he should take a look at the Lawyers' Room, that was quite a sight too. He would probably be shocked by the lot gathered there. The narrow, low room to which they were relegated was in itself an indication of the court's contempt for these people. Light enters the room only through a small hatch so high up that if someone wants to look out, and incidentally get a nose full of smoke and a sooty face from the chimney just outside, he first has to find a colleague who will hoist him up on his back. For over a year now—to give just one more example of the poor conditions—there's been a hole in the floor of the room, not large enough for a person to fall through, but big enough that one whole leg can sink in. The Lawyers' Room is in the upper level of the attic, so if someone slips through, his leg hangs down into the lower level, right into the hall where the parties are waiting. It's no exaggeration when such conditions are described in lawyers' circles as scandalous. Complaints to the administration don't have the slightest effect, yet lawyers are strictly forbidden from changing anything in the room at their own expense. But there's a reason they treat lawyers this way. They want to eliminate the defense as far as possible;

everything is to be laid upon the defendant himself. Basically that's not a bad position to take, but nothing would be more mistaken than to conclude from it that defendants have no need of lawyers before this court. On the contrary, there is no other court before which there is a greater need. For in general the proceedings are kept secret not only from the public but from the accused as well. Only insofar as possible of course, but to a very large extent it does prove possible. For even the accused has no access to the court records, and it's very difficult to ascertain during the interrogations which documents are involved, particularly for the defendant, who after all is timid and disconcerted, and distracted by all sorts of cares. This is where the defense enters in. In general defense lawyers are not allowed to be present at the interrogations and so must question the defendant about an interrogation immediately upon its conclusion, if at all possible at the very door of the inquiry room, and deduce from the defendant's often quite hazy accounts whatever might be of use to the defense. But that's not what's most important, since not much can be learned that way, though even here, as elsewhere, a skillful person can learn more than others. Nevertheless, the most important factor is still the lawyer's personal contacts; they are the most valuable aspect of a defense. Now K. had no doubt already learned from his own experience that the lowest level of the court system is not entirely perfect, that it includes some employees who forget their duty and can be bribed, which in turn produces breaches, so to speak, in the strictly closed system of the court. Now this is where the majority of lawyers push their way in, bribing people and pumping them for information; in fact in earlier days there were even cases of stolen files.

There's no denying a few momentary and even surprisingly positive results can be achieved on the defendant's behalf by such means, and petty lawyers parade them proudly to lure new customers, but as far as the future progress of the trial is concerned they're meaningless or worse. Only honest personal contacts are of true value, and with higher officials, by which is meant of course higher officials from the lower ranks. This is the sole means by which the progress of the trial can be influenced, imperceptibly at first, but more and more clearly as it moves along. Only a few lawyers can do that of course, and here K.'s choice had been fortunate indeed. There were only one or two lawyers who might possibly match Dr. Huld's contacts. Of course these paid no attention to the lot in the Lawyers' Room and had nothing to do with them. Their ties to the court officials, however, were correspondingly stronger. It wasn't even always necessary for Dr. Huld to go to court, wait in the outer offices for the chance appearance of examining magistrates, and then, according to their mood, achieve what was generally a merely apparent success, and perhaps not even that. No, as K. had seen himself, officials, and relatively high ones at that, came to him, offered information willingly that was clear or at least easily interpreted, discussed the recent progress of the trial, indeed in some cases even allowed themselves to be convinced, gladly taking on the other's point of view. Of course one didn't dare trust them too far with respect to this latter trait; no matter how decisively they state their new intent, which is favorable to the defense, they may well go straight to their office and issue a decision for the next day that conveys the exact opposite, and is perhaps even more severe with respect to the defendant than that which they had at first intended, and which they claimed to have entirely abandoned. Of course there was no way to protect oneself against that, for what was said in private conversation was exactly that, a private conversation with no public consequences, even if the defense had not been otherwise constrained to retain the favor of those gentlemen. On the other hand, of course, it was also true that these gentlemen were not moved simply by humanitarianism, or feelings of personal friendship, to establish contact with the defense, only a competent one naturally, but did so because they were in a certain sense dependent upon them. Here the disadvantage of a court system that was grounded from its very beginnings in secrecy came to the fore. The officials lack contact with the common people; they're well prepared for the normal, average trial, which rolls along its course almost on its own and needs only a push now and then, but faced with very simple cases or with particularly complex ones, they're often at a loss; because they're constantly constricted by the Law both night and day, they have no proper understanding of human relationships, and in such cases they feel that lack keenly. Then they come to the lawyer for advice, and behind them comes an assistant carrying the files, which are otherwise so secret. Many a gentleman one would least expect to find in such a situation might be discovered at this very window, gazing almost hopelessly out into the street, while at his desk the lawyer studies the files to offer his advice. Moreover one could see at such times how uncommonly seriously these gentlemen took their profession, and into what great despair they were thrown when, due to the very nature of the obstacles, they could not overcome them. In other ways too their position is no easy one, nor should one do them the injustice of regarding it as such. The gradations and ranks of the court are infinite, extending beyond the ken even of initiates. The proceedings in the courts of law are generally a mystery to the lower officials as well; therefore they can almost never follow the progress of the cases they are working on throughout their course; the case enters their field of vision, often they know not whence, and continues on, they know not where. The lessons to be learned from the study of the individual stages of a trial, the final verdict and its basis, are lost to these officials. Their involvement is limited to that part of the trial circumscribed for them by the Law, and they generally know less about what follows, and thus about the results of their own efforts, than the defense, which as a rule remains in contact with the accused almost to the very end of the trial. So in this respect too, they can occasionally learn something of value from the defense. Was K. still surprised then, bearing all this in mind, at the irritability of the officials, which sometimes expressed itself—as everyone soon learned—in an insulting manner toward the parties involved? All officials are irritable, even when they appear calm. Of course the petty lawyers suffer in particular from this. For instance the following story is told, and has every appearance of truth. An elderly official, a decent, quiet gentleman, had studied a difficult case, rendered particularly complex due to the lawyer's petitions, for one entire day and night without a break— these officials are truly the most industrious of people. Now as morning approached, after twenty-four hours of probably not very productive work, he went to the outer door, waited in ambush, and threw every lawyer who tried to enter down the steps. The lawyers gathered on the landing below and discussed what they should do; on the one hand they have no

real right to be admitted, so they can hardly start legal proceedings against the official, and as already mentioned, they
have to be careful not to arouse the ire of the bureaucracy.
On the other hand each day missed at court is a day lost, so it
was important to them to get in. Finally they decided to try to
wear the old gentleman down. One lawyer at a time would
rush up the stairs and, offering the greatest possible passive
resistance, allow himself to be thrown back down, where he
would then be caught by his colleagues. That lasted for about
an hour; then the old gentleman, who was already tired from
working all night, grew truly exhausted and went back into
his office. At first those below could hardly believe it, so they
sent someone up to check behind the door to make sure there
was really no one there. Only then did they enter, probably
not even daring to grumble. For the lawyers—and even the
least important of them has at least a partial overview of the
circumstances—are far from wishing to introduce or carry
out any sort of improvement in the court system, while—and
this is quite characteristic—almost every defendant, even the
most simple-minded among them, starts thinking up suggestions for improvement from the moment the trial starts, and
in doing so often wastes time and energy that would be better
spent in other ways. The only proper approach is to learn to
accept existing conditions. Even if it were possible to improve
specific details—which, however, is merely an absurd superstition—one would have at best achieved something for
future cases, while in the process damaging oneself immea-
surably by having attracted the attention of an always venge-
ful bureaucracy. Just don't attract attention! Keep calm, no
matter how much it seems counter to good sense. Try to realize that this vast judicial organism remains, so to speak, in a

state of eternal equilibrium, and that if you change something on your own where you are, you can cut the ground out from under your own feet and fall, while the vast organism easily compensates for the minor disturbance at some other spot— after all, everything is interconnected—and remains unchanged, if not, which is likely, even more resolute, more vigilant, more severe, more malicious. One should leave the task to the lawyers, instead of interfering with them. Reproaches are of little value, particularly when it seems the full import of what has caused them cannot be conveyed, but he must say how much K. had hurt his own affair by his behavior toward the chief clerk of the court. This influential man must almost certainly be crossed off the list of those to whom one might turn on K.'s behalf. He pointedly refused to acknowledge even passing references to K.'s trial. In many ways the officials were like children. They were often so hurt by seemingly minor matters, though K's behavior, unfortunately, did not fall into that category, that they stopped speaking even with close friends, turning aside when they met them, and opposing them in every possible way. But then, surprisingly and for no apparent reason, they would allow themselves a laugh at some small joke attempted only because the situation seemed so hopeless, and were reconciled once more. It was both difficult and easy to relate to them; there were hardly any guidelines to go by. Sometimes it seemed amazing that an average lifetime sufficed to learn enough to work here with a modicum of success. Of course there are always dark hours, everyone has them, when it seems that one has accomplished nothing, when it seems as if the only trials that turned out well were those that were destined to do so from the very beginning, without any help at

all, while all the others were lost in spite of following them so
closely, in spite of all the effort, all the small apparent victories that gave such pleasure. Then of course nothing seems
certain any longer, and if pressed specifically one does not
even dare deny that trials that by nature should have turned
out well were thrown off course precisely by the assistance
offered. That too is a type of belief in oneself after all, but it is
the only sort that remains. Lawyers are particularly suscepti-
ble to such attacks—they are of course mere attacks and
nothing more—when a trial they have conducted satisfacto-
rily up to a certain point is suddenly taken out of their hands.
That's probably the worst thing that can happen to a lawyer.
It's not the defendant who takes the trial from them, indeed
that probably never happens; once a defendant has engaged a
particular lawyer, he has to stick with him no matter what.
How could he possibly sustain himself alone, once he has
enlisted aid? So that doesn't happen, but it does indeed sometimes happen that the trial takes a direction the lawyer is not
permitted to follow. The trial, the defendant, everything is
simply withdrawn from the lawyer; in that case the best of
connections with the officials are of no use, for they themselves know nothing. The trial has entered a stage where no
further assistance can be given, where it is being handled by
inaccessible courts of law, where even the defendant is no
longer within reach of the lawyer. Then you come home one
day to find on your desk all the many petitions you submitted
so diligently and with such great hopes in the case; they've
been returned; since they can't be transferred to the new stage
of the trial, they're worthless scraps of paper. But that doesn't
mean the trial has been lost, not by any means, or at any rate
there is no definitive reason to assume so, one simply knows

nothing more about the trial, and won't learn anything more either. But fortunately such cases are exceptions, and even should K.'s trial turn out to be one of them, it was still far removed from such a stage at the moment. So there was still ample opportunity for the lawyer to take action, and K. could rest assured that those opportunities would be seized. As he had mentioned, the petition had not yet been submitted, but there was no hurry about that, the preliminary discussions with the officials in charge were of much greater importance, and those had already taken place. With varying degrees of success, it must be frankly admitted. It was far better for the time being not to reveal details which might only affect K. unfavorably and make him overly hopeful or all too anxious; suffice it to say that some of them had responded quite favorably and proved quite cooperative, while others had responded less favorably, while by no means refusing their assistance. The results were thus on the whole quite gratifying, although one mustn't draw too many conclusions from them, since preliminary proceedings always started out that way and only further developments would reveal their true value. At any rate nothing was lost as yet, and if it still proved possible to win over the chief clerk of the court in spite of everything—various steps had already been taken toward that end—then the whole matter, as the surgeons say, was a clean wound and one could await what was to follow with confidence.

In such and similar speeches the lawyer was inexhaustible. They were repeated at every visit. Progress had always been made, but the nature of this progress could never be specified. He was always at work on the first petition, but it was never finished, which generally proved at the next visit to have been a major advantage, since the last time, and there had been no way of foreseeing this, the circumstances had been quite unfavorable for its submission. If, on occasion, exhausted by these speeches, K. remarked that even considering all the difficulties, things seemed to be progressing quite slowly, he received the rejoinder that the progress was not at all slow but that things would doubtless be much further along had K. contacted the lawyer in a timely manner. Unfortunately he had neglected to do so, and this failure would result in further disadvantages, and not merely temporal ones.

The only welcome interruption during these visits was Leni, who always knew how to arrange things so that she served the lawyer's tea in K.'s presence. Then she would stand behind K., apparently watching the lawyer as he bowed deeply over his cup, almost greedily, to pour his tea and drink it, while she secretly allowed K. to grasp her hand. Total silence reigned. The lawyer drank, K. squeezed Leni's hand, and Leni sometimes dared to stroke K.'s hair softly. "You're still here?" asked the lawyer, when he had finished. "I wanted to clear away the dishes," said Leni, there was a last squeeze of the hand, the lawyer wiped his mouth and started speaking to K. again with renewed vigor.

Was it consolation or despair the lawyer sought to produce? K. didn't know, but he soon held it for an established fact that his defense was not in good hands. Everything the lawyer said might be true, although it was transparently clear he was primarily interested in emphasizing his own role and had probably never had a trial as important as he considered K.'s to be. But the constant emphasis on his personal contacts with officials remained suspicious. Were they being exploited solely to K.'s advantage? The lawyer never failed to remark that these were only lower-level officials, officials who were thus themselves in a position of dependence, and for whose advancement certain developments in the trials might presumably be of importance. Were they perhaps using the lawyer to effect such developments, which would of course be to the defendant's disadvantage? Perhaps they didn't do so in every trial, that would be unlikely; there were probably other trials in the course of which they allowed the lawyer certain advantages in exchange for his services, since they surely wished to maintain his good reputation undamaged. If that's how things really stood, however, what tack would they take in K.'s trial, which, as the lawyer explained, was a very difficult and important one that had excited a great deal of attention at court from the very start? There couldn't be much doubt about what they would do. Signs of it could already be seen in the fact that the first petition had still not been submitted, although the trial had already lasted for months, and that according to the lawyer everything was still in the beginning stages, which was of course admirably suited to lull the defendant to sleep and keep him in a state of helplessness, so that they could assault him suddenly with the verdict, or at least announce that the inquiry had concluded unfavorably for him and was being passed on to higher administrative authorities.

It was absolutely necessary for K. to intervene personally. It was precisely in states of extreme fatigue, as on this winter morning, when his thoughts were drifting aimlessly, that this conclusion seemed most inescapable. The contempt he had previously borne for the trial no longer applied. If he had been alone in the world he could have easily disregarded the trial, although then the trial would surely never have occurred at all. But now his uncle had already taken him to the lawyer, and family considerations were involved; his job was no longer totally independent of the course of the trial, he himself had been incautious enough to mention the trial to a few acquaintances with a certain inexplicable feeling of self-satisfaction, others had heard about it in unknown ways, his relationship to Fräulein Bürstner seemed to fluctuate with the trial itself—in short, it was no longer a matter of accepting or rejecting the trial, he was in the midst of it and had to defend himself. If he was tired, he was in trouble.

There was of course no reason to be overly concerned for the time being. He had managed to work his way up to a high position in the bank in a relatively short period of time, and, respected by all, maintain that position; all he had to do now was turn the abilities that had made that possible partially toward his trial and there was no doubt everything would turn out well. Above all, if he wanted to get anywhere, he had to reject the notion of any possible guilt right from the start. There was no guilt. The trial was no different than a major business deal of the sort he had often concluded advantageously for the bank, a deal in which, as was customary, various dangers lurked that must be avoided. To accomplish this, no notion of any sort of guilt dared be entertained of course, all thought must be focused as clearly as possible on one's own advantage. From this point of view it was also unavoidable that the lawyer be dismissed as soon as possible, preferably that very evening. It's true that was unheard of according to his stories, and no doubt quite insulting, but K. couldn't allow his own efforts in the case to run into hindrances that were perhaps occasioned by his own lawyer. Once he had shaken off his lawyer, however, he would need to submit the petition immediately, and to keep pressuring them, daily if possible, to consider it. To accomplish this K. would obviously have to do more than simply sit in the hall with the others and place his hat beneath the bench. He, or the women, or some other messengers, would have to besiege the officials day after day and force them to sit down at their desks and study K.'s petition, instead of staring through the grille into the hall. These efforts must be continuous, with everything organized and supervised; for once the court was going to run into a defendant who knew how to stand up for his rights.

But even though K. felt he could handle all this, the difficulty of composing the petition was overwhelming. At one point, about a week ago, it was only with a sense of shame that he could even contemplate having to prepare such a petition some day; that it might be difficult had not even occurred to him. He recalled how one morning, when he was inundated with work, he had suddenly shoved everything aside and taken out his notepad to have a try at drafting the general outlines of such a petition and perhaps making it available to his slow-witted lawyer, and how at that very moment the door of the head office had opened and the vice president had entered laughing heartily. That had been very embarrassing for K., even though the vice president was not, of course, laughing at the petition, of which he knew nothing, but at a stock market joke he'd just heard, a joke that could only be fully appreciated by means of a drawing, which, bending over K.'s desk and taking K.'s pencil from his hand, he sketched upon the notepad intended for the petition.

Today K. no longer thought of shame; the petition had to be written. If he couldn't find time for it at the office, which

was quite likely, he would have to do it nights at home. And if
the nights weren't sufficient, he would have to take a leave of
absence. Anything but stop halfway, that was the most senseless course of all, not only in business, but anywhere, at any
time. Admittedly, the petition meant an almost endless task.
One needn't be particularly faint of heart to be easily persuaded of the impossibility of ever finishing the petition. Not
because of laziness or deceit, the only things that kept the
lawyer from finishing, but because without knowing the
nature of the charge and all its possible ramifications, his
entire life, down to the smallest actions and events, would
have to be called to mind, described, and examined from
all sides. And what a sad job that was. Perhaps, someday
after retirement, it might provide a suitable occupation for a
mind turned childish, and help to while away the lengthening
days. But now, when K. needed all his wits for his work,
when, given that he was still on the rise and already a threat
to the vice president, every hour went speeding by, and when
he wished to enjoy the brief evenings and nights as a young
man, now he was supposed to start writing his petition. Once
more his thoughts ended in lament. Almost involuntarily,
simply to put an end to them, he felt for the button of the
buzzer connected to the waiting room. As he pressed it he
looked up at the clock. It was eleven o'clock; he had been
daydreaming for two hours, a long and valuable stretch of
time, and was of course even wearier than before. Nevertheless the time had not been wasted, he had reached decisions
that might prove of value. Along with assorted mail, the
assistant brought in two business cards from gentlemen who
had been waiting to see K. for some time. They were in fact
very important customers of the bank, who should not have

been left waiting on any account. Why had they shown up at such an inopportune time, and why, the gentlemen seemed to respond in turn from behind the closed door, did the industrious K. use prime business time for his private affairs. Tired from what he had already gone through, and tiredly awaiting what was yet to come, K. rose to greet the first of them.

He was a short, jovial gentleman, a manufacturer K. knew well. He apologized for interrupting K. in the midst of important work, while K. apologized in turn for keeping the manufacturer waiting so long. But even this apology was delivered so mechanically and with such false emphasis that the manufacturer, had he not been entirely engrossed in the business at hand, would surely have noticed it. Instead he hurriedly pulled figures and tables from every pocket, spread them before K., explained various entries, corrected a small error in the calculations that he'd caught in even this hasty survey, reminded K. of a similar transaction he had concluded with him around a year ago, mentioned in passing that this time another bank was making great sacrifices to secure the deal, and finally fell silent to hear K.'s reaction. K. had actually followed the manufacturer's explanations closely at first and had been caught up by the thought of a major business deal, but unfortunately not for long; he soon stopped listening, nodded a while longer at the more emphatic exclamations of the manufacturer, but in the end abandoned even that and limited himself to staring at the bald head bent over the papers, wondering when the manufacturer would finally realize that his entire presentation was in vain. As he now fell silent, K. actually believed at first it was meant to give him an opportunity to confess he could no longer listen. But to his regret he saw from the expectant gaze of the manufacturer, who was obviously prepared for any possible rejoinder, that the business conference was going to continue. So he ducked his head as if at an order and began moving his pencil back and forth above the papers, stopping here and there to stare at a number. The manufacturer sensed objections: perhaps the figures weren't really firm, perhaps they weren't truly conclusive, in any case the manufacturer placed his hand on the papers and, drawing right up against K., launched once more into a general description of the project. "It's complicated," K. said, pursing his lips, and since the papers, the only thing he could grasp, were covered, he slumped against the arm of his chair. He glanced up only weakly even when the door to the head office opened and, somewhat blurred, as if behind a gauzy veil, the figure of the vice president appeared. K. gave this no further thought, but simply observed the result, which pleased him greatly. For the manufacturer immediately jumped up from his chair and rushed toward the vice president; K. would have had him move ten times faster however, for he feared the vice president might disappear. His fear was unwarranted: the gentlemen met, shook hands, and walked together toward K.'s desk. The manufacturer complained because the financial officer had shown so little inclination for the project and pointed toward K. who, beneath the vice president's gaze, bent over the papers once more. As the two leaned against the desk and the manufacturer now began to try to win over the vice president, it seemed to K. as if the two men, whose size he mentally exaggerated, were negotiating with each other about him. Slowly he tried to ascertain with cautiously upturned eyes what was happening above him, took one of the sheets of paper from the desk without looking at it, placed it on the palm of his hand, and lifted it at last to the men as he himself stood up. He had nothing in particular in mind as he did so, but simply acted in the belief that he would have to behave thus when he finally prepared the grand petition that would totally exonerate him. The vice president, who had followed the conversation with the closest attention, simply glanced at the sheet, not even bothering to read it, since whatever was of importance to the financial officer was of no importance to him, took it from K.'s hand, said: "Thanks, I already know all about it," and laid it back calmly on the desk. K. gave him a bitter sidelong glance. But the vice president didn't notice at all, or if he did notice, it only amused him; he laughed aloud several times, put the manufacturer at an obvious loss once with a shrewd reply, but quickly smoothed things over by raising an objection to his own position, and finally invited him to join him in his office, where they could bring the matter to a close. "It's a very important project," he said to the manufacturer, "I see that quite clearly. And our chief financial officer"—even this remark was actually addressed only to the manufacturer—"will certainly be pleased if we take it off his hands. It's a matter that requires calm consideration. But he appears overburdened today, and a number of people have already been waiting hours for him in the outer office." K. retained just enough self-control to turn away from the vice president and direct his friendly but rigid smile solely to the manufacturer; otherwise he made no attempt to intervene, leaned forward slightly with both hands propped on his desk like a clerk at his station, and looked on as the two men continued talking, picked up the papers from the desk, and disappeared into the head office. While still in the doorway the manufacturer turned, said he wouldn't take his leave as yet, but would of course inform the financial officer of the outcome of the discussion, and that he still had one other small matter to mention to him.

At last K. was alone. He had no intention of admitting any other clients, and he was only vaguely conscious of how pleasant it was that the people outside believed he was still dealing with the manufacturer, so that no one, not even his assistant, could enter. He went to the window, sat down on the broad sill, held on tightly to the handle with one hand, and looked out onto the square. The snow was still falling; the day had not yet brightened.

He sat like that for a long time, without knowing what was actually troubling him, just glancing over his shoulder with a start from time to time at the door to the waiting room, where he mistakenly thought he heard a noise. But when no one arrived, he relaxed, went to the washbasin, washed his face with cold water, and returned to his place at the window with a clearer head. The decision to take charge of his own defense appeared more momentous now than he had originally assumed. So long as he had shifted the burden of his defense to his lawyer the trial had not affected him all that much; he had observed it from afar and could scarcely be touched by it directly; he could check up on his case whenever he wished, but he could also pull his head back whenever he wanted to. Now, on the other hand, if he intended to undertake his own defense, he would have to expose himself fully to the court for the moment; the result would eventually be his full and definitive release, but in order to achieve this, he must temporarily place himself in far greater danger than before. If he had any doubts on that score, today's meeting with the vice president and the manufacturer offered ample proof. How could he have just sat there, totally paralyzed by the mere decision to defend himself? What would things be like later? The days that lay ahead! Would he find the path that led through it all to a favorable end? Didn't a painstaking defense—and any other kind would be senseless—didn't a painstaking defense simultaneously imply the necessity of cutting himself off as far as possible from everything else? Would he successfully survive that? And how was he supposed to do that here at the bank? It wasn't just a matter of the petition, for which a leave might perhaps suffice, although requesting one just now would be taking a great chance; it was a matter of an entire trial, the length of which was unforeseeable. What an obstacle had suddenly been thrown in the path of K.'s career!

And now he was expected to work for the bank?—He glanced over at the desk.—Now he was supposed to admit clients and deal with them? While his trial rolled on, while the officials of the court were up there in the attic going over the trial documents, he was supposed to conduct bank business? Didn't that seem like a form of torture, sanctioned by the court, a part of the trial itself, accompanying it? And would anyone in the bank take his special situation into account when judging his work? No one, not ever. His trial was not entirely unknown, although it wasn't quite clear who knew about it and how much. He hoped, however, that the rumor had not yet reached the vice president; otherwise there would have already been some clear sign of how, without the least regard for collegiality or common decency, he would use it against K. And the president? There was no doubt that he was favorably inclined toward K., and if he were to learn about the trial, he would probably try to make things easier for K. as far as he could, but with little success to be sure, since now that the counterweight K. had offered up to this point was starting to weaken, he was falling increasingly under the influence of the vice president, who was also taking advantage of the president's precarious state of health to strengthen his own position. Then what hope was there for K.? Perhaps he weakened his own resistance by such reflections, and yet it was also necessary to avoid self-deception and to see everything as clearly as possible at that moment.

For no particular reason, simply to avoid returning to his desk for the time being, he opened the window. It was hard to open; he had to use both hands to turn the handle. Then fog mingled with smoke blew in through the window from top to bottom and filled the room with the faint smell of burning. A few flakes of snow drifted in as well. "A nasty autumn," the manufacturer said behind him, having entered the room unnoticed after leaving the vice president. K. nodded and looked nervously at the manufacturer's briefcase, from which he would now no doubt pull the papers to report the results of his discussion with the vice president. The manufacturer, however, followed K.'s gaze, tapped his briefcase, and said without opening it: "You want to hear how it turned out. Not too badly. I've practically got a signed contract in my pocket. A charming man, your vice president, but not without his dangerous side." He laughed, shook K.'s hand, and tried to get him to laugh as well. But now it struck K. as suspicious that the manufacturer didn't want to show him the papers, and he found nothing in the manufacturer's remarks to laugh about. "My dear sir," said the manufacturer, "you're probably suffering from the weather. You look so dejected today." "Yes," said K. and pressed his hand to his forehead, "a headache, family problems." "Yes, indeed," said the manufacturer, who was always in a hurry and could listen to no one patiently, "each of us has his cross to bear." K. had instinctively taken a step toward the door, as if he wished to see the manufacturer out, but the latter said: "I had one other small matter to mention, my dear sir. I'm afraid I may perhaps be adding to your burdens today with this, but I've already been here twice in the recent past and forgot it both times. If I put it off any longer it will probably lose its point altogether. But that would be too bad, since my information is perhaps not entirely without value." Before K. had time to reply, the manufacturer stepped up close to him, tapped him on the chest with his knuckle, and said quietly: "You're involved in a trial, right?" K. stepped back and exclaimed at once: "The vice president told you that." "Oh, no," said the manufacturer, "how would the vice president know?" "And you?" asked K., immediately calmer. "I find out things about the court now and then," said the manufacturer. "Such as the information I wanted to pass on to you." "So many people are connected with the court!" said K. with bowed head and led the manufacturer over to the desk. They sat down again as before and the manufacturer said: "I don't have much information to offer, unfortunately. But you shouldn't neglect even the smallest item in these matters. And I feel an urge to help you somehow, no matter how modest that help might be. We've been good business friends up to now, haven't we? Well, then." K. started to beg his pardon for the way he had behaved at that day's conference, but the manufacturer would not be interrupted; he shoved his briefcase high under his arm to show he was in a hurry and went on: "I know about your trial from a certain Titorelli. He's a painter;

Titorelli is just the name he goes by as an artist, I don't know his real one. He's been coming to my office off and on for years, bringing small paintings for which I always give him a sort of alms—he's almost a beggar. They're pretty pictures by the way, landscapes of heaths and the like. These sales— we're both long since used to them—go smoothly enough. But at one point he started repeating his visits too often, I raised objections, we started talking; I was interested in how he managed to support himself on his art alone and learned to my astonishment that his major source of income was portrait painting. He said he worked for the court. For which court, I asked. And then he told me about the court. You can no doubt well imagine how astonished I was at his stories. Since then, whenever he visits, I hear some item of news about the court, and so I've gradually gained a certain insight into the matter. Of course Titorelli gossips a lot, and I often have to turn him off, not simply because he surely lies as well, but above all because a businessman like myself, almost collapsing beneath the burdens of his own affairs, can't spend too much time worrying about those of others. But that's beside the point. Perhaps—it occurred to me now—Titorelli could be of some help to you; he knows several judges, and even if he doesn't have much influence himself, he could still advise you on how to gain access to various influential people. And even if this sort of advice is not in and of itself crucial, in my opinion it might take on great importance in your possession. After all, you're practically a lawyer. I always say: Chief Financial Officer K. is practically a lawyer. Oh, I have no worries about your trial. But would you like to visit Titorelli? With my recommendation he'll certainly try to do everything he can. I really think you should go. It doesn't

have to be today of course, some time or other, at your conve-
nience. Of course—let me add this—you mustn't feel obliged
to actually visit Titorelli just because I'm the one who advised
you to do so. No, if you think you can get along without him,
it would be better to leave him out of it entirely. Perhaps you
already have some precise plan Titorelli might disturb. Then
no, you most assuredly shouldn't go. A person is naturally
reluctant to allow himself to be advised by a fellow like that.
As you wish, then. Here's the letter of introduction and here's
the address."

Disappointed, K. took the letter and stuck it in his pocket.
Even in the most favorable of cases, any advantage he might
gain from the recommendation was small compared to the
harm that lay in the fact that the manufacturer knew about
his trial, and that the painter was spreading the news about.
He could hardly force himself to offer a few words of thanks
to the manufacturer, who was already on his way to the door.
"I'll go there," he said, as he saw the manufacturer off at the
door, "or, since I'm so busy right now, I'll write to say he
should come to my office sometime." "I knew you'd figure
out how best to handle it," said the manufacturer. "Of course
I thought you'd prefer to avoid inviting people like this
Titorelli to the bank to discuss your trial. It's not always a
good idea to send letters to such people either. But you've no
doubt thought everything over carefully and know what to
do." K. nodded and accompanied the manufacturer on
through the waiting room. In spite of his calm exterior, he
was shocked at himself. He'd only said he would write
Titorelli to show the manufacturer that he appreciated his
recommendation and that he would seriously consider the
possibility of getting together with Titorelli, but if he had

thought that Titorelli's assistance might be of use, he would not have hesitated to actually write to him. The resulting danger, however, had not occurred to him until the manufacturer made his remark. Could he really rely so little on his own judgment already? If he could allow himself to send an explicit letter of invitation to a man of questionable character to come to the bank, in order, separated only by a door from the vice president, to seek his advice on his trial, was it not possible, and even probable, that he was overlooking other dangers, or heading straight for them? There wouldn't always be someone standing at his side to warn him. And now of all times, when he should be gathering all his strength to act, previously unknown doubts about his own judgment had to arise. Were the difficulties he was having carrying out his office work going to begin in his trial as well? Certainly now he no longer understood how he could ever have considered writing to Titorelli and inviting him to the bank.

He was still shaking his head about it when the assistant stepped up beside him and pointed out three gentlemen sitting there in the outer room on a bench. They had been waiting to see K. for some time. Now that the assistant was speaking to K. they stood up, each seeking a favorable opportunity to approach K. before the others. Since the bank had been inconsiderate enough to waste their time in the waiting room, they were not about to show any further consideration themselves. "Sir," one of them was saying. But K. had asked the assistant to bring him his winter coat and, as the assistant helped him on with it, said to all three: "Pardon me, gentlemen, but unfortunately I have no time to receive you now. I do beg your pardon, but I have an urgent business errand to attend to and have to leave immediately. You see how long

I've been tied up. Would you be so kind as to come again tomorrow, or some other time? Or could we possibly handle the matter by phone? Or could you tell me briefly now what it is you wanted and I'll give you a full reply in writing. Of course the best thing would be to come again soon." K.'s suggestions so astonished the gentlemen, who had evidently waited entirely in vain, that they stared at each other in total speechlessness. "It's settled then?" asked K., turning to the assistant, who now brought him his hat as well. Through the open door of K.'s office one could see that the snow was falling much more heavily outside. Therefore K. turned up his coat collar and buttoned it up to his neck.

Just at that moment the vice president stepped out of the adjoining room, smiled as he saw K. in his winter coat conferring with the men, and asked: "Are you on your way out, Herr K.?" "Yes," said K., drawing himself up, "I have a business errand to attend to." But the vice president had already turned to the other men. "And these gentlemen?" he asked. "I believe they've been waiting a long time." "We've already worked that out," said K. But now the men could be held back no longer; they surrounded K. and declared that they wouldn't have waited all these hours if they hadn't had important business that needed to be discussed at once, in detail and privately, person to person. The vice president listened to them for a while, regarded K., who held his hat in his hand and was wiping a few spots of dust off it, and then said: "Gentlemen there's a simple solution. If you'll be kind enough to come along with me, I will gladly confer with you in place of the financial officer. Of course your business must be discussed at once. We're businessmen like yourselves, and we know how valuable a businessman's time is. Won't you come in?" And he opened the door that led into the waiting room of his office.

How good the vice president was at appropriating everything K. was forced to relinquish! But wasn't K. relinquishing more than was really necessary? While he was running off to an unknown painter with vague and, he must admit, quite slender hopes, his reputation here was suffering irreparable damage. It would probably have been much better to remove his winter coat and try to win back at least the two gentlemen who were still waiting in the next room. And K. might have tried to do so, had he not seen the vice president in his office, searching through the bookcase as if it were his own. As K. approached the door in agitation, the vice president exclaimed: "Oh, you haven't left yet." He turned his face toward him, its many deeply scored lines seeming to signal strength rather than age, and immediately renewed his search. "I was looking for the copy of a contract," he said, "that the firm's representative says you're supposed to have. Won't you help me look?" K. took a step, but the vice president said: "Thanks, I've just found it," and turned back into his office with a thick stack of documents that obviously contained much more than just the copy of the contract.

"I'm no match for him at the moment," K. said to himself, "but once I've dispensed with my personal difficulties, he's going to get it and get it good." Somewhat comforted by this thought, K. instructed the assistant, who had been holding the hall door open for him for some time, to inform the president when he got the chance that he was out on a business errand, then left the bank, almost happy to be able to devote himself totally to his case for a while.

He drove at once to the painter, who lived in a suburb that

lay in a completely opposite direction from the one with the law court offices. It was an even poorer neighborhood; the buildings were darker, the narrow streets filled with filth floating slowly about on the melting snow. In the building where the painter lived, only one wing of the great double door stood open; at the bottom of the other wing, however, near the wall, there was a gaping hole from which, just as K. approached, a disgusting, steaming yellow fluid poured forth, before which a rat fled into the nearby sewer. At the bottom of the steps a small child was lying face down on the ground, crying, but it could hardly be heard above the noise coming from a sheet-metal shop beyond the entranceway. The door of the workshop stood open; three workers were standing around some object in a half-circle, beating on it with hammers. A great sheet of tin hanging on the wall cast a pale shimmer that flowed between two workers, illuminating their faces and work aprons. K. merely glanced at all this; he wanted to finish up here as fast as possible, just see what he could learn from the painter with a few words and go straight back to the bank. If he had even the slightest success here, it would still have a good effect on that day's work at the bank. On the third floor he was forced to slow his pace; he was completely out of breath; the steps were unusually high and the flights unusually long, and the painter supposedly lived right at the top in an attic room. The air was oppressive as well; there was no stairwell, the narrow stairs were closed in on both sides by walls with only a few small windows here and there, high up near the ceiling. Just as K. paused for a moment, a few little girls ran out of an apartment and rushed on up the stairs laughing. K. followed them slowly, caught up with one of the girls, who had stumbled and remained behind the others, and asked as they continued to climb the stairs together: "Does a painter named Titorelli live here?" The girl, thirteen at most, and somewhat hunchbacked, poked him with her elbow and peered up at him sideways. Neither her youth nor her deformity had prevented her early corruption. She didn't even smile, but instead stared boldly and invitingly at K. Ignoring her behavior, K. asked: "Do you know the painter Titorelli?" She nodded and asked in turn: "What do you want with him?" K. thought it would be to his advantage to pick up a little quick knowledge about Titorelli: "I want him to paint my portrait," he said. "Paint your portrait?" she asked, opening her mouth wide and pushing K. lightly with her hand, as if he had said something extraordinarily surprising or gauche; then she lifted her little skirt, which was extremely short to begin with, with both hands and ran as fast as she could after the other girls, whose cries were already disappearing indistinctly above. At the very next landing, however, K. met up with all the girls again. They had evidently been informed of K.'s intentions by the hunchback and were waiting for him. They stood on both sides of the steps, pressed themselves against the walls so that K. could pass comfortably between them, and smoothed their smocks with their hands. Their faces as well as the guard of honor they formed conveyed a mixture of childishness and depravity. Above, at the head of the group of girls, who now closed around K. laughingly, was the hunchback, who took over the lead. It was thanks to her that K. found his way so easily. He had intended to go straight on up the stairs, but she showed him he had to take a stairway off to the side to reach Titorelli. The stairway that led to him was particularly narrow, extremely long, without a turn, visible along its entire length, and ended directly at Titorelli's door. This door, which compared to the rest of the stairway was relatively well illuminated by a small skylight set at an angle above it, was constructed of unfinished boards, upon which the name Titorelli was painted in red with broad brushstrokes. K. was barely halfway up the stairs with his retinue when the door above them opened slightly, apparently in response to the sound of all the feet, and a man appeared in the crack of the door, seemingly dressed only in his nightshirt. "Oh!" he cried as he saw the crowd approaching, and disappeared. The hunchback clapped her hands with joy and the rest of the girls pushed behind K. to hurry him along.

They weren't even all the way up yet, however, when the painter flung the door open wide and with a deep bow invited K. to enter. The girls, on the other hand, he fended off, he wouldn't let a single one in, no matter how they begged, no matter how hard they tried to push their way in, if not with his permission, then against his will. Only the hunchback managed to slip under his outstretched arm, but the painter raced after her, seized her by the skirts, whirled her once around him, and then set her back down in front of the door with the other girls, who had not dared cross the threshold when the painter abandoned his post. K. didn't know how to judge all this; it looked as if the whole thing was happening on friendly terms. The girls by the door craned their necks one after the other, called out various humorously intended remarks to the painter that K. couldn't catch, and the painter laughed as well while the hunchback almost flew in his hands. Then he shut the door, bowed to K. again, held out his hand, and introduced himself: "I'm Titorelli, the artist." K. pointed to the door, behind which the girls were whispering, and said: "You seem very popular here in the building." "Oh those brats!" said the painter, and tried in vain to button his nightshirt around his neck. He was barefoot as well, and otherwise wore nothing but a pair of roomy yellow linen trousers, tied with a belt whose long end dangled loosely. "Those brats are a real burden to me," he went on, giving up on his nightshirt, the last button of which had now come off, and fetching a chair, on which he made K. sit. "I painted one of them once—she isn't even here today—and they've been pestering me ever since. If I'm here, they only come in when I let them, but if I go away, there's always at least one of them here. They've had a key made to my door and lend it to each other. You can't imagine how annoying that is. For instance I come home with a lady I'm supposed to paint, open the door with my key, and find let's say the hunchback sitting at the little table there, painting her lips red with the brush, while her little sisters, the ones she's supposed to be watching, wander around making a mess in every corner of the room. Or, as happened only yesterday, I come home late at night—in light of which I hope you'll pardon my state and the disorder of the room—I come home late at night and start to get in bed when something pinches my leg; I look under the bed and pull out another one. Why they push themselves on me so I don't know; you'll have noticed yourself that I don't try to lure them in. Of course they disturb my work too. If this atelier weren't provided for me free, I would have moved out long ago." Just then a small voice called from behind the door, softly and timidly: "Titorelli, can we come in yet?" "No," answered the painter. "Not even just me?" it asked again. "Not even you," said the painter, walking over to the door and locking it.

In the meantime K. had been looking around the room; he would never have imagined that anyone could refer to this miserable little room as an atelier. You could scarcely take two long strides in any direction. Everything was made of wood, the floor, the walls, the ceiling; you could see narrow cracks between the boards. A bed stood against the wall across from K., piled high with bedding of various colors. On an easel in the middle of the room stood a painting covered by a shirt with its arms dangling to the floor. Behind K. was the window, through which one could see no farther in the fog than the snow-covered roof of the neighboring building.

The key turning in the lock reminded K. that he had intended to stay only a short while. So he pulled the manufacturer's letter from his pocket, handed it to the painter, and said: "I learned about you from this gentleman, whom you know, and I've come at his suggestion." The painter skimmed through the letter and tossed it onto the bed. Had the manufacturer not clearly spoken of Titorelli as someone he knew, a poor man dependent upon his alms, one might have easily believed Titorelli had no idea who the manufacturer was, or at any rate couldn't recall him. Moreover, the painter now asked: "Do you wish to buy paintings or to have your portrait painted?" K. looked at the painter in amazement. What was in that letter? K. had taken it for granted that the manufacturer's letter informed the painter that K. wished only to inquire about his trial. He had rushed over too quickly, without thinking! But now he had to give the painter some sort of answer, so he said with a glance at the easel: "Are you working on a painting now?" "Yes," said the painter and tossed the shirt that was hanging over the easel onto the bed alongside the letter. " It's a portrait. A nice job, but it's not quite finished yet." Luck was on K.'s side; the opportunity to talk about the court was being handed to him on a platter, for it was clearly the portrait of a judge. Moreover it was strikingly similar to the painting in the lawyer's study. Of course this was a completely different judge, a fat man with a black bushy beard that hung far down the sides of his cheeks, and that had been an oil painting, while this was faintly and indistinctly sketched in pastel. But everything else was similar, for here too the judge was about to rise up threateningly from his throne, gripping its arms. "That must be a judge," K. started to say, but then held back for a moment and approached the picture as if he wanted to study it in detail. He was unable to interpret a large figure centered atop the back of the throne and asked the painter about it. "I still have some work to do on it," answered the painter, taking a pastel crayon from the little table and adding a few strokes to the contours of the figure, without, however, making it any clearer to K. in the process. "It's the figure of Justice," the painter finally said. "Now I recognize it," said K., "there's the blindfold over her eyes and here are the scales. But aren't those wings on her heels, and isn't she in motion?" "Yes," said the painter, " I'm commissioned to do it that way, it's actually Justice and the goddess of Victory in one." "That's a poor combination," said K. smiling, "Justice must remain at rest, otherwise the scales sway and no just judgment is possible." "I'm just following the wishes of the person who commissioned it," said the painter. "Yes, of course," said K. who hadn't meant to hurt anyone's feelings by his remark. "You've painted the figure the way it actually appears on the throne." "No," said the painter, "I've seen neither the figure nor the throne, that's all an invention; but I was told what to paint." "What do you mean?" asked K., intentionally acting as if he didn't really understand the painter; "that's surely a judge sitting in a judge's chair." "Yes," said the painter, "but it's not a high judge, and he hasn't ever sat in a throne like that." "And yet he allows himself to be portrayed in such a solemn pose? He's sitting there like the president of the court." "Yes, the gentlemen are vain," said the painter. "But they have higher permission to be painted that way. There are precise instructions as to how each of them may be portrayed. But unfortunately it's impossible to judge the details of his attire and the chair in this picture; pastels aren't really suitable for these portraits." "Yes," said K., "it's strange that it's done in pastel." "The judge wanted it that way," said the painter, "it's intended for a lady." Looking at the painting seemed to have made him want to work on it; he rolled up the sleeves of his nightshirt, picked up a few pastels, and K. watched as, beneath the trembling tips of the crayons, a reddish shadow took shape around the judge's head and extended outward in rays toward the edges of the picture. Gradually this play of shadow surrounded the head like an ornament or a sign of high distinction. But, except for an imperceptible shading, brightness still surrounded the figure of Justice, and in this brightness the figure seemed to stand out strikingly; now it scarcely recalled the goddess of Justice, or even that of Victory, now it looked just like the goddess of the Hunt. The painter's work attracted K. more than he wished; at last, however, he reproached himself for having been there so long without having really undertaken anything for his own case. "What's the name of this judge?" he asked suddenly. "I'm not allowed to say," replied the painter; he was bent low over the painting and pointedly ignoring his guest, whom he had at first received so courteously. K. assumed this was a passing mood and was annoyed because it was causing him to lose time. "I take it you're a confidant of the court?" he asked. The painter laid aside his pastels at once, straightened up, rubbed his hands together, and looked at K. with a smile. "Just come straight out with the truth," he said, "you want to learn something about the court, as it says in your letter of introduction, and you discussed my paintings first to win me over. But I don't hold that against you, you had no way of knowing that doesn't work with me. Oh, come on!" he said sharply, as K. tried to object. And then continued: "By the way, your remark was quite accurate, I am a confidant of the court." He paused as if to allow K. time to come to terms with this fact. Now the girls could be heard again behind the door. They were probably crowding around the keyhole; perhaps they could see in through the cracks as well. K. made no attempt to excuse himself, not wishing to sidetrack the painter, but neither did he wish the painter to become too arrogant and move as it were beyond his reach, so he asked: "Is that an officially recognized position?" "No," said the painter curtly, as if that was all he had to say about it. But K. had no wish to see him fall silent and said: "Well, such unofficial positions often carry more influence than ones that are recognized." "That's how it is with mine," said the painter, and nodded with a frown. "I discussed your case yesterday with the manufacturer; he asked me whether I would be willing to help you, I replied: 'The man can come see me sometime,' and I'm pleased to see you here so soon. You seem to be taking the affair to heart, which doesn't surprise me in the least, of course. But wouldn't you like to take your coat off?" Although K. intended to stay for only a short while, the painter's suggestion was quite welcome. The air in the room had gradually become oppressive; he had glanced over several times at a small and obviously unlit iron stove in the corner; the closeness in the room was inexplicable. As he took off his winter coat and then unbuttoned his jacket as well, the painter said apologetically: "I have to keep it warm. It's cozy in here, isn't it? The room is well situated in that respect." K. did not reply to this, but actually it wasn't the warmth that made him uncomfortable, it was the muggy atmosphere that rendered breathing difficult; the room probably hadn't been aired for ages. This unpleasantness was intensified for K. by the fact that the painter had him sit on the bed, while he himself sat before the easel in the only chair in the room. Moreover the painter seemed to misunderstand K.'s reason for remaining perched on the edge of the bed; he even told K. to make himself comfortable and, when K. hesitated, he walked over and pressed him deep into the bedding and pillows. Then he returned to his chair and finally asked his first factual question, which made K. forget everything else. "Are you innocent?" he asked. "Yes," said K. Answering this question was a positive pleasure, particularly since he was making the statement to a private citizen, and thus bore no true responsibility. No one had ever asked him so openly. To savor this pleasure to the full, he added: "I am totally innocent." "Well then," said the painter, bowing his head and apparently considering this. Suddenly he lifted his head again and said: "If you're innocent, then the matter is really quite simple." K.'s face clouded over; this so-called confidant of the court was talking like an ignorant child. "My innocence doesn't simplify the matter," said K. He had to smile in spite of himself and shook his head slowly. "A number of subtle points are involved, in which the court loses its way. But then in the end it pulls out some profound guilt from somewhere where there was originally none at all." "Yes, yes, of course," said the painter, as if K. were needlessly interrupting his train of thought. "But you are innocent?" "Well, yes," said K. "That's the main thing," said the painter. He couldn't be swayed by counterarguments, but in spite of his decisiveness, it wasn't clear whether he was speaking from conviction or indifference. K. wanted to determine that first, and so he said: "You certainly know the court much better than I do; I don't know much more about it than what I've heard, from all sorts of people of course. But they're all in agreement that charges are never made frivolously, and that the court, once it brings a charge, is convinced of the guilt of the accused, and that it is difficult to sway them from this conviction." "Difficult?" asked the painter, throwing one hand in the air. "The court can never be swayed from it. If I were to paint all the judges in a row on this canvas and you were to plead your case before them, you would have more success than before the actual court." "Yes," K. said to himself, forgetting that he had only intended to sound out the painter.

Behind the door a girl started asking again: "Titorelli, isn't he going to leave pretty soon?" "Quiet," the painter yelled at the door, "can't you see that I'm having a conference with this gentleman?" But that didn't satisfy the girl, who instead asked: "Are you going to paint him?" And when the painter didn't reply she added: "Please don't paint him; he's so ugly." A confusion of unintelligible cries of agreement followed. The painter sprang to the door, opened it a crack—the clasped hands of the girls could be seen stretched out imploringly—and said: "If you don't be quiet, I'm going to throw you all down the stairs. Sit down on the steps and keep still." Apparently they didn't obey right away, so that he had to make it a command: "Down on the steps!" Only then was it quiet.

"Pardon me," said the painter, turning to K. again. K. had scarcely glanced toward the door; he'd left it entirely up to the painter whether and how he was to be protected. Even now he hardly moved as the painter bent down to him and, in order not to be heard outside, whispered in his ear: "Those girls belong to the court as well." "What?" asked K., jerking his head away and staring at the painter. But the latter sat down in his chair again and said half in jest, half in explanation: "Everything belongs to the court." "I hadn't noticed that," K. said curtly; the painter's general statement stripped the reference to the girls of any disturbing quality. Even so, K. gazed for a while at the door, behind which the girls were now sitting quietly on the steps. Only one had poked a piece of straw through a crack between the boards and was moving it slowly up and down.

"You don't seem to have a general overview of the court yet," said the painter; he had spread his legs wide and was tapping his toes on the floor. "But since you're innocent, you won't need one. I'll get you off on my own." "How are you going to do that?" asked K. "You said yourself just a moment ago that the court is entirely impervious to proof." "Impervious only to proof brought before the court," said the painter, and lifted his forefinger, as if K. had missed a subtle distinction. "But it's another matter when it comes to behind-the-scene efforts, in the conference rooms, in the corridors, or for example even here in the atelier." What the painter now said seemed less improbable to K.; on the contrary it stood in close agreement with what K. had heard from others as well. Yes, it was even filled with hope. If the judges could really be swayed as easily through personal contacts as the lawyer had suggested, then the painter's contacts with vain judges were particularly important and should by no means be underestimated. The painter would fit perfectly into the circle of helpers K. was gradually assembling about him. His organizational talents had once been highly praised at the bank; here, where he was entirely on his own, he had an excellent opportunity to test them to the full. The painter observed the effect of his explanation on K. and then asked with a certain anxiety: "Have you noticed I sound almost like a lawyer? It's constantly interacting with gentlemen of the court that influences me. Of course I profit greatly from it, but I tend to lose a good deal of artistic energy." "How did you first come in contact with the judges?" asked K.; he wanted to win the painter's confidence before directly enlisting his aid. "That was quite simple," said the painter, "I inherited the connection. My father himself was a court painter. It's one post that's always hereditary. New people are of no use for it. The rules for painting the various levels of officials are so numerous, so varied, and above all so secret, that they simply aren't known beyond certain families. There in that drawer, for example, I have my father's notes, which I show to no one. But only someone who knows them is equipped to paint the judges. Nevertheless, even if I were to lose them, I still carry so many rules in my head that no one could ever dispute my right to the post. Every judge wants to be painted like the great judges of old, and only I can do that." "That's an enviable situation," said K., who was thinking about his own position in the bank, "so your position is unshakable?" "Yes, unshakable," said the painter, proudly lifting his shoulders. "And that allows me to take a chance now and then helping a poor man with his trial." "And how do you do that?" asked K., as if he were not the one the painter had just called a poor man. But the painter wouldn't be sidetracked, saying instead: "In your case, for example, since you're entirely innocent, I plan to undertake the following." This repeated reference to his innocence was beginning to annoy K. At times it seemed to him as if, by such remarks, the painter was insisting upon a favorable outcome to the trial as a precondition for his help, which thus amounted to nothing on its own of course. But in spite of these doubts, K. controlled himself and didn't interrupt the painter. He didn't want to do without the painter's help, he was sure of that, and that help seemed no more questionable than the lawyer's. In fact K. far preferred the former, because it was offered more simply and openly.

The painter had pulled his chair closer to the bed and continued in a low voice: "I forgot to ask first what sort of release you want. There are three possibilities: actual acquittal, apparent acquittal, and protraction. Actual acquittal is best of course, but I don't have the slightest influence on that particular result. In my opinion there's not a single person anywhere who could have an influence on an actual acquittal. In that case the defendant's innocence alone is probably decisive. Since you're innocent, it would actually be possible to rely on your innocence alone. But then you wouldn't need help from me or anyone else."

This orderly presentation took K. aback at first, but then

he said, as quietly as the painter: "I think you're contradicting yourself." "How?" the painter asked patiently and leaned back with a smile. This smile made K. feel as if he were trying to reveal contradictions not so much in the words of the painter as in the legal process itself. Nevertheless he did not retreat, but said: "You remarked earlier that the court is impervious to proof; later you restricted this to the public aspect of the court, and now you even claim that an innocent man needs no help at all before the court. That's a contradiction in itself. Moreover you also stated earlier that judges can be personally influenced, although you now deny that actual acquittal, as you call it, can ever be achieved through personal influence. That's a second contradiction." "These contradictions can be easily explained," said the painter. "We're talking about two different things here, what the Law says, and what I've experienced personally; you mustn't confuse the two. In the Law, which I've never read, mind you, it says of course on the one hand that an innocent person is to be acquitted; on the other hand it does not say that judges can be influenced. My own experience, however, has been precisely the opposite. I know of no actual acquittals but know many instances of influence. Of course it's possible that in the cases I'm familiar with no one was ever innocent. But doesn't that seem unlikely? In all those cases not one single innocent person? Even as a child I listened closely to my father when he talked about trials at home, and the judges who came to his atelier discussed the court as well; in our circles no one talked of anything else; from the moment I was allowed to go to court I attended constantly, heard the crucial stages of innumerable trials, followed them insofar as they could be followed, and—I must admit—I never saw a single actual acquittal." "Not a single acquittal then," said K. as if speaking to himself and to his hopes. "That confirms the opinion I've already formed of this court. So it has no real point in that respect either. A single hangman could replace the entire court." "You mustn't generalize," said the painter, displeased, " I've spoken only of my own experience." " That's quite enough," said K., "or have you heard of acquittals in earlier times?" "Such acquittals are said to have occurred, of course," said the painter. "But that's extremely difficult to determine. The final verdicts of the court are not published, and not even the judges have access to them; thus only legends remain about ancient court cases. These tell of actual acquittals, of course, even in a majority of cases; you can believe them, but they can't be proved true. Nevertheless they shouldn't be entirely ignored; they surely contain a certain degree of truth, and they are very beautiful; I myself have painted a few pictures based on such legends." "Mere legends can't change my opinion," said K., "I assume these legends can't be cited in court?" The painter laughed. "No, they can't," he said. "Then it's useless talking about them," said K.; he was accepting all the painter's opinions for the time being, even if he considered them improbable and they contradicted other reports. He didn't have time right now to examine the truth of everything the painter said, let alone to disprove it; the best he could hope for was to induce the painter to help him somehow, even if it was not in any crucial way. So he said: "Let's leave actual acquittal aside then; you mentioned two further possibilities." "Apparent acquittal and protraction. It can only be one of those two," said the painter. "But don't you want to take off your jacket before we discuss them? You must be hot." "Yes," said K., who up

to then had been concentrating solely on the painter's explanations but whose forehead now broke out in heavy sweat as
he was reminded of the heat. "It's almost unbearable." The
painter nodded, as if he could well understand K.'s discomfort. "Couldn't we open the window?" K. asked. "No," said
the painter. "It's just a pane of glass set in the wall; it can't be
opened." K. now realized that he had been hoping the whole
time that either the painter or he would suddenly walk to the
window and throw it open. He was prepared to inhale even
the fog with an open mouth. The sense of being entirely cut
off from outside air made him dizzy. He struck the featherbed
beside him softly and said in a weak voice: "That's uncomfortable and unhealthy." "Oh, no," said the painter in
defense of his window. "Since it can't be opened, it holds in
the heat better than a double-paned window, even though it's
only a single sheet of glass. If I want to air things out, which
is hardly necessary, since air comes in through all the cracks
between the boards, I can open one of my doors, or even both
of them." Somewhat comforted by this explanation, K.
looked around for the second door. The painter noticed this
and said: "It's behind you; I had to block it with the bed."
Only then did K. see the little door in the wall. "This room is
really too small for an atelier," said the painter, as if wishing
to forestall a criticism on K.'s part. "I've had to arrange
things as best I could. Of course the bed is very poorly situated in front of the door. That's the door the judge I'm currently painting always uses, for example, and I've given him a
key to it so he can wait for me here in the atelier, even when
I'm not at home. But he generally arrives early in the morning
while I'm still asleep. Of course I'm always awakened from a
sound sleep when the door by the bed opens. You'd lose any

respect you have for judges if you could hear the curses I shower on him as he climbs across my bed in the morning. Of course I could take the key away from him, but that would only make matters worse. All the doors here can be torn off their hinges with a minimum of effort." Throughout these remarks, K. had been debating whether or not to take off his jacket; he finally realized that he wouldn't be able to stand it much longer if he didn't, so he removed his jacket, but laid it over his knee so that he could put it back on immediately in case the conversation came to an end. He had barely removed his jacket when one of the girls cried out: "He's taken off his jacket now," and they could all be heard rushing to the cracks to see the show for themselves. "The girls think I'm going to paint you and that's why you've taken off your jacket," said the painter. "I see," said K., only slightly amused, for he didn't feel much better than before, even though he was now sitting in his shirtsleeves. Almost grumpily, he asked: "What were the two other possibilities called?" He had already forgotten the terms. "Apparent acquittal and protraction," said the painter. "The choice is up to you. Both can be achieved with my help, not without an effort of course, the difference in that respect being that apparent acquittal requires a concentrated but temporary effort, while protraction requires a far more modest but continuous one. First, then, apparent acquittal. If that's what you want, I'll write out a certification of your innocence on a sheet of paper. The text of such certification was handed down to me by my father and is totally unchallengeable. Then I'll make the rounds of the judges I know with the certification. Let's say I start by submitting the certification to the judge I'm painting now, this evening, when he comes for his sitting. I submit the certification to him, explain to him that you're innocent, and act as a personal guarantor for your innocence. It's not a mere formality, it's a truly binding surety." In the painter's eyes lay something akin to reproach that K. would place the burden of such a surety upon him. "That would be very kind of you," said K. "And the judge would believe you and still not actually acquit me?" "Just as I said," answered the painter. "Nor is it absolutely certain that every judge would believe me; some judge or other, for example, might demand that I bring you to him personally. Then you would have to come along. In that case the battle is already half won, of course, particularly since I'd instruct you carefully in advance how to conduct yourself before the judge in question. Things are more difficult in the case of those judges who turn me away from the very start—and that will happen too. We'll just have to give up on those, not without trying several times of course, but we can afford that, since individual judges can't decide the issue. Now when I've gathered enough judges' signatures on the certification, I take it to the judge who's currently conducting your trial. Perhaps I have his signature already, then things go a little more quickly than usual. In general there aren't many more obstacles then, that's the period of highest confidence for the defendant. It's remarkable but true that people are more confident at this stage than after the acquittal. No further special effort is required. The judge has on the certification the surety of a number of judges; he can acquit you with no second thoughts, and, after going through various formalities, will no doubt do so, to please me and his other acquaintances. You, however, leave the court a free man." "So then I'm free," K. said hesitantly. "Yes," said the painter, "but only apparently free, or more accurately, temporarily free. Judges on the lowest level, and those are the only ones I know, don't have the power to grant a final acquittal, that power resides only in the highest court, which is totally inaccessible to you and me and everyone else. We don't know what things look like up there, and incidentally, we don't want to know. Our judges, then, lack the higher power to free a person from the charge, but they do have the power to release them from it. When you are acquitted in this sense, it means the charge against you is dropped for the moment but continues to hover over you, and can be reinstated the moment an order comes from above. Because I have such a close relationship with the court, I can also explain how the distinction between actual and apparent acquittal reveals itself in purely formal terms in court regulations. In an actual acquittal, the files relating to the case are completely discarded, they disappear totally from the proceedings, not only the charge, but the trial and even the acquittal are destroyed, everything is destroyed. An apparent acquittal is handled differently. There is no further change in the files except for adding to them the certification of innocence, the acquittal, and the grounds for the acquittal. Otherwise they remain in circulation; following the law court's normal routine they are passed on to the higher courts, come back to the lower ones, swinging back and forth with larger or smaller oscillations, longer or shorter interruptions. These paths are unpredictable. Externally it may sometimes appear that everything has been long since forgotten, the file has been lost, and the acquittal is absolute. No initiate would ever believe that. No file is ever lost, and the court never forgets. Someday—quite unexpectedly—some judge or other takes a closer look at the file, realizes that the case is still

active, and orders an immediate arrest. I'm assuming here
that a long time has passed between the apparent acquittal
and the new arrest; that's possible, and I know of such cases;
but it's equally possible that the acquitted individual leaves
the court, returns home, and finds agents already there, waiting to arrest him again. Then of course his life as a free man is
over." "And the trial begins all over again?" K. asked, almost
incredulously. "Of course," said the painter, "the trial begins
all over again, but it is again possible, just as before, to secure
an apparent acquittal. You must gather all your strength
again and not give up." Perhaps the painter added this final
remark because he had noticed that K. had slumped slightly.
"But isn't effecting a second acquittal more difficult than the
first?" K. said, as if he now wished to anticipate any further
revelations from the painter. "That can't be said for certain,"
replied the painter. "You mean, I take it, that the judges'
judgment might be unfavorably influenced with regard to the
defendant because of the second arrest. That's not the case.
The judges have foreseen this arrest from the moment of the
original acquittal. So in fact it has scarcely any effect. But
there are no doubt countless other reasons why the judge's
mood as well as his legal opinion on the case may differ, and
the efforts for a second acquittal must therefore be adapted
to the changed circumstances and be as strong in general as
they were for the first acquittal." "But this second acquittal
isn't final either," said K., turning his head away coldly. "Of
course not," said the painter, "the second acquittal is followed by a third arrest, the third acquittal by a fourth arrest,
and so on. That's inherent in the very concept of apparent
acquittal." K. was silent. "Apparent acquittal obviously
doesn't strike you as an advantage," said the painter, "per-

haps protraction would suit you better. Shall I explain to you the nature of protraction?" K. nodded. The painter had leaned back expansively in his chair, his nightshirt gaped open, he had shoved a hand inside it and was scratching his chest and sides. "Protraction," said the painter, gazing straight ahead for a moment, as if searching for a fully accurate explanation, "protraction is when the trial is constantly kept at the lowest stage. To accomplish this the defendant and his helper, in particular his helper, must remain in constant personal contact with the court. I repeat, this doesn't require the same effort it takes to secure an apparent acquittal, but it does require a much higher level of vigilance. You can't let the trial out of your sight; you have to visit the relevant judge at regular intervals, and any extra chance you get as well, and try to keep him as well disposed as possible in all ways; if you don't know the judge personally, you have to try to influence him through judges you do know, although you still don't dare dispense with the direct conferences. If nothing is omitted in this respect, you can be sufficiently assured that the trial will never progress beyond its initial stage. The trial doesn't end of course, but the defendant is almost as safe from a conviction as he would be as a free man. Compared with apparent acquittal, protraction offers the advantage that the defendant's future is less uncertain; he's spared the shock of sudden arrests, and he doesn't have to worry, at what may be precisely the worst time in terms of other circumstances, about taking on the stress and strain connected with securing an apparent acquittal. Of course protraction also has certain disadvantages for the accused that must not be underestimated. I don't mean the fact that the defendant is never free; he's not free in a true sense in the case of an apparent acquittal either. It's a different sort of disadvantage. The trial can't come to a standstill without some reason that's at least plausible. So something must happen outwardly in the trial. Therefore various measures must be taken from time to time, the defendant has to be interrogated, inquiries conducted, and so forth. The trial must be kept constantly spinning within the tight circle to which it's artificially restricted. Of course that involves certain inconveniences for the defendant, which on the other hand you mustn't imagine as all that bad. After all, it's a merely formal matter; for example the interrogations are quite brief; if you don't have the time or inclination to attend you can excuse yourself; with certain judges you can even set up a long-term schedule together in advance; in essence it's merely a matter of reporting to your judge from time to time, since you're a defendant." Even as these last words were being spoken, K. placed his jacket over his arm and rose. "He's standing up already," came an immediate cry from beyond the door. "Are you leaving so soon?" asked the painter, who had risen as well. "It must be the air here that's driving you away. I feel terrible about that. There was more I wanted to tell you. I had to sum things up briefly. But I hope it was all clear." "Oh, yes," said K., whose head ached from the effort he had made to force himself to listen. In spite of this assurance, the painter summed things up again, as if offering K. a word of comfort for the journey home: "Both methods have this in common: they prevent the accused from being convicted." "But they also prevent an actual acquittal," said K. softly, as if ashamed of the realization. "You've grasped the heart of the matter," the painter said quickly. K. placed his hand on his winter coat, but he couldn't even make up his mind to put on his jacket. He would have preferred to bundle them both up and rush out into the fresh air with them. The girls couldn't get him to put them on either, even though they called out to one another prematurely that he was doing so. The painter wished to get some sense of K.'s thoughts, so he said: "You probably still haven't reached a decision with regard to my suggestions. I approve of that. In fact I would have advised against a quick decision. There's only a hair's difference between the advantages and disadvantages. Everything has to be weighed quite carefully. Of course you don't want to lose too much time either." "I'll come again soon," said K., who, making an abrupt decision, put on his jacket, threw his coat over his shoulders, and hastened to the door, behind which the girls now began to shriek. K. felt as if he could see the shrieking girls through the door. "But you have to keep your word," said the painter, who hadn't followed him, "otherwise I'll come to the bank myself to inquire about it." "Unlock the door, will you," said K., pulling at the handle, which the girls, as he could tell from the counterpressure, were holding tight from the outside. "Do you want the girls bothering you?" asked the painter. "Why don't you use this way out instead?" and he pointed to the door behind the bed. That was fine with K., and he sprang back to the bed. But instead of opening the door, the painter crawled under the bed and asked from below: "Just a minute. Wouldn't you like to see a painting I could sell you?" K. didn't wish to be impolite; the painter really had taken his side and promised continued help, and due to K.'s own forgetfulness there had been no discussion of how K. might reimburse him for his help, so K. couldn't deny him now; he let him show his picture, even though he was trembling with impatience to leave the atelier.

From beneath the bed the painter dragged a pile of unframed paintings so deeply covered in dust that when the painter tried to blow it away from the one on top, the dust whirled up before K.'s eyes, and for some time he could scarcely breathe. "A landscape of the heath," said the painter, and handed K. the painting. It showed two frail trees, standing at a great distance from one another in the dark grass. In the background was a multicolored sunset. "Nice," said K., "I'll buy it." K. had spoken curtly without thinking, so he was glad when, instead of taking it badly, the painter picked up another painting from the floor. "Here's a companion piece to that picture," said the painter. It may have been intended as a companion piece, but not the slightest difference could be seen between it and the first one: here were the trees, here was the grass, and there the sunset. But that made little difference to K. "They're nice landscapes," he said, "I'll take both of them and hang them in my office." "You seem to like the subject," said the painter, and pulled out a third painting, "luckily enough, I have a similar one right here." It was not merely similar, however, it was exactly the same landscape. The painter was taking full advantage of the chance to sell his old pictures. "I'll take that one too," said K. "What do I owe you for the three of them?" "We'll talk about that next time," said the painter, "you're in a hurry now and we'll be keeping in touch, after all. By the way, I'm glad you like the paintings; I'll throw in all the pictures I have under here. They're all heath landscapes, I've painted a lot of heath landscapes. Some people are put off by paintings like these because they're too somber, but others, and you're among them, have a particular love for the somber." But K. was in no mood to discuss the mendicant artist's professional life just then. "Pack up all the paintings," he cried, interrupting the painter, "my assistant will come by tomorrow and pick them up." "That's not necessary," said the painter. "I think I can find a porter to go with you now." And at last he leaned across the bed and opened the door. "Don't be shy about stepping on the bed," said the painter, "everyone who comes in this way does." K. wouldn't have worried about it even without being told; he'd already put his foot in the middle of the featherbed; then he looked through the open door and drew his foot back again. "What's that?" he asked the painter. "What do you find so surprising?" he asked, himself surprised. "Those are the law court offices. Didn't you know there were law court offices here? There are law court offices in practically every attic, why shouldn't they be here too? In fact my atelier is part of the law court offices too, but the court has placed it at my disposal." K. wasn't so shocked at having found law court offices here; he was more shocked at himself, at his ignorance when it came to the court. It seemed to him a basic rule of behavior that the defendant should always be prepared, never be caught by surprise, never be looking blankly to the right when a judge was standing on his left—and it was precisely this basic rule that he was constantly breaking. A long corridor stretched before him, from which air drifted that made the air in the atelier seem refreshing by comparison. Benches stood on both sides of the hall, just as in the waiting room of K.'s court offices. There seemed to be precise guidelines for the furnishings of these offices. There weren't many parties there at the moment. A man sat there, half reclining; he had buried his face in his arm and seemed to be sleeping; another stood in semidarkness at the end of the hallway. K. now stepped across the bed; the painter followed him with the pictures. They soon met a court usher—K. had already learned to recognize the court ushers by the gold button they wore among the ordinary buttons on their civilian suits—and the painter instructed him to follow K. with the pictures. K. swayed rather than walked, with his handkerchief pressed to his mouth. They had almost reached the exit when the girls, from whom K. was not to be spared after all, stormed toward them. They had evidently seen the other door of the atelier being opened and had made a detour to force their way in from this side. "I can't accompany you any farther," said the painter, laughing beneath the press of girls. "Goodbye! And don't take too long thinking about it!" K. didn't even look back. On the street he took the first cab that came his way. He was anxious to be rid of the usher, whose gold button kept catching his eye, even though no one else probably noticed it. In his eagerness to serve, the usher even tried to take a seat on the coachbox, but K. chased him down. It was long past noon when K. arrived at the bank. He would have liked to leave the paintings in the cab, but he was afraid he might have to account for them to the painter at some point. So he ordered them taken into his office and locked them in the bottom drawer of his desk, to store them safely away from the vice president's eyes for at least the next few days.

BLOCK, THE MERCHANT

DISMISSAL OF THE LAWYER

At long last K. had decided to withdraw his case from the lawyer. Doubts as to whether it was the right thing to do could not be totally rooted out, but the firm conviction of its necessity outweighed them. This resolution drained K. of a great deal of energy the day he planned to visit the lawyer; he worked at an unusually slow pace, stayed late at the office, and it was past ten before he finally stood at the lawyer's door. Before actually ringing the bell, he asked himself if it might be better to dismiss the lawyer by telephone or letter; a personal discussion was bound to prove painful. But in the final analysis, K. did not want to forgo that opportunity; any other manner of dismissal might be accepted silently or with a few formal phrases and, unless Leni could perhaps learn something, K. would never find out how the lawyer took the dismissal and what, in his by no means insignificant opinion, the consequences of this action might be for K. But if the lawyer were sitting across from K. and the dismissal caught him by surprise, K. could easily learn everything he wanted to know from the lawyer's expression and demeanor, even if he couldn't coax much out of him. It was even possible he might be persuaded of the wisdom of leaving his defense in his lawyer's hands after all, and retract the dismissal.

The first ring at the lawyer's door was, as usual, in vain. "Leni could be a little quicker," thought K. But it would be good fortune enough just not to have a third party mix in, as they often did, whether it was the man in the dressing gown or someone else who started interfering. As K. pressed the button a second time, he looked back at the other door, but this time it too remained closed. Finally two eyes appeared at the peephole in the lawyer's door, but they weren't Leni's. Someone unlocked the door, braced himself against it for the moment, however, called back into the apartment "It's him," and only then opened the door wide. K. had pressed up against the door, for behind him he could hear the key being turned hastily in the lock of the door to the other apartment. Thus, when the door suddenly gave way before him, he practically stormed into the entranceway and caught sight of Leni, to whom the cry of warning from the man at the door had been directed, running off down the hall between the rooms in her slip. He stared after her for a moment and then turned to look at the man who had opened the door. He was a scrawny little man with a full beard, holding a candle in his hand. "Do you work here?" K. asked. "No," the man replied, "I'm not part of the household, the lawyer just represents me; I'm here on a legal matter." "Without a jacket?" K. asked, and indicated with a wave of his hand the man's inappropriate state of dress. "Oh, do forgive me," said the man, and cast the light of the candle upon himself, as if he were seeing his own state for the first time. "Is Leni your mistress?" K. asked curtly. His legs were slightly spread, his hands, in which he held his hat, were clasped behind him. The mere possession of a heavy overcoat made him feel quite superior to the short skinny man. "Oh goodness," said the other, and raised one hand before his face in shocked repudiation, "no, no, what are you thinking of?" "You look trustworthy," said K. with a smile, "but yet—let's go." He gestured with his hat for him to lead the way. "What's your name?" asked K. as they went along. "Block, Block the merchant," the little man said, turning around to K. as he introduced himself, but K. didn't allow him to stop. "Is that your real name?" asked K. "Of course," was the answer, "why would you doubt it?" "I thought you might have some reason to conceal it," said K. He felt totally at ease, the way one normally feels speaking with inferiors in a foreign country, avoiding everything personal, just talking indifferently about their interests, thereby elevating them in importance, but also in a position to drop them at will. K. stopped before the door of the lawyer's study, opened it, and called out to the merchant, who had continued docilely onward: "Not so fast! Bring the light here." K. thought Leni might have hidden herself there; he had the merchant check all the corners, but the room was empty. Before the painting of the judge, K. held the merchant back by his suspenders. "Do you know him?" he asked, and pointed upward. The merchant lifted the candle, squinted up, and said: "It's a judge." "A high judge?" asked K. and stepped to the side of the merchant to observe the impression the picture made on him. The merchant gazed up in admiration. "It's a high judge," he said. "You don't know much," said K. "He's the lowest of the lower examining magistrates." "Now I remember," said the merchant and lowered the candle, "I've already heard that." "But of course," cried K., "yes I forgot, of course you would have already heard that." "But why, why?" asked the merchant as he moved toward the door, impelled by K.'s hands. In the hall outside K. said: "You know where Leni's hidden herself, don't you?" "Hidden herself?" said the merchant, "no, but she may be in the kitchen cooking soup for the lawyer." "Why didn't you say so in the first place?" asked K. "I was taking you there, but you called me back," replied the merchant, as if confused by the contradictory orders. "You probably think you're pretty clever," said K., "lead on then!" K. had never been in the kitchen; it was surprisingly spacious and well equipped. The stove alone was three times the size of a normal stove, but no other details were visible, for the kitchen was illuminated at the moment only by a small lamp hanging by the door. Leni was standing at the stove in her usual white apron, breaking eggs into a saucepan over an alcohol flame. "Good evening, Josef," she said with a sidelong glance. "Good evening," said K. and pointed to a chair off to the side that the merchant was to sit on, which he did. K., however, went up close behind Leni, bent over her shoulder and asked: "Who is this man?" Leni grasped K. with one hand while the other stirred the soup, pulled him forward, and said: "He's a pitiful fellow, a poor merchant named Block. Just look at him." They both looked back. The merchant was sitting in the chair K. had indicated; he had blown out the candle, its light now unnecessary, and was pinching the wick to stop the smoke. "You were in your slip," said K., turning her head back to the stove with his hand. She was silent. "Is he your lover?" asked K. She started to lift the soup pan, but K. seized both her hands and said: "Answer me!" She said: "Come into the study, I'll explain everything." "No," said K. "I want you to explain here." She clung to him, wanting to give him a kiss, but K. fended her off and said: "I don't want you kissing me now." "Josef," said Leni, staring at K. imploringly yet frankly, "you're surely not jealous of Herr Block." "Rudi," she said then, turning to the merchant, "help me out, you can see I'm under suspicion, put that candle down." One might have thought he hadn't been paying attention, but he knew just what she meant. "I really don't know what you have to be jealous about," he said, not very quick-wittedly. "I really don't know either," said K., and regarded the merchant with a smile. Leni laughed aloud, took advantage of K.'s distraction to slip her arm in his, and whispered: "Let him alone now, you see what sort of a man he is. I took a little interest in him because he's a major client of the lawyer, for no other reason. And you? Do you want to speak to the lawyer yet today? He's very sick today, but if you wish, I'll let him know you're here. But you'll stay overnight with me, that's definite. You haven't been here for such a long time that even the lawyer asked about you. Don't neglect your trial! And I've learned a few things I want to tell you about. But first take off your coat!" She helped him off with it, removed his hat, ran into the hall with them to hang them up, then came back and checked on the soup. "Shall I first tell him you're here, or bring him his soup first?" "First tell him

I'm here," said K. He was annoyed; he'd originally intended
to discuss his situation with Leni, particularly the question of
dismissal, but given the presence of the merchant he no
longer wished to. But now he felt his case was after all too
important for this small-time merchant to have any decisive
influence on it, so he called Leni, who was already in the hall,
back again. "Go ahead and take him his soup first," he said,
"he should gather his strength for our conference; he's going
to need it." "You're one of the lawyer's clients too," the merchant said softly from his corner, as if to confirm it. But it
wasn't well received. "What difference does it make to you?"
said K., and Leni said: "Will you be quiet." "I'll take him the
soup first then," said Leni to K. and poured the soup into a
bowl. "The only worry is he might fall asleep then; he usually
drops off to sleep right after he eats." "What I have to say
will keep him awake," said K.; he wanted to keep intimating
that he had something of major importance to discuss with
the lawyer; he wanted Leni to ask what it was and only then
seek her advice. But she merely carried out his spoken
instructions promptly. As she passed by with the bowl she
deliberately nudged him softly and whispered: "As soon as
he's eaten his soup, I'll tell him you're here; that way I'll get
you back as quickly as possible." "Go on," said K., "just go
on." "Try being a little friendlier," she said, turning around
once again in the doorway, bowl in hand.

K. watched her go; now that he had definitely decided to
dismiss the lawyer, it was probably just as well that he hadn't
managed to discuss the matter further with Leni beforehand;
she hardly had a sufficient grasp of the whole, and would certainly have advised against it; she might even have actually
prevented K. from announcing the dismissal at this point; he

would have remained upset and unsure, and yet in the end, after a period of time, he would still have carried out his decision, for the decision itself was all too compelling. The sooner it was carried out, however, the more damage it would prevent. Perhaps the merchant might have something to say about it.

K. turned around; the moment the merchant noticed, he began to rise. "Don't get up," said K., and drew a chair up beside him. "You're an old client of the lawyer?" asked K. "Yes," said the merchant, "a very old client." "How many years has he been representing you then?" asked K. "I don't know in what sense you mean that," said the merchant, "he's been representing me in my business affairs—I'm a grain dealer—ever since I took over the firm, for about twenty years now, and in my own trial, to which you're no doubt alluding, he's represented me right from the start as well, for more than five years now." "Yes, much longer than five years," he went on to add, and pulled out an old wallet, "I've written it all down here; if you wish I can give you the exact dates. It's hard to keep track of it all. No doubt my trial has been going on much longer than that; it began shortly after the death of my wife and that was more than five and a half years ago." K. drew nearer to him. "So the lawyer handles ordinary legal affairs as well?" he asked. This alliance of the court with jurisprudence seemed to K. unusually comforting. "Of course," said the merchant, and then whispered to K.: "They say he's even better in legal affairs than he is in the others." But then he seemed to regret his words; he placed a hand on K.'s shoulder and said: "Please don't betray me." K. patted him comfortingly on the thigh and said: "No, I'm no traitor." "He's vindictive, you see," said the merchant.

"Surely he wouldn't do anything to such a faithful client," said K. "Oh, yes he would," said the merchant, "when he's upset he draws no distinctions, and what's more I'm not really faithful to him." "What do you mean?" K. asked. "Should I confide in you?" the merchant asked doubtfully. "I believe you may," said K. "Well," said the merchant, "I'll confide it in part, but you have to tell me a secret too, so that we both have something to hold over the other with regard to the lawyer." "You're certainly cautious," said K., "but I'll tell you a secret that will put you entirely at ease. So, in what way are you unfaithful to the lawyer?" "Well," said the merchant hesitantly, in a tone as if he were confessing something dishonorable, "I have other lawyers besides him." "That's really nothing very bad," said K., a little disappointed. "Yes it is, here," said the merchant, still breathing heavily after his confession, but gaining confidence from K.'s remark. "It's not allowed. And the last thing you're allowed to do is take on shysters in addition to one designated as a lawyer. And that's just what I've done; in addition to him I have five shysters." "Five!" K. exclaimed, astonished above all by the number; "five lawyers besides him?" The merchant nodded: "I'm negotiating with a sixth right now." "But why do you need so many lawyers," asked K. "I need them all," said the merchant. "Won't you tell me why?" asked K. "Gladly," said the merchant. "First of all I don't want to lose my trial, that goes without saying. So I mustn't overlook anything that might be of use; even if there's only a slight hope in a given instance that it might be of use, I still don't dare discard it. So I've spent everything I have on my trial. For example, I've withdrawn all my capital from the business; my firm's offices used to almost fill an entire floor; now one small room in the back suffices, where I work with an apprentice. Of course this decline resulted not only from a withdrawal of funds, but even more from the withdrawal of my energy. If you're trying to work on your trial, you have little time for anything else." "So you deal directly with the court yourself?" asked K. "I'd like to know more about that." "There's not much to tell," said the merchant, "I tried it at first, but soon gave it up. It's too exhausting, with too few results. At any rate I found I just couldn't work there and deal with them myself. Just sitting and waiting is a major strain. You know yourself how stuffy it is in the offices." "How do you know I was there?" asked K. "I was in the waiting room when you passed through." "What a coincidence!" cried K., carried away and completely forgetting how ridiculous the merchant had once seemed. "So you saw me! You were in the waiting room when I passed through. Yes, I did pass through there once." "It's not that great a coincidence," said the merchant, "I'm there practically every day." "I'll probably have to go there fairly often now," said K., "but I doubt I'll be received as respectfully as I was back then. Everyone stood up. They probably thought I was a judge." "No," said the merchant, "we were greeting the court usher. We knew you were a defendant. News like that travels fast." "So you already knew that," said K., "then my behavior may have struck you as arrogant. Didn't anyone mention it?" "No," said the merchant, "on the contrary. But that's all nonsense." "What sort of nonsense?" asked K. "Why do you ask?" the merchant said irritably, "You don't seem to know the people there and might take it wrong. You have to realize that a great number of things are discussed in these proceedings that the mind just can't deal with, people are simply too tired and distracted, and by way of compensation they resort to superstition. I'm talking about the others, but I'm no better. One such superstition, for example, is that many people believe they can predict the outcome of the trial from the face of the defendant, and in particular from the lines of his lips. Now these people claimed that according to your lips, you were certain to be convicted soon. I repeat, it's a ridiculous superstition, and completely disproved in a majority of cases, but when you live in such company, it's difficult to avoid these beliefs. Just think how strong the effect of such a superstition can be. You spoke to someone there, didn't you? But he could hardly answer you. Of course there are all sorts of reasons for getting confused there, but one was the sight of your lips. He told us later he thought he'd seen the sign of his own conviction on your lips as well." "My lips?" asked K., taking out a pocket mirror and regarding his face. "I can't see anything unusual about my lips. Can you?" "Neither can I," said the merchant, "absolutely nothing at all." "These people are so superstitious!" K. exclaimed. "Didn't I tell you so?" asked the merchant. "Do they spend so much time together then, exchanging opinions?" said K. "I've avoided them totally up to now." "They generally don't spend much time together," said the merchant, "they couldn't, there are too many of them. And they don't have many interests in common. When a group occasionally begin to believe they share some common interest, it soon proves a delusion. Group action is entirely ineffective against the court. Each case is investigated on its own merits; the court is, after all, extremely meticulous. So group action is entirely ineffective, it's only individuals who sometimes manage something in secret; only when it's been achieved do others learn of it; no one knows how it happened. So there's no sense of community; people meet now and then in the waiting room, but there's not much conversation there. These superstitions have been around for ages, and multiply totally on their own." "I saw the gentlemen there in the waiting room," said K., "their waiting seemed to me so pointless." "Waiting isn't pointless," said the merchant, "the only thing that's pointless is independent action. As I mentioned, I have five lawyers besides this one. One would think—and I thought so myself at first—that I could now turn the case over to them completely. But that's totally mistaken. I'm even less able to turn it over to them than if I had only one. You probably don't understand why?" "No," said K., placing his hand soothingly on that of the merchant to slow down his all too rapid speech, "I just wonder if you could speak a little more slowly; all of these things are very important to me, and I can't really follow you." "I'm glad you reminded me," said the merchant, "you're a newcomer, after all, a mere youth. Your trial is six months old, right? Yes, I've heard about it. Such a young trial! I, on the other hand, have thought these things through innumerable times; to me they're the most self-evident matters in the world." "You're no doubt happy your trial's so far along?" K. inquired; he didn't want to ask straight out how the merchant's case was coming. But he didn't receive a straightforward answer either. "Yes, I've been pushing my trial along for five years," said the merchant, bowing his head, "that's no small accomplishment." Then he fell silent for a moment. K. listened to hear if Leni was return-ing yet. On the one hand he didn't want her to come, for he still had many questions to ask and didn't want Leni to dis-cover him in intimate conversation with the merchant; on the other hand, he was annoyed that in spite of his presence, she

was remaining so long with the lawyer, much longer than
necessary to hand him his soup. "I still remember clearly,"
the merchant continued, and K. was immediately all ears,
"when my trial was about as old as yours is now. Back then I
had only this one lawyer, but I wasn't particularly satisfied
with him." "I'm finding out everything here," thought K.,
and nodded vigorously as if to encourage the merchant to tell
him everything worth knowing. "My trial," the merchant
went on, "was getting nowhere; inquiries were taking place
all right, and I attended every one of them, gathered material,
and turned all my business records over to the court, which I
discovered later wasn't even necessary; I kept running to my
lawyer, and he was submitting various petitions as well—"
"Various petitions?" asked K. "Yes, of course," said the merchant. "That's very important to me," said K., "in my case
he's still preparing the first petition. He hasn't done anything
yet. I see now that he's neglecting me shamefully." "There
may be various valid reasons why the petition isn't finished
yet," said the merchant. "And my petitions, by the way, later
proved to be entirely worthless. I even read one of them
myself through the good graces of a court clerk. It was scholarly all right, but in fact contained nothing of substance. A
lot of Latin for the most part, which I don't understand, then
several pages of general appeals to the court, then flattery of
certain individual officials, who weren't in fact named but
could have been deduced by anyone familiar with the court,
then self-praise on the lawyer's part, combined with an
almost canine servility before the court, and finally analyses
of legal cases from ancient times that were supposedly similar
to mine. Of course these analyses, so far as I could tell, were
very carefully done. I don't mean to judge the lawyer's work

in saying all this, and the petition I read was only one of many; nevertheless, and this is what I want to get to, I couldn't see that my trial was making any progress." "What sort of progress did you expect to see?" asked K. "That's a very sensible question," said the merchant with a smile, "you seldom see any sort of progress at all in such proceedings. But I didn't know that then. I'm a merchant, and was much more of one then than I am today; I wanted to see tangible results; I expected the whole matter to be moving toward a conclusion, or at least to advance at a steady pace. Instead there were nothing but hearings, most of which went over the same old material; I already had the answers prepared like a litany; several times a week, court messengers would come to my firm or to my lodgings, or wherever they could find me; that was disturbing of course (things are much better these days, at least in that respect; a telephone call causes far less disruption), and rumors about my trial were starting to spread, among my colleagues in particular, but among my relatives as well, so that damage was being done on all sides, without the least indication that even the first session of the trial would take place anytime soon. So I went to my lawyer and complained. He offered long explanations of course, but steadfastly refused to take the action I desired; no one could influence the setting of a firm date for the trial, to make such a demand in a petition—as I was asking—was simply unheard of and would ruin both him and me. I thought to myself: what this lawyer either can't or won't do, some other lawyer can and will. So I looked around for other lawyers. Let me say right away: not one of them asked for or succeeded in getting a firm date set for the main hearing; it turns out that, with one reservation, which I'll come to, it's truly impossible to do so; on this point the lawyer had not deceived me; for the rest however I had no regrets about having turned to other lawyers. You've probably already heard something about shysters from Dr. Huld; no doubt he portrayed them as contemptible, and in fact they are. Of course whenever he talks about them, and compares himself and his colleagues with them, a small error always creeps in, which I wish simply to point out to you in passing. He always refers to his own circle of lawyers, by way of contrast, as the 'great' lawyers. That's inaccurate; anyone can call himself 'great' if he wants to, of course, but in this case court usage is decisive. According to that there are, in addition to the shysters, both petty lawyers and great lawyers. This lawyer and his colleagues are only petty lawyers, however; the great lawyers, whom I've merely heard of but never seen, stand incomparably higher in rank above the petty lawyers than those do over the despised shysters." "The great lawyers?" asked K. "Who are they then? How can they be contacted?" "So you've never heard of them," said the merchant. "There's scarcely a single defendant who doesn't dream of them for a time after learning about them. Don't fall prey to that temptation. I don't know who the great lawyers are, and it's probably impossible to contact them. I don't know of a single case in which they can be said with certainty to have intervened. They do defend some people, but it's not possible to arrange that on one's own, they only defend those they wish to defend. The cases they take on, however, have no doubt already advanced beyond the lower court. On the whole it's best not to think about them, otherwise consultations with other lawyers, their advice and assistance, all seem so disgusting and useless that, as I myself know from experience, what you would like most to do would be to pitch the whole affair, go home to bed, and hear nothing more of it. But of course that would be equally stupid; nor would you be left at peace in bed for long." "So you didn't think about the great lawyers back then?" asked K. "Not for long," said the merchant, and smiled again, "you can never quite forget them, unfortunately, nights are particularly conducive to such thoughts. But back then I wanted immediate results, so I went to the shysters."

"Look at the two of you sitting together," cried Leni, who had returned with the bowl and paused at the door. In fact they were sitting quite close to one another; the slightest turn and they would bump their heads; the merchant, who apart from his short stature also stooped, had forced K. to bend low if he wanted to hear everything. "Just give us another minute," K. said, putting Leni off, and the hand he still left placed on the merchant's twitched impatiently. "He wanted me to tell him about my trial," the merchant said to Leni. "Go ahead and tell him," she said. She spoke tenderly to the merchant, but condescendingly as well, which didn't please K; after all, as he now realized, the man had some merit, at least he had experience in these matters and could communicate it. Leni probably judged him unfairly. He watched with annoyance as Leni took the candle from the merchant, who had been gripping it firmly the whole time, wiped his hand with her apron, and then knelt down beside him to scratch away some wax that had dripped onto his trousers. "You were going to tell me about the shysters," K. said, pushing Leni's hand away without comment. "What do you think you're doing?" asked Leni, giving K. a small tap and resuming her task. "Yes, the shysters," said the merchant, and passed his hand across his brow, as if he were thinking. K. tried to prompt him by saying: "You wanted immediate results and so you went to the shysters." "That's right," said the merchant, but didn't continue. "Perhaps he doesn't want to talk about it in front of Leni," thought K., suppressing his impatience to hear the rest at once and pressing him no further.

"Did you tell him I was here?" he asked Leni. "Of course," she said, "he's waiting for you. Now leave Block alone; you can always talk with Block later; he's staying here after all." K. hesitated a moment longer. "You're staying here?" he asked the merchant; he wanted him to answer for himself, not to have Leni talking about the merchant as if he weren't there; he was filled with hidden resentment against Leni today. Again only Leni answered: "He often sleeps here." "Sleeps here?" cried K.; he'd thought the merchant would simply wait for him while he dealt quickly with the lawyer, and that they would then leave together and discuss everything thoroughly, without interruption. "Yes," said Leni, "not everyone is allowed to see the lawyer whenever they wish, like you, Josef. You don't seem at all surprised that the lawyer is receiving you at eleven o'clock at night, in spite of his illness. You take what your friends do for you too much for granted. Well, your friends do it gladly, or at least I do. I don't want or need any other thanks than that you're fond of me." "Fond of you?" K. thought for a moment, and only then did it occur to him: "Well, I am fond of her." Nevertheless he said, ignoring all the rest: "He receives me because I'm his client. If I needed outside help for that too, I'd be bowing and scraping at every step." "He's being very bad today, isn't he?" Leni asked the merchant. "Now I'm the one who isn't here," thought K., and almost grew angry with the merchant as well, as the latter, adopting Leni's rude manner, said: "The lawyer has other reasons for receiving him too. His case is much more interesting than mine. And his trial is in its beginning stages, and therefore probably not particularly muddled yet, so the lawyer still enjoys dealing with it. Things will be different later on." "Yes, yes," said Leni, and glanced at the merchant with a smile, "how he rattles on! You don't dare believe him at all," here she turned to K., "he's as gossipy as he is sweet. Maybe that's why the lawyer doesn't like him. At any rate, he only sees him if he's in a good mood. I've been trying hard to change that, but it's impossible. Just think, sometimes I tell him Block's here and it's three days before he receives him. If Block isn't on the spot when called, however, all is lost, and he has to be announced anew. That's why I let Block sleep here; he's been known to ring for him in the night. So now Block is ready nights as well. Sometimes, of course, if Block does prove to be here, the lawyer then retracts the order to admit him." K. threw a questioning glance at the merchant. The merchant nodded and said as frankly as he had in speaking with K. earlier, perhaps forgetting himself in his embarrassment: "Yes, you grow very dependent on your lawyer later on." "He's just making a show of complaining," said Leni. "He enjoys sleeping here, as he's often confessed to me." She walked over to a little door and pushed it open. "Do you want to see his bedroom?" she asked. K. walked over and gazed from the threshold into the low, windowless room, completely filled by a narrow bed. The only way to get into the bed was to climb over the bedposts. At the head of the bed was a niche in the wall in which a candle, inkwell and quill, as well as a sheaf of papers, probably trial documents, were meticulously arranged. "You sleep in the maid's room?" asked K. and turned back toward the merchant. "Leni lets me have it," answered the merchant, "it's very convenient." K. took a long look at him; perhaps his first impression of the merchant had been correct after all; he was experienced in these matters, since his trial had been under way for a long time, but he had paid dearly for that experience. Suddenly K. could no longer stand the sight of the merchant. "Put him to bed," he cried to Leni, who seemed to have no idea what he meant. He himself wanted to see the lawyer, and by dismissing him, to free himself not only from the lawyer, but from Leni and the merchant as well. But before he reached the door, the merchant addressed him softly: "Herr K." K. turned around with an angry look. "You've forgotten your promise," said the merchant, and leaned forward imploringly from his chair toward K., "you were going to tell me a secret." "That's true," said K., glancing at Leni as well, who regarded him attentively, "well, listen: it's hardly a secret by now of course. I'm going to see the lawyer now to dismiss him." "He's dismissing him," cried the merchant, jumping up from his chair and racing about the kitchen with his arms in the air. Again and again he cried out: "He's dismissing his lawyer." Leni immediately started for K., but the merchant got in her way and she struck him with her fists. Still clenching her fists, she ran after K., who, however, had a sizable lead. He had already entered the lawyer's room when Leni caught up with him. He'd almost shut the door behind him, but Leni, who held the door open with her foot, grabbed him by the arm and tried to pull him back. He squeezed her wrist so hard, however, that she groaned and let him go. She didn't dare enter the room at once, and K. locked the door with the key.

"I've been waiting a long time for you," said the lawyer

from his bed, placing on the nightstand a document he'd been reading by candlelight and donning a pair of glasses, through which he peered sharply at K. Instead of apologizing, K. said: "I'll be leaving soon." Because K.'s remark was not an apology, the lawyer ignored it and said: "I'll not see you again at such a late hour." "That's in accord with my desires," said K. The lawyer looked at him inquisitively. "Sit down," he said. "As you wish," said K., pulling a chair up to the nightstand and sitting down. "It looked to me like you locked the door," said the lawyer. "Yes," said K., "because of Leni." He intended to spare no one. But the lawyer asked: "Was she being too forward again?" "Too forward?" K. asked. "Yes," said the lawyer with a chuckle, fell prey to a fit of coughing, then started chuckling again once it had passed. "You've no doubt noticed how forward she is?" he asked, patting K. on the hand he'd braced distractedly on the nightstand and now quickly withdrew. "You don't attach much importance to it," said the lawyer as K. remained silent, "so much the better. Otherwise I might have had to offer you my apologies. It's a peculiarity of hers I've long since forgiven her for, and I wouldn't bring it up at all if you hadn't locked the door just now. This peculiarity, and of course you're probably the last person I need to explain this to, but you look so perplexed that I will, this peculiarity consists in the fact that Leni finds most defendants attractive. She's drawn to all of them, loves all of them, and of course appears to be loved by them in turn; she occasionally amuses me with stories about it, when I let her. I'm not nearly as surprised as you seem to be. If you have an eye for that sort of thing, defendants are indeed often attractive. It is of course remarkable, in a sense almost a natural phenomenon. It's clear no obvious change in appearance is noticeable once a person has been accused. The situation differs from a normal court case; most defendants continue to lead a normal life and, if they find a good lawyer who looks out for them, they aren't particularly hampered by the trial. Nevertheless, an experienced eye can pick out a defendant in the largest crowd every time. On what basis? you may ask. My reply won't satisfy you. The defendants are simply the most attractive. It can't be guilt that makes them attractive, for—at least as a lawyer I must maintain this—they can't all be guilty, nor can it be the coming punishment that renders them attractive in advance, for not all of them will be punished; it must be a result, then, of the proceedings being brought against them, which somehow adheres to them. Of course some are even more attractive than others. But they're all attractive, even that miserable worm, Block."

By the time the lawyer had finished, K. had completely regained his composure; he even nodded emphatically at his final words, which reconfirmed his original conviction that the lawyer, now as always, was attempting to divert his attention from the main question by conveying general information having nothing to do with the matter at hand, which was what he had actually accomplished in K.'s case. The lawyer no doubt noticed that K. was putting up more resistance than usual on this occasion, for he now fell silent in order to allow K. a chance to speak, and when K. said nothing, he asked: "Have you come with some special purpose in mind today?" "Yes," said K., shading the candle with his hand slightly, so he could see the lawyer better, "I wanted to tell you that as of today I no longer wish for you to represent me." "Do I understand you correctly?" the lawyer asked, rising halfway up in bed and propping himself with one hand on the pillows.

"I assume so," said K., who was sitting there tensely, on the alert. "Well now, we can discuss this plan," said the lawyer after a pause. "It's no longer a plan," said K. "That may be," said the lawyer, "but still we mustn't be too hasty." He used the word "we" as if he had no intention of freeing K, as if he were still his advisor, even if he were no longer his legal representative. "There's nothing hasty about it," said K., standing up slowly and stepping behind his chair, "it's been carefully considered, perhaps at even too great a length. The decision is final." "Then permit me just a few more remarks," said the lawyer, pulling off the quilt and sitting up on the edge of the bed. His bare, white-haired legs trembled in the cold. He asked K. to pass him a blanket from the divan. K. fetched the blanket and said: "There's no reason to risk catching cold." "The cause is important enough," said the lawyer as he pulled the quilt around his upper body and then wrapped the blanket around his legs. "Your uncle is my friend, and I've grown fond of you as well over the course of time. I admit that openly. I needn't be ashamed of it." These emotional sentiments on the old man's part were not welcomed by K., for they forced him to a more detailed explanation he would have preferred to avoid, and they disconcerted him as well, as he admitted openly to himself, although they could never, of course, cause him to retract his decision. "I appreciate your kind feelings," he said, "and I realize you did as much as you could in my case, and in a manner you thought was in my interest. Recently, however, I've become convinced that isn't enough. Naturally I would never attempt to persuade you, a much older and more experienced man, to adopt my point of view; if I've sometimes tried to do so instinctively, please forgive me, but as you say, the cause is important enough, and

I'm convinced it's necessary to intervene much more actively in the trial than has been done to this point." "I understand," said the lawyer, "you're impatient." "I'm not impatient," said K., slightly irritated and choosing his words less carefully now. "You may have noticed during my first visit, when I came here with my uncle, that I wasn't particularly concerned about the trial; when I wasn't forcibly reminded of it, so to speak, I forgot it entirely. But my uncle insisted I ask you to represent me, and I did it to oblige him. One would have thought the trial would weigh less heavily upon me then; the point of engaging a lawyer is to shift the burden of the trial in part from one's self. But the opposite occurred. I never had as many worries about the trial as I did from the moment you began to represent me. When I was on my own I did nothing about my case, but I hardly noticed it; now, on the other hand, I had someone representing me, everything was set so that something was supposed to happen, I kept waiting expectantly for you to take action, but nothing was done. Of course you passed on various bits of information about the court I might not have garnered from anyone else. But I don't find that sufficient when the trial is positively closing in on me in secret." K. had pushed the chair away and was standing there with his hands in his pockets. "From a certain point onward in one's practice," the lawyer said softly and calmly, "nothing really new ever happens. How many clients at a similar stage in their trial have stood before me as you do now and spoken similar words." "Then all those similar clients," said K. "were as much in the right as I am. That doesn't refute what I say." "I wasn't trying to refute you," said the lawyer, "but I was about to add that I expected better judgment from you than from the others, particularly since

I've given you a greater insight into the workings of the court and my own actions than I normally do for clients. And now I'm forced to realize that in spite of everything, you have too little confidence in me. You don't make things easy for me." How the lawyer was humbling himself before K.! With no consideration at all for the honor of his profession, which was doubtless most sensitive on this point. And why was he doing it? He appeared to be a busy lawyer and a rich man as well, so the loss of the fee itself or of one client couldn't mean that much to him. And given his illness, he should be thinking about reducing his workload anyway. Nevertheless, he was holding on tight to K. Why? Was it out of personal consideration for his uncle, or did he truly find K.'s trial so extraordinary that he hoped to distinguish himself on K.'s behalf, or—the possibility could never be entirely dismissed—on behalf of his friends at court? His demeanor revealed nothing, no matter how sharply K. scrutinized him. You might almost think he was awaiting the effect of his words with a deliberately blank expression. But he evidently interpreted K.'s silence all too positively, for he now continued: "You will have noticed I have a large office but employ no staff. Things used to be different; there was a time when several young lawyers worked for me, but today I work alone. That's due in part to a change in my practice, in that I restrict myself increasingly to legal matters like yours, in part to a deepening insight I've gained through such cases. I found I didn't dare delegate this work to anyone else if I wished to avoid sinning against my client and the task I'd undertaken. But the decision to handle everything myself had certain natural consequences: I had to turn down most requests to represent clients and could only relent in cases I found of particular interest—well, there are plenty of wretched creatures, even right in this neighborhood, ready to fling themselves on the smallest crumb I cast aside. And I fell ill from overwork as well. Nevertheless, I don't regret my decision; perhaps I should have refused more cases than I did, but devoting myself entirely to the trials I did take on proved absolutely necessary and was rewarded by success. I once read an essay in which I found the difference between representing a normal case and representing one of this sort expressed quite beautifully. It said: one lawyer leads his client by a slender thread to the judgment, but the other lifts his client onto his shoulders and carries him to the judgment and beyond, without ever setting him down. That's how it is. But I wasn't quite accurate when I said I never regretted this difficult task. When, as in your case, it's so completely misunderstood, well then, I almost do regret it." This speech, instead of convincing K., merely increased his impatience. From the lawyer's tone, he gathered some sense of what awaited him if he gave in, the vain promises that would begin anew, the references to progress on the petition, to the improved mood of the court officials, but also to the immense difficulties involved—in short, everything K. already knew ad nauseam would be trotted out once again to lure him with vague hopes and torment him with vague threats. He had to put a clear stop to that, and so he said: "What steps will you take in my case if you continue to represent me?" The lawyer bowed to even this insulting question and answered: "I'll continue along the lines I've already taken." "I knew it," said K., "well, there's no need to waste another word." "I'll make one more attempt," said the lawyer, as if what was upsetting K. was affecting to him instead. "I suspect that what's led both to your false judgment of my legal assistance and to your general behavior is that, in spite of being an accused man, you've been treated too well, or to put it more accurately, you've been treated with negligence, with apparent negligence. There's a reason for this as well; it's often better to be in chains than to be free. But I'd like to show you how other defendants are treated; perhaps you'll be able to draw a lesson from it. I'm going to call Block in now; unlock the door and sit down here beside the nightstand." "Gladly," said K. and did as the lawyer asked; he was always ready to learn. But as a general precaution, he asked as well: "You do understand, however, that I'm dispensing with your services?" "Yes," said the lawyer, "but you can still retract that decision today." He lay back down in bed, pulled the quilt up to his chin, and turned toward the wall. Then he rang.

Leni appeared almost simultaneously with the sound of the bell; she tried to ascertain what had happened with a few quick glances; the fact that K. was sitting quietly by the lawyer's bed seemed to reassure her. She nodded with a smile to K., who stared fixedly at her. "Get Block," said the lawyer. But instead of going to get him, she simply stepped outside the door, called out: "Block! To the lawyer!" and then, no doubt because the lawyer was still turned toward the wall and paying no attention, slipped behind K.'s chair. She kept distracting him from that point on, leaning over the back of his chair, or running her fingers, quite gently and surreptitiously of course, through his hair, and stroking his cheeks. Finally K. tried to stop her by grabbing her hand, which, after a brief resistance, she surrendered to him.

Block arrived immediately in response to the summons but stopped at the door and seemed to be debating whether or

not he should enter. He raised his eyebrows and inclined his
head, as if listening to hear if the order to see the lawyer
might be repeated. K. might have encouraged him to enter,
but he had decided to make a clean break, not only with his
lawyer, but with everything that went on in his apartment,
and so he remained motionless. Leni too was silent. Block
saw that at least he wasn't being driven away and entered on
tiptoe, his face tense, his hands clenched behind him. He had
left the door open for a possible retreat. He didn't even glance
at K. but instead gazed only at the puffy quilt beneath which
the lawyer, who had moved right against the wall, could not
even be seen. Then, however, his voice was heard: "Block
here?" he asked. This query delivered a virtual blow to Block,
who had already advanced a good way forward, striking him
in the chest and then in the back so that he stumbled, came to
a stop with a deep bow, and said: "At your service." "What
do you want?" asked the lawyer; "you've come at an inopportune time." "Wasn't I summoned?" asked Block, more to
himself than to the lawyer, lifting his hands protectively and
ready to retreat. "You were summoned," said the lawyer,
"but you've still come at an inopportune time." And after a
pause he continued: "You always come at inopportune
times." Once the lawyer began speaking, Block no longer
looked at the bed, but instead stared off somewhere into a
corner and merely listened, as if the sight of the speaker was
too blinding to bear. Listening was difficult too, however, for
the lawyer was speaking to the wall, softly and rapidly. "Do
you wish me to leave?" asked Block. "You're here now," said
the lawyer. "Stay!" One would have thought the lawyer had
threatened to flog Block, not grant his wish, for now Block
began to tremble in earnest. "Yesterday," said the lawyer, "I

visited the third judge, my friend, and gradually brought the conversation around to you. Do you want to know what he said?" "Oh, please," said Block. Since the lawyer didn't reply at once, Block repeated his entreaty, and stooped as if to kneel. But then K. lashed out at him: "What are you doing?" he cried. Since Leni tried to stop his outburst, he seized her other hand as well. It was no loving embrace in which he held them; she groaned several times and tried to pull her hands away. Block was the one punished for K.'s outburst, however, for the lawyer asked him: "Who's your lawyer?" "You are," said Block. "And other than me?" asked the lawyer. "No one but you," said Block. "Then don't listen to anyone else," said the lawyer. Block accepted this totally; he measured K. with an angry glance and shook his head vigorously. Translated into words, his gestures would have constituted a tirade of abuse. And this was the man K. had wished to engage in friendly conversation about his own case! "I won't disturb you further," said K., leaning back in his chair, "kneel down or crawl around on all fours, do just as you like, it makes no difference to me." But Block did have a sense of honor after all, at least as far as K. was concerned, for he headed toward him, brandishing his fists and crying out as loudly as he dared in the lawyer's presence: "You can't talk to me like that, it's not allowed. Why are you insulting me? And in front of the lawyer, who tolerates both you and me merely out of compassion? You're no better a person than I am, for you're a defendant too and also on trial. But if you remain a gentleman in spite of that, then I'm as much a gentleman as you, if not a greater one. And I wish to be addressed as one, especially by you. But if you think you're privileged because you're allowed to sit here quietly and listen while I, as you put it, crawl around on all fours, then let me remind you of the old legal maxim: a suspect is better off moving than at rest, for one at rest may be on the scales without knowing it, being weighed with all his sins." K. said nothing; he simply stared fixedly in astonishment at this flustered man. How many transformations he had undergone in just this past hour! Was it the trial that cast him about so, and kept him from distinguishing his friends from his enemies? Couldn't he see that the lawyer was intentionally humiliating him, with no other goal on this occasion but to parade his power before K. and by so doing perhaps intimidate K. as well? But if Block was incapable of recognizing that, or feared the lawyer so much that this knowledge was of no help, how was he clever or bold enough to deceive the lawyer and conceal the fact that he had other lawyers working for him as well. And how did he dare to attack K., who could betray his secret at any time. But he dared more than this; he approached the lawyer's bed and began complaining about K. there as well: "Herr Huld," he said, "you've heard how this man speaks to me. His trial can still be reckoned in hours and he's already trying to give me advice, me, a man who's been on trial for five years. He even abuses me. Knows nothing and abuses me, a man who has studied closely, to the best of my poor abilities, what decency, duty, and court custom demand." "Don't worry about anyone else," said the lawyer, "just do what seems right to you." "Certainly," said Block, as if building up his own courage, and, with a quick sidelong glance, he knelt at the side of the bed. "I'm on my knees, sir," he said. But the lawyer said nothing. Block caressed the quilt cautiously with one hand. In the silence that now reigned Leni said, as she freed herself from K.'s hands: "You're hurting me. Leave me alone. I'm going to Block." She went over and sat down on the edge of the bed. Block was greatly pleased by her arrival; he begged her at once with urgent but silent gestures to plead his cause with the lawyer. He evidently needed the lawyer's information badly, perhaps only so that it could be used by his other lawyers. Leni apparently knew just how to approach the lawyer; she pointed to the lawyer's hand and pursed her lips as if for a kiss. Block immediately kissed it and at Leni's prompting, did so twice more. But still the lawyer said nothing. Then Leni leaned over the lawyer, displaying her fine figure as she stretched forward and bent down close to his face to stroke his long white hair. That finally wrested a response from him. "I hesitate to tell him," said the lawyer, and you could see how he shook his head slightly, perhaps to enjoy the touch of Leni's hand more fully. Block listened with bowed head, as if he were breaking some rule by doing so. "Why do you hesitate?" asked Leni. K. had the feeling he was listening to a carefully rehearsed dialogue that had occurred many times before, and would occur many times again, one that would remain forever fresh only to Block. "How has he behaved today?" asked the lawyer, instead of answering. Before replying, Leni looked down at Block for a few moments as he raised his hands to her and wrung them imploringly. At last she nodded gravely, turned to the lawyer, and said: "He's been quiet and industrious." An elderly merchant, a man with a long beard, begging a young woman to put in a good word for him. Even if he had his own ulterior motives, nothing could justify his actions in the eyes of his fellow man. It almost dishonored the onlooker. K. didn't see how the lawyer could possibly have believed this performance would win him over. If he had not already dri-

ven him away, this scene would have done so. So the lawyer's
methods, to which K., fortunately, had not been long enough
exposed, resulted in this: that the client finally forgot the
entire world, desiring only to trudge along this mistaken path
to the end of his trial. He was no longer a client, he was the
lawyer's dog. If the lawyer had ordered him to crawl under
the bed, as into a kennel, and bark, he would have done so
gladly. K. listened critically and coolly, as if he had been commissioned to mentally record everything, render an account
of it at a higher level, and file a report. "What did he do all
day?" asked the lawyer. "I locked him in the maid's room,
where he generally stays anyway," said Leni, "so that he
wouldn't bother me while I was working. I checked on what
he was doing from time to time through the peephole. He
was always kneeling on the bed with the documents you
loaned him open on the windowsill, reading them. That
made a positive impression on me; the window opens only
onto an air shaft and offers hardly any light. That Block was
reading in spite of this made me realize how obedient he is."
"I'm glad to hear it," said the lawyer. "But did he understand
what he was reading?" Block moved his lips constantly during this conversation, apparently formulating the replies he
hoped Leni would give. "Of course I can't really say for
sure," said Leni. "At any rate I could see he was reading carefully. He spent the whole day reading the same page, and
would move his finger along the lines as he read. Whenever I
looked in he was sighing, as if he were finding it hard to read.
The texts you gave him are probably hard to understand."
"Yes," said the lawyer, "of course they are. And I don't imagine he does understand any of them. They're simply meant to
give him some idea of the difficulty of the battle I'm waging

in his defense. And for whom am I waging this difficult battle? For—ludicrous as it may sound—for Block. He must learn the full import of that as well. Did he study without a break?" "Almost without a break," said Leni, "there was just one time when he asked me for a drink of water. I passed him a glass through the peephole. Then at eight o'clock I let him out and gave him something to eat." Block gave K. a sidelong glance, as if something praiseworthy had been said about him and must surely have impressed K. as well. He seemed quite hopeful now; he moved more freely and shifted about on his knees. It was therefore all the more obvious when he froze at the following words from the lawyer: "You're praising him," said the lawyer. "But that's just why I find it hard to speak. For the judge's remarks were not at all favorable, for Block or his trial." "Not favorable?" asked Leni. "How could that be?" Block looked at her expectantly, as if he thought her capable of turning to his favor the words long since spoken by the judge. "Not favorable," said the lawyer. "He was annoyed that I even brought up Block's name. 'Don't talk about Block,' he said. 'He's my client,' I said. 'You're letting him take advantage of you,' he said. 'I don't consider his case a lost cause,' I said. 'You're letting him take advantage of you,' he repeated. 'I don't believe it,' I said. 'Block works hard on his trial and always tries to keep up with it. He practically lives with me in order to stay current. One doesn't always find such commitment. It's true he's an unpleasant person, has bad manners and is dirty, but with regard to procedural matters he's irreproachable.' I said irreproachable; I was intentionally exaggerating. To which he replied: 'Block is simply cunning. He's gained a good deal of experience and knows how to protract a trial. But his ignorance far outweighs his cunning. What do you think he would say if he were to learn that his trial hasn't even begun yet, if someone were to tell him that the bell that opens the trial still hasn't rung.' Quiet, Block," said the lawyer, for Block was starting to rise up on his wobbly knees and was apparently about to ask for an explanation. Now for the first time the lawyer addressed Block directly at length. His tired eyes roamed about, at times aimlessly, at times focusing on Block, who slowly sank to his knees again beneath his gaze. "The judge's remark is of no importance for you," said the lawyer. "Don't go into shock at every word. If you do it again, I won't disclose anything further to you. I can't even begin a sentence without having you stare at me as if I were about to deliver your final judgment. You should be ashamed here in front of my client! You'll undermine his faith in me as well. What is it you want? You're still alive, you're still under my protection. It's senseless anxiety! You've read somewhere that in some cases the final judgment comes unexpectedly from some chance person at some random moment. With numerous reservations that's true of course, but it's equally true that your anxiety disgusts me and that I see in it a lack of necessary faith. What have I said after all? I've repeated a judge's remark. You know that various views pile up around these proceedings until they become impenetrable. For instance this judge assumes a different starting point for the trial than I do. A difference of opinion, that's all. There is an old tradition that a bell is rung at a certain stage in the trial. In this judge's view it marks the beginning of the trial. I can't tell you everything that speaks against this at the moment, nor would you understand it all; suffice it to say a great deal speaks against it." Embarrassed, Block ran his fingers through the fur of the bedside rug; the anxiety caused by the judge's statement caused him to forget for a moment his own subservience to the lawyer; he now thought only of himself, turning the judge's words over, examining them from all sides. "Block," said Leni in a tone of warning, lifting him up a bit by the collar. "Leave that fur alone and listen to the lawyer."

IN THE CATHEDRAL

An Italian business associate of major importance to the bank was visiting the city for the first time, and K. had been assigned to show him a few of its artistic treasures. At any other time he would have considered the assignment an honor, but now that he was expending so much effort defending his prestige at the bank, he accepted it reluctantly. Every hour away from the office troubled him; it was true he could no longer use his office time as efficiently as before; he spent many an hour in only the most superficial appearance of actual work, but that made him all the more worried when he was away from the office. He pictured the vice president, who was always lurking about, entering his office from time to time, sitting down at his desk, rifling through his papers, receiving customers who over the years had almost become K.'s friends, luring them away, yes, perhaps even discovering errors, which K. felt threatened by from a thousand directions as he worked, errors he could no longer avoid. So no matter how much it honored him, whenever he was given any assignment that required a business call or even a short trip—as chance would have it, the number of such assignments had mounted recently—the suspicion was never far removed that they were trying to get him out of the office for a while to check on his work, or at the very least, that they thought they could spare him easily at the office. He could have turned down most of the assignments with no difficulty, but he didn't dare, for if there was any justification at all for his fear, refusing the assignment would be taken as an admission of his anxiety. For this reason he accepted such assignments with apparent equanimity, even concealing a bad cold when faced with a strenuous two-day business trip, so that there would be no risk of his being held back due to the prevailing rainy autumn weather. Returning from the trip with a raging headache, he discovered he was supposed to host the Italian colleague the following day. The temptation to refuse, at least on this occasion, was strong, particularly since what he was being asked to do bore no direct relationship to his work at the bank; fulfilling this social duty for a business colleague was doubtless important in itself, but not to K., who was well aware that only success in the office could protect him, and that if he couldn't manage that, even proving unexpectedly charming to the Italian would be of no value at all; he didn't want to be forced away from work even for a day, for the fear that he might not be allowed to return was too great, a fear that he knew all too well was far-fetched but that nonetheless oppressed him. In this case of course it was almost impossible to invent a plausible excuse; K.'s Italian was not particularly fluent, but it was adequate; the decisive argument, however, was that K. had some knowledge of art history, acquired in earlier days; this had become known at the bank and blown far out of proportion because for a time, and solely for business reasons as it happened, K. had belonged to the Society for the Preservation of Municipal Works of Art. Since rumor had it that the Italian was an art lover, the choice of K. as a guide had been obvious.

It was a very wet and windy morning as K., full of irritation at the day before him, entered his office at seven o'clock in hopes of accomplishing at least some work before the visitor took him away from everything. He was very tired, having spent half the night preparing himself somewhat by poring over an Italian grammar; the window at which he was accustomed to sit all too often in recent days attracted him more than his desk, but he resisted and sat down to work. Unfortunately his assistant entered immediately and announced that the president had asked him to see if K. was in yet; if he was, would he be so kind as to come over to the reception room, since the gentleman from Italy had already arrived. "I'll be right there," said K., stuck a small dictionary in his pocket, tucked an album of city sights he had brought for the visitor under his arm, and walked through the vice president's office into the head office. He was happy that he'd arrived at the office so early and was immediately available, which no one could seriously have expected. The vice president's office was still empty of course, as in the depths of night; the assistant had probably been asked to call him to the reception room too, but without success. As K. entered the reception room the two men rose from their deep arm-chairs. The president wore a friendly smile and was obviously delighted at K.'s arrival; he handled the introductions at once, the Italian shook K.'s hand warmly, and laughingly called someone an early riser; K. wasn't sure exactly whom he meant, for it was an odd expression, and it took K. a moment or so to guess its sense. He answered with a few smooth sentences that the Italian responded to with another laugh, nervously stroking his bushy, gray-blue mustache several times. This mustache was obviously perfumed, one was almost tempted to draw near and sniff it. When they were all seated and had launched into a brief preliminary conversation, K. realized with discomfort that he understood only bits and pieces of what the Italian was saying. When he spoke slowly, he could understand almost everything, but those were rare exceptions; for the most part the words literally poured from his lips, and he shook his head in seeming pleasure as they did so. At such times, however, he kept falling into some dialect or other that didn't really sound like Italian to K., but that the president not only understood but also spoke, something K. should have predicted, of course, since the Italian came from southern Italy, and the president had spent a few years there himself. At any rate K. realized he would have little chance of understanding the Italian, for his French was hard to follow too, and his mustache hid the movement of his lips, the sight of which might otherwise have helped him out. K. began to foresee various difficulties; for the moment he'd given up trying to follow the Italian—given the presence of the president, who understood him so easily, it was an unnecessary strain—and limited himself to observing peevishly the way he sat so deeply yet lightly in the

armchair, how he tugged repeatedly at his short, sharply tailored jacket, and how once, lifting his arms and fluttering his
hands, he tried to describe something K. couldn't quite follow, even though he leaned forward and stared at his hands.
In the end K., who was now simply glancing mechanically
back and forth during the conversation, began to fall prey to
his earlier fatigue and at one point to his horror caught himself, just in time fortunately, starting to rise absentmindedly,
turn around, and leave. Finally the Italian glanced at his
watch and jumped up. After he had taken leave of the president, he pressed up so near to K. that K. had to shove his
armchair back in order to move at all. The president, who
had surely seen in K.'s eyes the difficulty in which he found
himself with the Italian, intervened in their conversation so
delicately and cleverly that it seemed as if he were only making minor suggestions, while in reality he was succinctly
conveying the sense of everything the Italian, who kept on
interrupting him, was saying. K. gathered from him that the
Italian still had a few business errands to attend to, that his
time was unfortunately limited, that it was certainly not his
intention to try to rush through every sight, and that he had
decided—provided, of course, it met with K.'s approval, the
decision was entirely up to him—to visit just the cathedral,
but to take a really good look at it. He was looking forward
to visiting it in the company of such a learned and amiable
companion—by this he meant K., who was interested in
nothing but trying to tune out the Italian and quickly grasp
the president's words—and if it was convenient, he would
like to meet him at the cathedral about two hours from now,
say around ten. He thought he could surely make it there by
then. K. responded appropriately, the Italian shook hands,

first with the president, then with K., then with the president
again, and walked to the door accompanied by them both,
still half turned to them, not quite finished talking even yet.
K. remained for a short time with the president, who appeared to be feeling worse than usual today. He thought he
owed some sort of apology to K. and said—they were standing in close intimacy—that at first he'd intended to accompany the Italian himself, but then—he offered no specific
reason why—he'd decided to send K. instead. If he didn't
understand the Italian at first, he mustn't let that bother him,
he would soon begin to catch on, and even if there was a lot
he didn't understand, that wouldn't be so terrible, since it
really didn't matter that much to the Italian whether anyone
understood him or not. Moreover, K.'s Italian was surprisingly good and he was certain everything would go fine. With
that K. was dismissed. He spent his remaining free time copying down various special terms he would need for the tour of
the cathedral from the dictionary. It was a terribly tedious
task; assistants brought in mail, clerks came with various
inquiries, pausing at the door when they saw K. was busy, but
refusing to stir until K. had heard them out, the vice president
missed no opportunity to disturb K., entering several times,
taking the dictionary from his hand and leafing through it,
obviously at random; clients even appeared in the semidarkness of the waiting room when the door opened, bowing
hesitantly, trying to attract his attention, but unsure whether
or not they had been seen—all this revolved around K. as if
he were an axis, while he himself listed the words he would
need, looked them up in the dictionary, copied them down,
practiced pronouncing them, and finally tried to learn them
by heart. But his once excellent memory seemed to have

abandoned him totally; at times he got so mad at the Italian for causing all this trouble that he buried the dictionary under stacks of paper with the firm intention of making no further preparations; but then he would realize that he couldn't just parade past the artworks in the cathedral in total silence with the Italian, and he would pull the dictionary out again in even greater rage.

At nine-thirty, just as he was preparing to leave, he received a phone call; Leni said good morning and asked how he was doing; K. thanked her hurriedly and said he couldn't possibly talk now because he had to go to the cathedral. "To the cathedral?" asked Leni. "Yes, that's right, to the cathedral." "Why the cathedral?" asked Leni. K. started to give a brief explanation, but he'd hardly begun when Leni suddenly said: "They're hounding you." K. could not stand pity that he neither desired nor expected; he broke off the conversation with a word or two, but as he replaced the receiver he said, partly to himself, partly to the distant young woman he could no longer hear: "Yes, they're hounding me."

By now it was getting late; there was almost a danger he might not arrive in time. He went there by cab; at the last moment he remembered the album, which he'd found no opportunity to hand over earlier, and took it along. He held it on his knees and drummed on it restlessly throughout the trip. The rain had let up, but it was damp, cool, and dark; it would be hard to see much in the cathedral, and K.'s cold would surely get worse from his standing so long on the cold flagstones.

The cathedral square was totally deserted; K. recalled how even as a small child he'd been struck by the fact that the houses on this narrow square always had most of their window curtains lowered. Of course given today's weather that made more sense than usual. The cathedral appeared deserted as well; naturally no one thought of visiting it now. K. walked down both side aisles and saw only an old woman, wrapped in a warm shawl, kneeling before a painting of the Virgin Mary and gazing up at it. Then in the distance he saw a limping sexton disappear through a door in the wall. K. had arrived punctually; it was striking eleven just as he entered, but the Italian wasn't there yet. K. went back to the main entrance, stood there a while indecisively, then circled the cathedral in the rain to see if the Italian might be waiting at one of the side entrances. He was nowhere to be seen. Could the president have misunderstood the time? How could anyone understand the man? Be that as it may, K. should wait for him at least half an hour. Since he was tired he wanted to sit down; he walked back into the cathedral, found a small carpetlike remnant on a step, dragged it with his toe over to a nearby pew, wrapped his overcoat more tightly around him, turned up his collar, and sat down. To pass the time he opened the album and leafed through it a while, but soon had to stop, for it had grown so dark that when he looked up he could scarcely distinguish a single detail in the nearby side aisle.

In the distance a large triangle of candle flames gleamed on the high altar; K. couldn't say for certain if he had seen them before. Perhaps they had just been lighted. Sextons are stealthy by profession, one hardly notices them. K. happened to turn around and saw not far behind him a tall, thick candle affixed to a column, burning as well. Lovely as it was, it was an entirely inadequate illumination for the altarpieces, most of which were hanging in the darkness of the side chapels; it actually increased the darkness. The Italian had been as right as he was impolite not to come; there would have been nothing to see, and they would have had to rest content with examining a few paintings inch by inch with K.'s pocket flashlight. To try this out, and discover what they might expect to see, K. approached a small nearby chapel, climbed a few steps to a low marble balustrade and, leaning forward over it, illuminated the altarpiece with his flashlight. The sanctuary lamp dangled annoyingly in the way. The first thing K. saw, and in part surmised, was a tall knight in armor, portrayed at the extreme edge of the painting. He was leaning on his sword, which he had thrust into the bare earth—only a few blades of grass sprang up here and there—before him. He seemed to be gazing attentively at a scene taking place directly in front of him. It was amazing that he simply stood there without moving closer. Perhaps he was meant to stand guard. K., who hadn't seen any paintings for a long time, regarded the knight at length, in spite of the fact that he had to keep squinting, bothered by the green glare of the flashlight. Then, as he passed the light over the remaining portion of the painting, he discovered it was a conventional depiction of the entombment of Christ, and moreover a fairly recent one. He put his flashlight away and returned to his seat.

There was probably no point in waiting any longer for the Italian, but it must be pouring rain outside, and since it wasn't as cold inside as K. had expected, he decided to remain for the time being. The main pulpit was nearby; two bare golden crosses were placed aslant on its small round dome, their tips crossed. The front of the balustrade and its juncture with the supporting column were formed of green foliage clutched by little angels, now lively, now serene. K. stepped before the pulpit and examined it from all sides; the stonework had been carved with extraordinary care, the profound darkness between and behind the leaves seemed captured and held fast; K. placed his hand in one such gap and carefully felt along the stone; he had never known this pulpit existed. Then he happened to notice a sexton standing behind the nearest row of pews in a long, loosely hanging, pleated black robe, holding a snuffbox in his left hand and staring at him. "What does the man want?" thought K. "Do I seem suspicious to him? Does he want a tip?" When the sexton realized K. had noticed him, he pointed with his right hand, still holding a pinch of snuff between two fingers, in some vague direction. His behavior was almost incomprehensible; K. waited a while longer, but the sexton kept pointing at something and nodding emphatically. "What does he want?" K. asked under his breath, not daring to call out there; but then he pulled out his wallet and squeezed his way through the next pew to reach the man. The man, however, made an immediate dismissive gesture, shrugged his shoulders, and limped away. With just such a hasty limp had K. attempted, as a child, to imitate a man riding a horse. "A childish old man," thought K., "with just enough wits about him to handle the job of a sexton. Look how he pauses whenever I do, watching to see if I intend to continue." Smiling, K. followed the old man along the entire side aisle almost to the high altar; the old man kept pointing, but K. refused to turn around, the pointing had no other purpose than to throw him off the old man's track. At last he relented, however; he didn't want to frighten him too greatly, and he didn't want to scare away this apparition completely, in case the Italian arrived after all.

As he stepped into the nave to find the place where he'd left the album, he noticed, almost immediately adjoining the benches for the choir, a column with a small auxiliary pulpit of pale bare stone. It was so small that from the distance it appeared to be an empty niche intended for a statue. The preacher would not have room to step even one full pace back from the balustrade. Moreover the stone vaulting of the pulpit began at an unusually low point and rose, bare of any decoration it's true, but curved inward so sharply that a man of average height could not stand upright there, but instead would have to bend forward over the balustrade the entire time. The whole arrangement seemed designed to torture the preacher; there was no conceivable reason why this pulpit was needed at all, since the other large and finely decorated one was available.

Nor would K. have even noticed this small pulpit, had not a lamp been placed above it, as is the custom shortly before a sermon is to begin. Was there going to be a sermon? In the empty church? K. peered down at the steps that hugged the column and led up to the pulpit; they were so narrow they appeared merely decorative, not meant for human use. But at the foot of the pulpit, K. smiled with astonishment, a priest actually stood, his hand on the railing, ready to ascend, and stared at K. Then he nodded slightly, at which K. crossed himself and bowed, as he should have done earlier. The priest swung forward and ascended to the pulpit with short, quick steps. Was a sermon really about to begin? Perhaps the sexton was not quite so witless as he seemed and had wished to guide K. toward the preacher, which would certainly be necessary given the empty church. And there was still an old woman somewhere in front of a picture of the Virgin Mary who should come too. And if it was going to be a sermon, why wasn't it being introduced by the organ? But the organ remained silent, gleaming faintly in the gloom of its great height.

K. considered leaving as quickly as possible; if he didn't go now there was no chance of doing so during the sermon, he would have to remain for as long as it lasted, losing a great deal of time at the office, and he was certainly no longer obliged to wait for the Italian; he looked at his watch: it was eleven. But could there really be a sermon? Could K. alone represent the congregation? What if he were merely a stranger who wanted to see the church? Basically that's all he was. It was senseless to believe there was going to be a sermon, now, at eleven o'clock, on a workday, in the dreariest of weather. The priest—he was clearly a priest, a young man with a smooth, dark face—was obviously climbing up simply to extinguish the lamp that had been lighted in error.

But that wasn't the case; in fact the priest inspected the lamp and screwed it a bit higher, then turned slowly to the balustrade, grasping the angular border at its front with both hands. He stood for a while thus and gazed about without moving his head. K. had retreated some distance and was resting his elbows against the foremost pew. Vaguely, without knowing precisely where, he saw the sexton huddling peacefully, his back bent, as if his task had been accomplished. What silence now reigned in the cathedral! But K. was going to have to disturb it, for he had no intention of staying; if it was the priest's duty to deliver a sermon at a given hour without regard to the circumstances, he was free to do so; it could take place just as well without K.'s support, just as K.'s presence would in no way intensify the effect. So K. began to move off slowly; he tiptoed along the pew, entered the broad central aisle, and proceeded down it undisturbed, except that the stone floor rang beneath the softest tread, and the vaulted roof echoed the sounds faintly but steadily, continuing to multiply them in regular progression. K. felt somewhat forlorn walking along alone between the empty rows, perhaps observed by the priest, and the cathedral's size seemed to border on the limits of human endurance. When he came to his earlier seat, he reached out and grabbed the album lying there without even slowing down. He had almost left the area of the pews and was approaching the open space between them and the outer door when he heard the voice of the priest for the first time. A powerful, well-trained voice. How it filled the waiting cathedral! It was not the congregation that the priest addressed, however; it was completely clear, and there was no escaping it; he cried out: "Josef K.!"

K. hesitated and stared at the floor. At the moment he was still free; he could walk on and leave through one of the three small dark wooden doors not far from him. That would mean he hadn't understood or that he had indeed understood but couldn't be bothered to respond. But if he turned around he was caught, for then he would have confessed that he understood quite well, that he really was the person named, and that he was prepared to obey. If the priest had called out again, K. would surely have walked out, but since all remained still, however long K. waited, he finally turned his head a bit, for he wanted to see what the priest was doing now. He was standing quietly in the pulpit as before, but he had clearly noticed K.'s head turn. It would have been a childish game of hide-and-seek for K. not to turn around completely now. He did so and the priest beckoned him to approach. Now that everything could be done openly, he

walked with long, rapid strides toward the pulpit—out of
curiosity as well, and to cut this business short. He paused by
the first pews, but that still seemed too great a distance to the
priest, who stretched out his hand and pointed sharply down-
ward toward a spot just in front of the pulpit. K. obeyed this
gesture as well; from this position he had to lean his head far
back in order to see the priest. "You're Josef K.," said the
priest, and lifted one hand from the balustrade in a vague gesture. "Yes," said K.; he recalled how openly he had always
said his name; for some time now it had been a burden, and
people he met for the first time already knew his name; how
good it felt to introduce oneself first and only then be known.
"You stand accused," said the priest in a very low voice.
"Yes," said K. "I've been notified about it." "Then you're the
one I'm seeking," said the priest. "I'm the prison chaplain."
"I see," said K. "I had you brought here," said the priest, "so
I could speak with you." "I didn't know that," said K. "I
came here to show the cathedral to an Italian." "Forget such
irrelevancies," said the priest. "What's that in your hand? Is
it a prayer book?" "No," replied K., "it's an album of city
sights." "Put it aside," said the priest. K. threw it down so
violently that it flew open and skidded some distance across
the floor, its pages crushed. "Do you realize your trial is going
badly?" asked the priest. "It seems that way to me too," said
K. "I've tried as hard as I can, but without any success so far.
Of course I haven't completed my petition yet." "How do
you imagine it will end," asked the priest. "At first I thought
it would surely end well," said K., "now sometimes I even
have doubts myself. I don't know how it will end. Do you?"
"No," said the priest, "but I fear it will end badly. They think
you're guilty. Your trial may never move beyond the lower

courts. At least for the moment, your guilt is assumed proved." "But I'm not guilty," said K. "It's a mistake. How can any person in general be guilty? We're all human after all, each and every one of us." "That's right," said the priest, "but that's how guilty people always talk." "Are you prejudiced against me too?" asked K. "I'm not prejudiced against you," said the priest. "Thank you," said K. "But everyone else involved with the proceedings is prejudiced against me. And they instill it in those who aren't involved. My position is becoming increasingly difficult." "You misunderstand the facts of the matter," said the priest. "The judgment isn't simply delivered at some point; the proceedings gradually merge into the judgment." "So that's how it is," said K. and bowed his head. "What will you do next in your case?" asked the priest. "I intend to seek additional help," said K., and raised his head to see how the priest judged this. "There are still certain possibilities I haven't taken advantage of." "You seek too much outside help," the priest said disapprovingly, "particularly from women. Haven't you noticed that it isn't true help." "Sometimes, often even, I'd have to say you're right," said K., "but not always. Women have great power. If I could get a few of the women I know to join forces and work for me, I could surely make it through. Particularly with this court, which consists almost entirely of skirt chasers. Show the examining magistrate a woman, even at a distance, and he'll knock over the courtroom table and the defendant to get to her first." The priest lowered his head to the balustrade; only now did the pulpit's roof seem to weigh down upon him. What sort of a storm could there be outside? It was no longer a dull day, it was already deep night. No pane of stained glass within the great window emitted even a shimmer of light to interrupt the wall's darkness. And this was the moment the sexton chose to start extinguishing the candles on the main altar one by one. "Are you angry with me?" K. asked the priest. "Perhaps you don't know the sort of court you serve." He received no reply. "Of course that's just my own personal experience," said K. Still only silence from above. "I didn't mean to insult you," said K. Then the priest screamed down at K.: "Can't you see two steps in front of you?" It was a cry of rage, but at the same time it was the cry of someone who, seeing a man falling, shouts out in shock, involuntarily, without thinking.

Now both were silent for a long time. Of course the priest could barely distinguish K. in the darkness reigning below, while K. could see the priest clearly by the light of the little lamp. Why didn't the priest come down? He hadn't delivered a sermon, but instead merely told K. a few things that would probably harm him more than help if he paid any attention to them. Nevertheless, the priest's good intentions seemed clear to K.; it was not impossible that they might come to terms if he would come down, it was not impossible that he might receive some form of decisive and acceptable advice from him, something that might show him, for example, not how to influence the trial, but how to break out of it, how to get around it, how to live outside the trial. Surely that possibility existed; K. had thought about it often in the recent past. If the priest knew of such a possibility, he might reveal it if asked, even though he himself was part of the court, and even though when K. attacked the court, he had suppressed his gentle nature and actually shouted at K.

"Won't you come down now?" asked K. "There's no sermon to deliver. Come down to me." "Now I can come," said the priest, perhaps regretting having yelled at him. As he removed the lamp from its hook, he said: "I had to speak to you first from a distance. Otherwise I'm too easily influenced and forget my position."

K. awaited him at the bottom of the steps. The priest stretched out his hand to him while still on the upper steps as he descended. "Do you have a little time for me?" asked K. "As much time as you need," said the priest, and handed the little lamp to K. for him to carry. Even up close, there was still a certain aura of solemnity about him. "You're very friendly toward me," said K. They walked side by side up and down the dark side aisle. "You're an exception among those who belong to the court. I trust you more than I do any of them I've met so far. I can speak openly with you." "Don't deceive yourself," said the priest. "How am I deceiving myself?" asked K. "You're deceiving yourself about the court," said the priest, "in the introductory texts to the Law it says of this deception: Before the Law stands a doorkeeper. A man from the country comes to this doorkeeper and requests admittance to the Law. But the doorkeeper says that he can't grant him admittance now. The man thinks it over and then asks if he'll be allowed to enter later. 'It's possible,' says the doorkeeper, 'but not now.' Since the gate to the Law stands open as always, and the doorkeeper steps aside, the man bends down to look through the gate into the interior. When the doorkeeper sees this he laughs and says: 'If you're so drawn to it, go ahead and try to enter, even though I've forbidden it. But bear this in mind: I'm powerful. And I'm only the lowest doorkeeper. From hall to hall, however, stand doorkeepers each more powerful than the one before. The mere sight of the third is more than even I can bear.' The man from the country has not anticipated such difficulties; the Law should be accessible to anyone at any time, he thinks, but as he now examines the doorkeeper in his fur coat more closely, his large, sharply pointed nose, his long, thin, black tartar's beard, he decides he would prefer to wait until he receives permission to enter. The doorkeeper gives him a stool and lets him sit down at the side of the door. He sits there for days and years. He asks time and again to be admitted and wearies the doorkeeper with his entreaties. The doorkeeper often conducts brief interrogations, inquiring about his home and many other matters, but he asks such questions indifferently, as great men do, and in the end he always tells him he still can't admit him. The man, who has equipped himself well for his journey, uses everything he has, no matter how valuable, to bribe the doorkeeper. And the doorkeeper accepts everything, but as he does so he says: 'I'm taking this just so you won't think you've neglected something.' Over the many years, the man observes the doorkeeper almost incessantly. He forgets the other doorkeepers and this first one seems to him the only obstacle to his admittance to the Law. He curses his unhappy fate, loudly during the first years, later, as he grows older, merely grumbling to himself. He turns childish, and since he has come to know even the fleas in the doorkeeper's collar over his years of study, he asks the fleas too to help him change the doorkeeper's mind. Finally his eyes grow dim and he no longer knows whether it's really getting darker around him or if his eyes are merely deceiving him. And yet in the darkness he now sees a radiance that streams forth inextinguishably from the door of the Law. He doesn't have much longer to live now. Before he dies, everything he has experienced over the years coalesces in his mind into a single question he has never asked the doorkeeper. He motions to him, since he can no longer straighten his stiffening body. The doorkeeper has to bend down to him, for the difference in size between them has altered greatly to the man's disadvantage. 'What do you want to know now,' asks the doorkeeper, 'you're insatiable.' 'Everyone strives to reach the Law,' says the man, 'how does it happen, then, that in all these years no one but me has requested admittance.' The doorkeeper sees that the man is nearing his end, and in order to reach his failing hearing, he roars at him: 'No one else could gain admittance here, because this entrance was meant solely for you. I'm going to go and shut it now.' "

"So the doorkeeper deceived the man," K. said at once, strongly attracted by the story. "Don't be too hasty," said the priest, "don't accept another person's opinion unthinkingly. I've told you the story word for word according to the text. It says nothing about deception." "But it's clear," said K., "and your initial interpretation was quite correct. The doorkeeper conveyed the crucial information only when it could no longer be of use to the man." "He wasn't asked earlier," said the priest, "and remember he was only a doorkeeper and as such fulfilled his duty." "What makes you think he fulfilled his duty?" asked K.; "he didn't fulfill it. It may have been his duty to turn away anyone else, but he should have admitted this man for whom the entrance was meant." "You don't have sufficient respect for the text and are changing the story," said the priest. "The story contains two important statements by the doorkeeper concerning admittance to the Law, one at the beginning and one at the end. The one passage says: 'that he can't grant him admittance now'; and the other: 'this entrance was meant solely for you.' If a contradiction existed between these two statements you would be right, and the doorkeeper would have deceived the man. But there is no contradiction. On the contrary, the first statement even implies the second. One could almost argue that the doorkeeper exceeded his duty by holding out to the man the prospect of a possible future entry. At that time his sole duty appears to have been to turn the man away. And indeed, many commentators on the text are surprised that the doorkeeper intimated it at all, for he appears to love precision and the strict fulfillment of his duty. He never leaves his post once in the course of all those years, and he waits till the very end to close the gate; he's well aware of the importance of his office, for he says 'I'm powerful'; he respects his superiors, for he says 'I'm only the lowest doorkeeper'; when it comes to fulfilling his duty he can neither be moved nor prevailed upon, for it says of the man 'he wearies the doorkeeper with his entreaties'; he is not garrulous, for in all those years he only asks questions 'indifferently'; he can't be bribed, for he says of a gift 'I'm taking this just so you won't think you've neglected something'; finally even his external appearance hints at his pedantic nature, the large, sharply pointed nose and the long, thin, black tartar's beard. Can there be a more conscientious doorkeeper? But certain other elements enter into the basic character of the doorkeeper which are quite favorable to the person seeking to enter, and which, in spite of everything, help us understand how and why the doorkeeper might exceed his duty somewhat by the intimation of that future possibility. For it can't be denied that he's somewhat simpleminded, and consequently somewhat conceited as well. Even if his remarks about his own power and that of the other doorkeepers, and about how unbearable their sight is even for him—I say even if all these remarks are correct in themselves, the manner in which he brings them forth shows that his understanding is clouded by simplemindedness and presumption. The commentators tell us: the correct understanding of a matter and misunderstanding the matter are not mutually exclusive. At any rate one must assume that this simplemindedness and presumption, trivial as their manifestations might be, could still weaken his defense of the entrance; they are breaches in the doorkeeper's character. To this may be added the fact that the doorkeeper seems friendly by nature; he's by no means always the official. Within the first few minutes he allows himself the jest of inviting the man to enter, in spite of the fact that he has strictly forbidden it; and he doesn't send him away, but instead, we are told, gives him a stool and lets him sit at the side of the door. The patience with which he endures the man's entreaties over the years, the brief interrogations, the acceptance of the gifts, the polite sensitivity with which he permits the man beside him to curse aloud the unhappy fate which has placed the doorkeeper in his way—all this points toward feelings of compassion. Not every doorkeeper would have acted thus. And finally he bends down low when the man motions to him, to give him the opportunity to ask a final question. Only a slight impatience—after all, the doorkeeper knows the end is at hand—is expressed in the words 'you're insatiable.' Some go so far in such commentaries as to maintain that the words 'you're insatiable' express a sort of friendly admiration, which of course is not entirely free of condescension. At any rate the figure of the doorkeeper that emerges is quite different from your perception of him." "You know the story much better than I do, and have known it for a longer time," said K. They fell silent for a while. Then K. said: "So you think the man wasn't deceived?" "Don't misunderstand me," said the priest, "I'm just pointing out the various opinions that exist on the matter. You mustn't pay too much attention to opinions. The text is immutable, and the opinions are often only an expression of despair over it. In this case there's even an opinion according to which the doorkeeper is the one deceived." "That's an extreme opinion," said K. "What's it based on?" "It's based," answered the priest, "on the simple-mindedness of the doorkeeper. It's said that he doesn't know the interior of the Law, but only the path he constantly patrols back and forth before it. His ideas about the interior are considered childish, and it's assumed that he himself fears the very thing with which he tries frighten the man. Indeed he fears it more than the man, for the latter wants nothing more than to enter, even after he's been told about the terrifying doorkeepers within, while the doorkeeper has no wish to enter, or at any rate we hear nothing about it. Others say that he must indeed have already been inside, for after all he has been taken into the service of the Law, and that could only have happened within. To this it may be replied that he might well have been named a doorkeeper by a shout from within, and at any rate could not have progressed far into the interior, since he is unable to bear the sight of even the third doorkeeper. Moreover there is no report of his saying anything over the years about the interior, other than the remark about the doorkeepers. Perhaps he was forbidden to do so, but he never mentions such a prohibition either. From all this it is concluded that he knows nothing about the appearance and significance of the interior, and is himself deceived about it. But he is also in a state of deception about the man from the country, for he is subordinate to him and doesn't know it. It's evident in several places that he treats the man as a subordinate, as I'm sure you'll recall. But it is equally clear, according to this opinion, that he is in fact subordinate to him. First of all, the free man is superior to the bound man. Now the man is in fact free: he can go wherever he wishes, the entrance to the Law alone is denied to him, and this only by one person, the doorkeeper. If he sits on the stool at the side of the door and spends the rest of his life there, he does so of his own free will; the story mentions no element of force. The doorkeeper, on the other hand, is bound to his post by his office; he is not permitted to go elsewhere outside, but to all appearances he is not permitted to go inside either, even if he wishes to. Moreover he is in the service of the Law but serves only at this entrance, and thus serves only this man, for whom the entrance is solely meant. For this reason as well he is subordinate to him. It can be assumed that for many years, as long as it takes for a man to mature, his service has been an empty formality, for it is said that a man comes, that is, a mature man, so that the doorkeeper had to wait a long time to fulfill his duty, and in fact had to wait as long as the man wished, who after all came of his own free will. But the end of his service is also determined by the end of the man's life, and he therefore remains subordinate to him until the very end. And it is constantly emphasized that the doorkeeper apparently realizes none of this. But nothing striking is seen in this, for according to this opinion, the doorkeeper exists in an even greater state of deception with regard to his office. For at the very end he speaks of the entrance and says 'I'm going to go now and shut it,' but at the beginning it's said that the gate to the Law always stands open; if it always stands open, however, that is, independent of how long the man lives for whom it is meant, then even the doorkeeper can't shut it. Opinions vary as to whether the doorkeeper intends the announcement that he is going to shut the gate merely as an answer, or to emphasize his devotion to duty, or because he wants to arouse remorse and sorrow in the man at the last moment. Many agree, however, that he will not be able to shut the gate. They even think that, at least at the end, he's subordinate to the man in knowledge as well, for the former sees the radiance which streams forth from the entrance to the Law, while the doorkeeper, by profession, is probably standing with his back to the entrance, nor does he show by anything he says that he might have noticed a change." "That's well reasoned," said K., who had repeated various parts of the priest's explanation to himself under his breath. "It's well reasoned, and now I too believe that the doorkeeper is deceived. But that doesn't change my earlier opinion, for in part they coincide. It makes no difference if the doorkeeper sees clearly or is deceived. I said the man was deceived. If the doorkeeper sees clearly, one might have doubts about that, but if the doorkeeper is deceived, the deception must necessarily carry over to the man. In that case the doorkeeper is indeed no deceiver, but is so simpleminded that he should be dismissed immediately from service. You have to realize that the state of deception in which the doorkeeper finds himself doesn't harm him but harms the man a thousandfold." "You run up against a contrary opinion there," said the priest. "Namely, there are those who say that the story gives no one the right to pass judgment on the doorkeeper. No matter how he appears to us, he's still a servant of the Law; he belongs to the Law, and thus is beyond human judgment. In that case one can't see the doorkeeper as subordinate to the man. To be bound by his office, even if only at the entrance to the Law, is incomparably better than to live freely in the world. The man has only just arrived at the Law, the doorkeeper is already there. He has been appointed to his post by the Law, to doubt his dignity is to doubt the Law itself." "I don't agree with that opinion," said K., shaking his head, "for if you accept it, you have to consider everything the doorkeeper says as true. But you've already proved conclusively that that's not possible." "No," said the priest, "you don't have to consider everything true, you just have to consider it necessary." "A depressing opinion," said K. "Lies are made into a universal system."

K. said that with finality, but it was not his final judgment. He was too tired to take in all of the consequences of the story; they led him into unaccustomed areas of thought, toward abstract notions more suited for discussion by the officials of the court than by him. The simple tale had become shapeless; he wanted to shake off the thought of it, and the priest, who now showed great delicacy of feeling, allowed him to do so, accepting his remark in silence, although it surely was at odds with his own opinion.

They walked on for a while in silence; K. stayed close to the priest, not knowing in the darkness where he was. The lamp in his hand had long since gone out. Once, directly before him, the silver statue of a saint glimmered briefly, with only the gleam of its silver, then fell back at once into the darkness. Not wishing to remain entirely dependent on the priest, K. asked him: "Are we near the main entrance now?" "No," said the priest, "we're a long way from it. Do you want to leave already?" Although K. hadn't been thinking of that at the moment, he said at once: "Of course, I have to go. I'm the chief financial officer of a bank, and they're expecting me; I only came here to show the cathedral to a colleague from abroad." "Well," said the priest, holding his hand out to K., "go on then." "But I can't find my way in the dark alone," said K. "Go left to the wall," said the priest, "then just keep to the wall all the way and you'll find a way out." The priest had moved just a few steps away, but K. called out in a loud voice: "Please, wait a moment." "I'm waiting," said the priest. "Do you want anything else from me?" asked K. "No," said the priest. "You were so friendly to me before," said K., "and explained everything, but now you're leaving as if I meant nothing to you." "But you have to go," said the priest. "Yes," said K., "you must see that." "First you must see who I am," said the priest. "You're the prison chaplain," said K. and drew nearer to the priest; his immediate return to the bank wasn't so important as he'd thought, he could easily stay here longer. "Therefore I belong to the court," said the priest. "Why should I want something from you. The court wants nothing from you. It receives you when you come and dismisses you when you go."

THE END

On the eve of his thirty-first birthday—it was around nine in the evening, when the streets are quiet—two gentlemen entered K.'s lodgings. In frock coats, pale and fat, with top hats that seemed immovable. After brief formalities at the outer door over who would enter first, the same formalities were repeated more elaborately before K.'s door. Without having been informed of their visit, K., also dressed in black, was sitting in an armchair near the door, slowly pulling on new gloves that stretched tightly over his fingers, with the look of someone expecting guests. He stood up immediately and regarded the gentlemen curiously. "So you are meant for me?" he asked. The gentlemen nodded, each pointing with the top hat in his hand toward the other. K. admitted to himself that he had been expecting different visitors. He went to the window and looked out again into the dark street. Almost all the windows across the way were still dark, in many the curtains had been lowered. In a lighted window on that floor two small children were playing together behind a grille, reaching out toward each other with their little hands, not yet capable of moving from the spot. "They've sent old supporting actors for me," K. said to himself, and looked around again to confirm his impression. "They want to finish me off cheaply." K. turned to them abruptly and asked: "Which theater are you playing at?" "Theater?" one of them asked, the corners of his mouth twitching, turning to the other for help. His companion gestured like a mute man struggling with his stubborn vocal cords. "They're not prepared for questions," K. said to himself, and went to get his hat.

The men wanted to take hold of K.'s arms on the stairway, but K. said: "Wait till we're in the street, I'm not ill." Just beyond the entrance, however, they took his arms in a manner K. had never before experienced in walking with anyone. They held their shoulders right behind his, didn't crook their arms, but instead wrapped them about the whole length of his, seizing K.'s hands below with a well-trained, practiced, and irresistible grip. K. walked along stiffly between them; now they formed such a close unit that had one of them been struck down they would all have fallen. It was a unit of the sort seldom formed except by lifeless matter.

Beneath the street lamps K. tried several times, in spite of the difficulty imposed by their tight formation, to see his escorts more clearly than he had in the semidarkness of his room. "Perhaps they're tenors," he thought as he regarded their thick double chins. He was nauseated by the cleanliness of their faces. You could practically still see the cleansing hand that had wiped the corners of their eyes, rubbed their upper lips, scrubbed the folds of their chins.

When K. noticed that, he stopped, causing the others to stop as well; they were on the edge of an open, deserted square decorated with flower beds. "Why did they send you of all people?" he shouted more than asked. The men were apparently at a loss for an answer; they waited with their free arms dangling, like male nurses with a patient who needs to rest. "I'm not going any farther," said K. to see what would happen. The men didn't need to reply; they simply maintained their grip and tried to pry K. from the spot, but K. resisted. "I won't need my strength much longer, I'll use all I have now," he thought. He pictured flies, tearing their tiny legs off as they struggled to escape the flypaper. "These gentlemen have their work cut out for them."

At that moment, coming up a small flight of stairs to the square from a narrow lane below, Fräulein Bürstner appeared before them. He couldn't be absolutely sure it was her; there was certainly a strong resemblance. But it made no difference to K. whether it was really Fräulein Bürstner; the futility of resistance was suddenly clear to him. There would be nothing heroic in resistance, in making trouble for these men, in trying to enjoy a final vestige of life by fighting back. He started moving again, and part of the pleasure he gave the men by doing so was transmitted back to him. Now they allowed him to choose the direction they should take, and he chose to follow in the steps of the young woman ahead of them, not because he wanted to catch up with her, and not because he wanted to keep her in sight for as long as possible, but simply not to forget the reminder she signified for him. "The only thing I can do now," he said to himself, and the way his steps matched those of the other three confirmed his thoughts, "the only thing I can do now is keep my mind calm and analytical to the last. I've always wanted to seize the world with twenty hands, and what's more with a motive that was hardly laudable. That was wrong; do I want to show now that even a yearlong trial could teach me nothing? Do I want to leave the parting impression that I'm slow-witted? Shall they say of me that at the beginning of my trial I wanted to end it, and now, at its end, I want to begin it again? I don't want them to say that. I'm grateful they've sent these half-mute, insensitive men to accompany me on this journey, and that it's been left to me to say myself what needs to be said."

In the meantime the young woman had turned into a side street, but K. could do without her now and submitted to the men escorting him. Now all three of them, in total accord, crossed a bridge in the moonlight, the men yielding willingly to K.'s slightest move, and when he turned slightly toward the railing they too turned, presenting a solid front. Glittering and trembling in the moonlight, the water parted around a small island upon which the foliage of trees and shrubbery rose in masses, as if crowded together. Beneath the foliage, invisible now, were gravel paths with comfortable benches where for many a summer K. had relaxed and stretched his legs. "I didn't really want to stop," K. said to his escorts, shamed by their ready compliance. One of them seemed to be gently reproaching the other behind K.'s back for the mistaken stop, then they went on.

They walked along a few narrow, steeply rising lanes in which policemen were standing or walking about, at times in the distance and at times quite near to them. One of them with a bushy mustache and his hand on the hilt of his saber stepped up to the not entirely unsuspicious-looking group with what appeared to be a purposeful stride. The men hesitated, the policeman seemed about to open his mouth, then K. pulled the men forward forcibly. He turned around cautiously several times to make sure the policeman wasn't following; but when they had a corner between them and the policeman, K. started to run and the men had to run with him, although they were gasping for breath.

They were thus soon out of the city, which in this direction bordered on open fields with almost no transition. A small stone quarry, abandoned and desolate, lay beside a building which was still quite urban. Here the men halted, either because this spot had been their goal from the beginning, or because they were too tired to go any farther. Now they released K., who waited silently as they removed their top hats and wiped the perspiration from their foreheads with their handkerchiefs while they looked about the quarry. Moonlight lay everywhere with the naturalness and serenity no other light is granted.

After a brief polite exchange about who was responsible for the first of the tasks to come—the men seemed to have received their assignment without any specific division of labor—one of them went to K. and removed his jacket, his vest, and finally his shirt. K. shivered involuntarily, whereupon the man gave him a gentle, reassuring pat on the back. Then he folded the clothes carefully, as if they would be needed again, though not in the immediate future. In order not to leave K. standing motionless, exposed to the rather chilly night air, he took him by the arm and walked back and forth with him a little, while the other man searched for some suitable spot in the quarry. When he had found it, he waved, and the other gentleman led K. over to it. It was near the quarry wall, where a loose block of stone was lying. The men sat K. down on the ground, propped him against the stone, and laid his head down on it. In spite of all their efforts, and in spite of the cooperation K. gave them, his posture was still quite forced and implausible. So one of the men asked the other to let him work on positioning K. on his own for a while, but that didn't improve things either. Finally they left K. in a position that wasn't even the best of those they had already tried. Then one man opened his frock coat and, from a sheath on a belt that encircled his vest, drew forth a long, thin, double-edged butcher knife, held it up, and tested its sharpness in the light. Once more the nauseating courtesies began, one of them passed the knife across K. to the other, who passed it back over K. K. knew clearly now that it was his duty to seize the knife as it floated from hand to hand above him and plunge it into himself. But he didn't do so; instead he twisted his still-free neck and looked about him. He could not rise entirely to the occasion, he could not relieve the authorities of all their work; the responsibility for this final failure lay with whoever had denied him the remnant of strength necessary to do so. His gaze fell upon the top story of the building adjoining the quarry. Like a light flicking on, the casements of a window flew open, a human figure, faint and insubstantial at that distance and height, leaned far out abruptly, and stretched both arms out even further. Who was it? A friend? A good person? Someone who cared? Someone who wanted to help? Was it just one person? Was it every-one? Was there still help? Were there objections that had been

forgotten? Of course there were. Logic is no doubt unshakable, but it can't withstand a person who wants to live.
Where was the judge he'd never seen? Where was the high
court he'd never reached? He raised his hands and spread out
all his fingers.

But the hands of one man were right at K.'s throat, while
the other thrust the knife into his heart and turned it there
twice. With failing sight K. saw how the men drew near his
face, leaning cheek-to-cheek to observe the verdict. "Like a
dog!" he said; it seemed as though the shame was to outlive
him.

FRAGMENTS

B.'S FRIEND

O ver the next few days K. was unable to exchange even a few words with Fräulein Bürstner. He tried any number of approaches, but she always managed to avoid him. He came straight home from the office, sat on the divan in his room without turning on the light, and concentrated all his attention on the hall. If the maid happened to pass by and shut the door to the apparently empty room, he would get up after a moment or so and open it again. He rose an hour earlier than usual each morning on the chance that he might meet Fräulein Bürstner alone as she was leaving for the office. But none of these attempts succeeded. Then he wrote a letter, both to her office and to her lodgings, in which he tried again to justify his behavior, offered to make whatever amends he could, promised never to transgress whatever boundaries she might choose to set, and asked only for a chance to speak with her, particularly since he couldn't settle things with Frau Grubach without first conferring with her, and finally, informed her that he would spend the entire day in his room that coming Sunday, waiting for some sign she might grant his request, or at least explain to him why she couldn't, in spite of the fact that he had promised to do as she wished in all respects. The letters were not returned, but neither were they answered. On Sunday, however, he was given a sign whose meaning was sufficiently clear. Early that morning, K. observed through the keyhole an odd commotion in the hall which was soon clarified. A French teacher, a German by the name of Montag, a weak, pale young woman with a slight limp who had been living in a room of her own till then, was moving in with Fräulein Bürstner. For hours she could be seen shuffling back and forth in the hall. There was always some piece of laundry, or a coverlet, or a book that had been forgotten, for which a special trip to the new room had to be made.

When Frau Grubach brought K. his breakfast—ever since she had angered K. so, she no longer entrusted the maid with even the smallest task—K. couldn't resist speaking to her for the first time in five days. "Why is there such a racket in the hall today?" he asked as he poured his coffee. "Isn't there some way to stop it? Must we have housecleaning on a Sunday?" Even though K. didn't glance up at Frau Grubach, he noticed that she seemed to sigh in relief. Even these stern queries on K.'s part she read as forgiveness, or the initial stage of forgiveness. "It's not a housecleaning, Herr K.," she said, "Fräulein Montag is simply moving in with Fräulein

Bürstner and she's carrying her things over." She said nothing more, waiting to see K.'s reaction and whether he would permit her to go on talking. But K. put her to the test, stirring his coffee pensively and saying nothing. Then he looked up at her and said: "Have you put aside your earlier suspicions about Fräulein Bürstner yet?" "Herr K.," cried Frau Grubach, who had been waiting for just this question and now stretched her clasped hands toward him, "you took a casual remark so seriously then. I hadn't the least intention of offending you or anyone else. You've known me long enough to know that, Herr K. You don't know how I've suffered the last few days! That I would slander my boarders! And you thought I had, Herr K.! And said I should give you notice! Give you notice!" Her final exclamation was already choked by tears; she raised her apron to her face and sobbed aloud.

"Please don't cry, Frau Grubach," said K., gazing out the window; he was thinking only of Fräulein Bürstner and that she was taking a stranger into her room. "Please don't cry," he said again, as he turned back toward the room and Frau Grubach continued to weep. "I didn't mean to be so harsh either then. We just misunderstood one another. That happens sometimes, even to old friends." Frau Grubach lowered the apron from her eyes to see if K. was truly appeased. "That's all it was," said K., and ventured to add, since he gathered from Frau Grubach's behavior that the captain hadn't told her anything: "Do you really think I'd let some young woman I don't really know come between us?" "That's just it, Herr K.," said Frau Grubach, whose misfortune it was to say something awkward the moment she began to relax in the least, "I kept asking myself: Why is Herr K. taking such an interest in Fräulein Bürstner? Why is he arguing with me about her, when he knows I lose sleep over every angry word he says? After all, all I said about Fräulein Bürstner was what I'd seen with my own eyes." K. made no reply; it would have meant driving her from the room at the very first word, and he didn't want to do that. He was content to drink his coffee and allow Frau Grubach to feel superfluous. Outside, the dragging steps of Fräulein Montag could be heard once more along the entire length of the hall. "Do you hear that?" asked K., pointing toward the door. "Yes," Frau Grubach said with a sigh, "I wanted to help her, and have the maid help too, but she's stubborn, she wants to move everything herself. I'm surprised at Fräulein Bürstner. I regret having Fräulein Montag as a boarder often enough, and now Fräulein Bürstner is taking her into her own room." "That shouldn't bother you," said K., crushing the sugary residue in his cup. "Do you lose anything by it?" "No," said Frau Grubach, "it's even good as far as I'm concerned; it leaves a room free for my nephew, the captain. I've been worried he might have bothered you the last few days while I had to let him sleep next door in the living room. He's not particularly considerate." "What an idea!" said K., standing up; "not in the least. You seem to think I'm overly sensitive just because I can't stand listening to Fräulein Montag—there she goes back again—making all those trips." Frau Grubach found herself at a loss. "Should I tell her to postpone the rest of the move, Herr K.? I'll do so at once if you wish." "But she's moving in with Fräulein Bürstner!" said K. "Yes," said Frau Grubach, not quite seeing K.'s point. "Well, then," said K., "she has to take her things there." Frau Grubach merely nodded. This silent helplessness, which had the surface appearance of stubbornness, irritated K. even further. He began pacing back and forth in the room from window to door, giving Frau Grubach no opportunity to slip away, which she would otherwise no doubt have done.

K. had just reached the door again when there was a knock. It was the maid, who reported that Fräulein Montag would like a few words with Herr K. and requested that he join her for that purpose in the dining room, where she was awaiting him. K. listened pensively to the maid, then turned with an almost scornful look to a startled Frau Grubach. His look seemed to say he'd long since expected Fräulein Montag's invitation and that it fit in quite well with the general annoyance he was being forced to suffer at the hands of Frau Grubach's boarders this Sunday morning. He sent the maid back to say that he would come at once, then went to his wardrobe to change his jacket, responding to Frau Grubach, who was complaining under her breath about the irksome young woman, merely by asking her to please clear away the breakfast dishes. "But you've hardly touched anything," said Frau Grubach. "Oh, just take it away," cried K; it seemed to him as if Fräulein Montag were somehow mixed up with it all, making it disgusting.

As he passed through the hall, he looked over at the closed door to Fräulein Bürstner's room. He hadn't been invited there, however, but to the dining room instead, where he pulled the door open without knocking.

It was a very long but narrow room with a single window. There was only enough space to place two cupboards at an angle in the corners on the wall at the door, while the remainder of the room was totally occupied by the long dining table, which began near the door and extended almost to the large window, practically blocking it off. The table was already set, and for several people, since almost all the boarders took their midday meal there on Sunday.

As K. entered, Fräulein Montag left the window and approached him along one side of the table. They greeted each other in silence. Then Fräulein Montag, as always holding her head unusually erect, said: "I don't know if you know me." K. regarded her with a frown. "Of course," he said, "you've been living at Frau Grubach's for some time now." "But I don't think you pay much attention to the affairs of the boardinghouse," said Fräulein Montag. "No," said K. "Won't you sit down," said Fräulein Montag. In silence, they both drew out chairs from the very end of the table and sat down across from each other. But Fräulein Montag rose again immediately, for she had left her little handbag on the windowsill and went back to get it; she limped the whole length of the room. When she returned, gently swinging the little handbag, she said: "I just want to have a few words with you on behalf of my friend. She wanted to come herself, but she's not feeling very well today. She asks you to forgive her and to hear me out instead. She couldn't have said anything to you but what I'm going to say anyway. On the contrary, I think I can say more, since I'm relatively uninvolved. Don't you think?" "Well, what is there to say!" replied K., who was tired of seeing Fräulein Montag stare so fixedly at his lips. By this means she already assumed control over what he had yet to say. "Apparently Fräulein Bürstner doesn't wish to grant me the personal discussion I requested." "That's right," said Fräulein Montag, "or rather, that's not it at all, you put it much too strongly. As a general rule, discussions are neither granted nor denied. But they may be considered unnecessary, as in this case. Now after what you've said I can speak frankly. You asked my friend, either in writing or orally, to discuss something with you. But my friend knows what this discussion would concern, or so I at least assume, and is therefore convinced, for reasons unknown to me, that it would be to no one's benefit for the discussion to actually take place. She mentioned it to me for the first time yesterday, by the way, and then only in passing; she said among other things that the discussion couldn't be all that important to you, for you could only have hit upon such an idea by chance, and that, even without a specific explanation, you would soon see how pointless the whole thing was, if you hadn't realized it already. I replied that she might be right, but nonetheless I felt that, in order to make everything perfectly clear, it might still be preferable to give you some explicit answer. I offered to take on this task myself, and after some hesitation my friend yielded. I hope I've acted as you would have wished too, for even the slightest uncertainty in the most minor matter is always annoying, and if, as in this case, the uncertainty can be dispelled so easily, it's best to do so at once." "I thank you," K. replied at once, rose slowly, gazed at Fräulein Montag, then across the table, then out the window—the building opposite stood in sunlight—and walked toward the door. Fräulein Montag followed him for a few steps as if she didn't trust him completely. But at the door they both had to draw back, for it opened and Captain Lanz entered. K. saw him for the first time up close. He was a tall man of about forty, with a tanned, fleshy face. He made a slight bow, which was meant for K. as well, then went up to Fräulein Montag and kissed her hand respectfully. He moved with easy assurance. His politeness toward Fräulein Montag differed strikingly from the treatment K. had accorded her.

Even so, Fräulein Montag didn't seem angry with K., for as far as he could tell, she was about to introduce him to the captain. But K. had no desire for introductions; he felt incapable of showing any friendliness toward either the captain or Fräulein Montag, for in his eyes the kiss of her hand had united them as a pair that desired, beneath the appearance of utmost inoffensiveness and unselfishness, to keep him from seeing Fräulein Bürstner. K. not only believed this but felt as well that Fräulein Montag had selected an excellent, albeit two-edged, weapon to accomplish her aim. She exaggerated the importance of the relationship between Fräulein Bürstner and K., and above all the importance of the discussion he sought, while at the same time attempting to twist things around so that K. seemed to be the one exaggerating everything. She would be proved wrong; K. had no desire to exaggerate anything; he knew that Fräulein Bürstner was an ordinary little typist who couldn't resist him for long. In this connection, he deliberately omitted any consideration of what he had learned about Fräulein Bürstner from Frau Grubach. He was thinking about all this as he left the room with scarcely a nod. He intended to go straight to his room, but a little laugh he heard coming from Fräulein Montag in the dining room gave him an idea that would give both the captain and Fräulein Montag a surprise. He looked around and listened to see if an interruption might be expected from any of the adjoining rooms; it was quiet everywhere; the only sound was the conversation in the dining room and, from the hall leading to the kitchen, Frau Grubach's voice. It seemed like a good opportunity; K went to Fräulein Bürstner's door and knocked softly. Since nothing stirred, he knocked again, but there was still no response. Was she asleep? Or was she

truly ill? Or just pretending she wasn't there because she
sensed that only K. would knock so softly? K. decided she
was pretending and knocked more loudly, and since his
knocking went unanswered, finally opened the door cautiously, not without the feeling he was doing something
wrong, and pointless as well. There was no one in the room.
Moreover it scarcely resembled the room as K. knew it. Two
beds were now placed in a row against the wall, three arm-
chairs near the door were piled high with clothes and undergarments, a wardrobe stood open. Fräulein Bürstner had
probably departed while Fräulein Montag was talking to K.
in the dining room. K. was not particularly thrown by this, he
had hardly expected to find Fräulein Bürstner so easily; he
had made this attempt largely to spite Fräulein Montag.
That, however, made it all the more embarrassing when, as
he was reclosing the door, he saw Fräulein Montag and the
captain conversing in the open doorway of the dining room.
They might have been standing there since the moment K.
first opened the door; they avoided any appearance of having
been watching K.; they were talking softly and merely followed K.'s movements with occasional glances as people do
without thinking in the midst of a conversation. But their
glances weighed heavily upon K., and he hurried along the
wall to reach his room.

PUBLIC PROSECUTOR

In spite of the human insight and worldly experience K. had acquired during his long period of service in the bank, the company at his regular table had always seemed to him unusually worthy of respect, and he never denied in his own mind that it was a great honor to belong to such a group. It consisted almost exclusively of judges, public prosecutors, and lawyers, to which were added a few quite young clerks and legal assistants, who, however, sat at the very end of the table and were only allowed to join in the debates when questions were put directly to them. For the most part such queries were intended only for the company's amusement, and Public Prosecutor Hasterer, who generally sat next to K., took particular pleasure in embarrassing the young men in this way. Whenever he spread out his strong, hairy hand in the middle of the table and turned toward its lower end, they all immediately pricked up their ears. And when someone there took up his question but either failed from the very start to decipher it, or stared thoughtfully into his beer, or instead of speaking simply clamped his jaw shut, or even—that was the worst—broke into an impetuous flood of words to back up some erroneous or unverified opinion, then the older men shifted about in their chairs with a smile and seemed to be really enjoying themselves for the first time. Truly serious professional conversations remained their exclusive preserve.

K. had been introduced into this company by a lawyer, the bank's legal representative. At one period, K. had been involved in several long conferences with this lawyer which kept them at the bank late into the evening, and so it happened that he joined the lawyer for supper at his regular table and took pleasure in the company he found there. He considered them all scholarly, respectable, and relatively powerful gentlemen, whose relaxation consisted in trying to solve complex questions far removed from everyday life, and who worked hard to do so. If, as was natural, he was unable to join in to any great degree, he could still make use of the opportunity to learn a great deal that might sooner or later be of advantage to him at the bank, while establishing the sort of personal contacts with the court that were always useful. And those present seemed to enjoy his company as well. He was soon acknowledged as an expert in business, and his views on such matters were accepted—though not without a touch of irony—as the final word. It was by no means rare for two members who disagreed on some legal question to request K.'s view of the matter, and for K.'s name to recur in their subsequent statements and rejoinders, and be brought even into the most abstract analyses, which K. had long since ceased to follow. Of course he gradually came to understand a good deal, particularly since he had a good advisor at his side in Hasterer, the public prosecutor, who also drew closer to him as a friend. K. even often accompanied him home at night. But it took a long time for him to grow used to walking arm in arm with this giant of a man, who could have hidden him quite unobtrusively in his cycling cape.

In the course of time, however, they grew so intimate that all distinctions of education, profession, and age were gradually effaced. They acted as if they had always been together, and if one occasionally appeared superior to the other in the relationship, it was not Hasterer but K., for in the end his practical experience usually proved correct, since it was gained so directly, as almost never happens at the courtroom table.

This friendship was of course soon generally recognized at the table, and no one really remembered who had first introduced K. into the company; by now at any rate it was Hasterer who stood behind K.; if K.'s right to sit there was ever questioned, he was fully justified in calling on Hasterer for support. K. thus achieved a particularly privileged position, for Hasterer was as respected as he was feared. The power and skill of his legal thought were no doubt admirable, but in this there were many who were at least his equal, yet no one matched the savagery with which he defended his opinions. K. had the impression that if Hasterer couldn't convince his opponent, he at least frightened him, for many drew back when he merely raised his outstretched finger. It seemed as if the opponent had forgotten he was in the company of old acquaintances and colleagues, that the questions under discussion were after all merely theoretical, that there was no way anything could actually happen to him—instead he fell silent, and even shaking his head took courage. It was an almost painful sight when his opponent was sitting so far away, Hasterer realized, that no agreement was possible at such a distance, when he would shove back his plate of food and slowly rise to approach the man himself. Those close by would lean their heads back to observe his face. Of course these incidents were relatively rare; for the most part only legal questions excited him, and in particular those concerning trials he himself had conducted, or was conducting. When such questions were not involved he was friendly and calm, his laugh was kindly, and his passion devoted to food and drink. On occasion he even ignored the general conversation, turned toward K., placed his arm on the back of his chair, questioned him in an undertone about the bank, then spoke of his own work or even told stories about women he knew who kept him almost as busy as the court did. He was not to be seen conversing thus with any other person among the company and in fact if someone wanted to ask a favor of Hasterer—generally it was to effect a reconciliation with some colleague—they came first to K. and asked him to intercede, which he always did gladly and easily. He was in general quite polite and modest toward everyone, without exploiting his relationship with Hasterer in any way, and, more important than politeness or modesty, he was capable of accurately assessing the rank of the various gentlemen, and knew how to treat each according to his station. Of course Hasterer constantly instructed him in this regard; it was the only set of rules Hasterer himself never violated, even in the most heated debate. Thus Hasterer never addressed the young men at the end of the table, who had almost no rank at all, in any but the most general of terms, as if they were not individuals but merely an aggregate mass. But it was precisely these gentlemen who showed him the greatest respect, and when he arose around eleven o'clock to go home, there was always someone there to help him on with his heavy coat, and another who opened the door for him with a low bow, and who of course still held it open as K. left the room behind Hasterer.

While in the beginning K. would walk part way home with Hasterer, or Hasterer with K., later such evenings generally ended with Hasterer inviting K. up to his apartment for a while. There they would sit for another hour over brandy and cigars. Hasterer enjoyed these evenings so much that he didn't even want to forgo them when he had a woman by the name of Helene living with him for a few weeks. She was a thickset older woman with a yellowish complexion and black curls ringing her forehead. At first K. saw her only in bed; she usually lay there shamelessly, reading a serial novel and paying no attention to the gentlemen's conversation. Only when it grew late would she stretch, yawn, and, if she could get his attention by no other means, even throw an installment of her novel at Hasterer. Then he would rise with a smile and K. would take his leave. Later of course, when Hasterer began to tire of Helene, she was a major irritant during their evenings together. Now she always awaited the men fully clothed, and usually in a dress she no doubt considered expensive and becoming, but which was in reality an old, overly ornate ball gown with several embarrassing rows of long fringe dangling from it for decoration. K. was unaware of the precise appearance of this dress, since he more or less refused to look at it, sitting for hours with eyes lowered while she swayed through the room or sat somewhere nearby; later, in desperation as her position became even less tenable, she even tried to make Hasterer jealous by showing a preference for K. It was simply desperation, and not spite, that made her lean her bare, fat round back across the table and bring her face close to K. to get him to look up. All this accomplished was to keep K. from going near Hasterer's for a while, and when after a time he did come again, Helene had been sent away once and for all; K. accepted that as a matter of course. That evening they spent a particularly long time together, drank a pledge to brotherhood at Hasterer's suggestion, and K. was almost a little tipsy on the way home from all the smoking and drinking.

The very next morning in the course of a business discussion, the president of the bank mentioned he thought he'd seen K. the previous evening. If he wasn't mistaken, K. had been walking arm in arm with Hasterer, the public prosecutor. The president seemed to find this so striking that—totally in keeping with his usual precision of course—he named the church beside which, near the fountain, the encounter had taken place. Had he wished to describe a mirage, he would not have expressed himself differently. K. now explained that the public prosecutor was his friend and that they had in fact passed by the church that evening. The president smiled in astonishment and asked K. to take a seat. It was one of those moments that so endeared the president to K., moments in which a certain concern for K.'s well-being and his future surfaced in this weak, ill, coughing man weighed down with work of the highest responsibility, a concern that some of course might call cold and superficial, as other officers who had similar experiences with the president tended to do, simply a good way to bind valuable officers to him for years by sacrificing two minutes of his time—be that as it may, K. succumbed to the president in such moments. Perhaps the president spoke to K. somewhat differently than he did to the others; it wasn't that he ignored his superior position and dealt with K. on an equal footing—something he generally tended to do in everyday business affairs—but rather he seemed to disregard K.'s position altogether, speaking to him as if he were a child, or as if he were an inexperienced young man seeking his first job, who for some unknown reason had awakened the president's good will. K. would certainly never have allowed himself to be spoken to in this way by anyone else, or even by the president himself, had the president's solicitude not appeared to him genuine, or at least had the possibility of this solicitude as it appeared in such moments not cast such a total spell upon him. K. recognized his weakness; perhaps it was based on the fact that in this respect there was indeed still something childlike about him, since without ever having experienced the care of his own father, who had died quite young, he had left home early, and had always tended to reject rather than elicit the tenderness of his mother, whom he had last visited some two years ago, and who, half blind, still lived out in the small, unchanging village.

"I knew nothing of this friendship," said the president, and only a faint friendly smile softened the severity of these words.

One evening shortly before quitting time, K. was instructed by phone to appear immediately at the law court offices. He was warned against any failure to obey. His outrageous statements—that the interrogations were useless, that they could and would yield nothing, that he would refuse to appear again, that he would ignore all summons, whether by phone or in writing, and throw any messengers out the door—all these statements had been entered into the record and had already done him considerable damage. Why was he refusing to cooperate? After all, weren't they attempting to straighten out his complex case, regardless of the time and cost? Was he going to wantonly disturb this process and force them to violent measures he had thus far been spared? Today's summons was a final attempt. He could do as he wished, but he should bear in mind that the high court could not permit itself to be mocked.

Now K. had set up his visit with Elsa for that evening, and this alone was reason enough not to appear in court; he was pleased he could justify his failure to appear before the court, although of course he would never make use of this excuse, and what's more would probably have refused to appear in court even if he'd had no other obligation of any kind that evening. Nevertheless, fully aware he had a good excuse, he asked over the phone what would happen if he didn't come. "We'll know how to find you," was the reply. "And will I be punished for failing to come of my own free will?" asked K. and smiled in anticipation of what he would hear. "No," was the reply. "Splendid," said K., "but then what possible reason do I have to comply with today's summons?" "People generally avoid inciting the court to exercise its powers on them," said the voice, becoming fainter and finally dying away. "It would be very unwise not to incite them," thought K. as he left, "after all, one should try to get to know those powers."

He drove directly to Elsa without delay. Leaning back comfortably in the corner of the cab, his hands in his coat pockets—it was already turning cool—he observed the busy streets. He meditated with a certain satisfaction on the fact that if the court was truly in session, he was causing it no small difficulty. He hadn't said clearly whether or not he would appear in court; thus the judge was waiting, perhaps the entire assembly was waiting; K. alone would fail to appear, to the particular disappointment of the gallery. Unperturbed by the court, he was heading exactly where he wanted to go. For a moment he couldn't be sure that he hadn't absentmindedly given the driver the court's address, so he called out Elsa's address loudly to him; the driver nodded, he had been given no other. From then on K. gradually forgot about the court, and thoughts of the bank began to occupy him fully once more, as in earlier times.

STRUGGLE WITH THE VICE PRESIDENT

One morning K. felt much fresher and more resistant than usual. He scarcely thought about the court at all; when it did come to mind, however, it seemed to him as if there must be some grip, hidden of course, one would have to feel about in the dark, by means of which this huge and totally obscure organization could easily be seized, pulled up, and destroyed. His unusual state even tempted K. to invite the vice president into his office to discuss a business matter that had been pending for some time. On such occasions the vice president always acted as if his relationship to K. had not changed in the least over the past months. He would enter calmly, just as in the early period of his continuous rivalry with K., listen equally calmly to K.'s exposition, show his interest by brief remarks of a confidential and even comradely nature, and would confuse K., but not necessarily intentionally, only by refusing to allow himself to be deflected in any way from the main business at hand and devoting himself to the affair literally to the depths of his being, while in the face of this model of conscientiousness K.'s thoughts would begin at once to swarm in every direction, forcing him to turn the matter itself over to the vice president with scarcely any show of resistance. On one occasion things got so bad that K. finally took notice only when the vice president stood up abruptly and returned to his office without a word. K. didn't know what had happened; it was possible that the conference had come to a proper conclusion, but it was equally possible that the vice president had broken it off because K. had unknowingly offended him, or said something nonsensical, or because it had become abundantly clear to the vice president that K. was no longer listening and had his mind on other things. It was even possible that K. had made some ludicrous decision, or that the vice president had elicited it from him and was now rushing to put it into effect, to K.'s detriment. The affair had not been brought up again either; K. had no wish to recall it and the vice president himself remained taciturn; there were no further visible consequences of course, at least for the time being. In any case K. was not intimidated by the incident, and whenever a suitable opportunity arose and he felt even partially up to it, he would be right at the vice president's door, ready to enter or to invite him into his own office. Now was not the time to hide from him, as he had done in the past. He no longer hoped for a quick and decisive victory that would free him all at once from every care and automatically reestablish his old relationship to the vice president. K. realized he didn't dare let up; if he retreated, as the state of things perhaps demanded, there was a chance he might never be able to advance again. The vice president must not be left with the impression that K. had been disposed of; he mustn't be allowed to sit quietly in his office under that impression, he had to be disturbed, he had to be made aware as often as possible that K. was alive, and that, like all living things, he might one day show surprising new capabilities, no matter how harmless he appeared at the moment. Indeed K. sometimes told himself that he was simply struggling to protect his honor, for in actuality it could do him little good in his present state of weakness to keep confronting the vice president, strengthening the latter's feeling of power and giving him the opportunity to make observations and take measures precisely suited to the immediate circumstances. But K. could not change his behavior; he succumbed to self-deception: he sometimes believed quite firmly that he could now compete with the vice president without worrying; the most disheartening practical experiences taught him nothing, and if he failed at a thing ten times, he thought he could succeed on the eleventh try, in spite of the fact that everything went wrong with unvarying regularity. When, after such a confrontation, he came away exhausted, perspiring, his mind empty, he no longer knew if it had been hope or despair that had driven him to the vice president, but next time it was again totally clear that hope alone impelled him toward the vice president's door.

So it was today as well. The vice president entered at once, then paused near the door, polished his pince-nez in a newly adopted habit, and regarded first K. and then, in order not to be too obviously concerned with K., the whole room as well, in greater detail. He seemed to be taking advantage of the opportunity to test his vision. K. withstood his gaze, even smiled slightly, and invited the vice president to sit down. He himself dropped into his armchair, moved it as close as possible to the vice president, picked up the necessary papers immediately from his desk, and began his report. At first the vice president scarcely seemed to listen. The surface of K.'s desk was bordered by a low carved balustrade. The entire desk was splendid work and even the balustrade was firmly set into the wood. But the vice president acted as if he had just discovered it was coming loose and attempted to correct the problem by banging on the balustrade sharply with his index finger. K. started to break off his report, but the vice president urged him to go on, since, as he explained, he was listening carefully and following it all. But while K. was unable in the meantime to elicit a single pertinent remark from him, the balustrade appeared to call for special measures, for the vice president now pulled out his pocket knife, took K.'s ruler as a counterlever, and attempted to pry up the balustrade, in all likelihood to make it easier to push it back in more firmly. K. had incorporated a completely new type of proposal in his report, one he expected would make a major impression on the vice president, and as he now came to this proposal he could hardly contain himself, so caught up was he in his own work, or rather so pleased was he to enjoy the increasingly rare conviction that he still was of importance to the bank, and that his ideas had the power to vindicate him. Perhaps this way of defending himself was best, not only in the bank but in his trial as well, much better perhaps than any other defense he had tried thus far or planned. Since he was speaking rapidly, K. had no time to draw the vice presi-

dent explicitly away from his work on the balustrade; he
merely stroked the balustrade two or three times with his free
hand as he read aloud, as if in reassurance, to show the vice
president, almost without realizing it, that there was no problem with the balustrade and that even if there were, it was
more important at the moment for him to listen, and more
proper than any repair work. But, as is often the case with
active men who devote themselves solely to mental labor, this
small practical task had excited the zeal of the vice president;
a section of the balustrade had at last indeed been lifted, and
it was now a case of reinserting the little pegs in their respec-
tive holes. This was the most difficult task yet. The vice president had to stand up and try to press the balustrade back into
the desktop with both hands. But in spite of all his efforts it
wouldn't go in. While he had been reading aloud—ad-libbing
a good deal as well—K. had only dimly perceived that the
vice president had arisen. Although he had almost never lost
sight of the vice president's activities, he had nonetheless
assumed that the vice president's movements were still
related in some way to his presentation, so he stood up as
well, and with his finger pressed beneath a figure he held out
a sheet of paper to the vice president. In the meantime, however, the vice president had come to realize that the pressure
of his hands was insufficient, and so with sudden decisiveness
he sat on the balustrade with his full weight. Of course that
did it; now the little pegs went squeaking into the holes, but
in the rush one peg broke off and in another place the delicate
upper strip broke in two. "Poor-quality wood," said the vice
president with annoyance, got off the desk and sat

THE BUILDING

With no definite purpose in mind at first, K. had tried on various occasions to discover the location of the office from which the initial notification of his case had been issued. He found out without difficulty; both Titorelli and Wolfhart gave him the exact number of the building the first time he asked. Later, with a smile that he always held in reserve for secret plans that K. had not submitted for his assessment, Titorelli filled in this information by maintaining that the office was not of the slightest importance, that it simply communicated whatever it was instructed to, and was merely the external agent of the vast Office of Prosecution itself, which was of course inaccessible to the parties involved. So if you wished something from the Office of Prosecution—there were always many wishes of course, but it wasn't always wise to express them—then naturally you had to turn to the lower office in question, but in doing so you could neither make your way to the actual Office of Prosecution, nor ever convey your wish to them.

K. was already familiar with the painter's nature, so he didn't contradict him, nor inquire further, but simply nodded and took note of what had been said. Again it seemed to him, as so often in the recent past, that as far as torture went, Titorelli was filling in quite amply for the lawyer. The only difference consisted in the fact that K. was less dependent on Titorelli, and could get rid of him easily if he liked, further that Titorelli was extremely communicative, indeed even garrulous, though less so now than formerly, and finally that K. for his part could certainly torture Titorelli as well.

And so he did in this matter, often speaking of the building in a tone that implied he was hiding something from Titorelli, as if he had established contacts with the office, which, however, had not yet been developed to the point where they could be revealed without danger; but if Titorelli then pressed him for further details, K. suddenly changed the subject and didn't mention it again for a long time. He took pleasure in these small victories; he felt then that he understood the people on the periphery of the court much better; now he could toy with them, almost join them himself, gaining for the moment at least the improved overview afforded, so to speak, by standing on the first step of the court. What difference did it make if he were to end up losing his place on the level below? A further possibility of escape was offered here as well, he need only slip in among the ranks of these people; if, due to their inferior status or for any other reason, they were unable to aid him in his trial, they could at least take him in and hide him; indeed if he thought it all through carefully and carried it out secretly, he felt they could scarcely refuse to serve him in this way, particularly not Titorelli, since K. was after all his benefactor now, and a close acquaintance.

K. did not nourish hopes of such and similar nature on a daily basis; in general he still was quite discerning and was careful not to overlook or skip over any difficulty, but at times—mostly states of total exhaustion in the evening after work—he found consolation in the most trifling and, what is more, equivocal incidents of the day. Then he would generally lie on the divan in his office—he could no longer leave his office without an hour's rest on the divan—and mentally assemble his observations. He did not restrict himself narrowly to those people connected with the court, for here in half sleep they all mingled; he forgot then the magnitude of the court's tasks, it seemed to him as if he were the only defendant and all the others were walking about as officials and lawyers in the halls of a courthouse, even the dullest of them with his chin resting on his chest, his lips pursed, and the fixed stare of someone meditating on matters of great account. Then the tenants of Frau Grubach always stepped forward as a closed group, standing side by side, their mouths gaping like an accusing chorus. There were many strangers among them, for K. had long since ceased paying the least attention to the affairs of the boardinghouse. Because so many of them were strangers he felt uncomfortable regarding the group more closely, but he had to do so from time to time when he sought among them for Fräulein Bürstner. For example, as he scanned the group quickly, two totally unknown eyes suddenly gleamed at him and brought him to a stop. Then he couldn't find Fräulein Bürstner; but when, in order to avoid any mistake, he searched again, he found her right in the middle of the group, her arms around two men standing on either side of her. That made absolutely no impression on him, particularly because this sight was nothing new, but merely the indelible memory of a photograph on the beach he had once seen in Fräulein Bürstner's room. All the same this sight drove K. away from the group, and even though he often returned there, now he hurried back and forth through the courthouse with long strides. He still knew his way around the rooms quite well, forlorn passages he could never have seen seemed familiar to him, as if he had been living there forever; details kept impressing themselves upon his brain with painful clarity: for example, a foreigner strolling through a lobby, dressed like a bullfighter, his waist carved inward as if by knives, with a short stiff little jacket of coarse yellow lace, a man who allowed K. to gaze at him in unremitting astonishment, without ever pausing in his stroll for an instant. K. slipped around him, stooping low, and stared at him wide-eyed. He knew all the patterns of the lace, all the frayed fringes, every swing of the little jacket, and still he hadn't seen enough. Or rather he had long since seen more than enough, or even more accurately had never wanted to see it in the first place, but it held him fast. "What masquerades foreign countries offer!" he thought, and opened his eyes still wider. And he trailed after this man until he rolled over on the divan and pressed his face into the leather.

JOURNEY TO HIS MOTHER

Suddenly at lunch it occurred to him that he ought to visit his mother. Spring was drawing to a close, and with it the third year since he'd seen her. She'd asked him at that time to visit her on his birthday, and in spite of several obstacles he had complied with her wish, and even made her a promise to spend every birthday with her, a promise, it must be said, that he had already broken twice. Now, however, to make up for it, he wouldn't wait until his birthday, although it was just two weeks away, but would go at once. He did tell himself there was no particular reason to go just now; on the contrary, the reports he received every two months from his cousin, who owned a shop in the village and administered the money K. sent for his mother, were more reassuring than ever before. His mother's vision was failing, to be sure, but K. had been expecting that for years after what the doctors had said; other than that her condition had improved and various ailments of old age had abated rather than worsening, or at any rate she complained less. In his cousin's judgment this might be connected with the fact that over the past few years—K. had already noticed, almost with repugnance, minor signs of this during his last visit—she had become excessively pious. His cousin had described quite vividly in a letter how the old woman, who had previously struggled to drag herself about, now positively strode along on his arm when he took her to church on Sunday. And K. could trust his cousin, for he was normally overanxious, and tended to exaggerate the negative aspects of his report rather than the positive ones.

Be that as it may, K. had now decided to go; among other distressing things, he had recently noted a certain tendency toward self-pity, an almost irresistible urge to give in to every desire—well, in this case his weakness was at least serving a good purpose.

He stepped to the window to gather his thoughts, then had his meal cleared away at once, sent his assistant to Frau Grubach to inform her of his departure and bring back an attaché case in which Frau Grubach was to pack whatever she thought necessary, then gave Herr Kühne a few business assignments to handle in his absence, scarcely even irritated this time by Herr Kühne's rude manner, which had now become habitual, of receiving assignments with his face averted, as if he knew quite well what needed to be done and endured the communication of these assignments merely for form's sake, and last of all went to see the president. When he requested a two-day leave of absence because he needed to visit his mother, the president naturally asked if K.'s mother were ill. "No," said K., without further explanation. He was standing in the middle of the room, his hands clasped behind his back. Frowning, he thought things over. Had he perhaps made preparations for departure too hastily? Wouldn't it be better to remain here? What did he want there? Was he going out of mere sentimentality? And out of sentimentality possibly neglecting some important matter here, an opportunity to intervene, which might turn up any day or hour now, since the trial seemed to have been at a standstill for weeks and scarcely a single piece of concrete news about it had reached him? And might he not shock the old woman as well, without wishing to of course, but against his will, since so many things were happening now against his will. And his mother was not even asking for him. Previously, pressing invitations from his mother had appeared regularly in his cousin's letters, but for some time now they had not. He wasn't going for his mother's sake then, that was clear. But if he was going in hopes of something, for his own sake, then he was a total fool and would reap only final despair as a reward for his foolishness. But as if all these doubts were not his own, but being pushed upon him instead by strangers, he suddenly snapped out of his reverie and stuck with his decision to go. In the meantime the president, either by chance, or more likely out of special consideration for K., had bent over a newspaper; now he raised his eyes, held his hand out to K. as he arose, and without a single further question wished him a pleasant journey.

K. then waited in his office for his assistant, pacing up and down; saying as little as possible, he warded off the vice president, who came in several times to try to discover the reason for K.'s departure; when K. finally had his attaché case, he hurried straight down to the cab, which he had ordered in advance. He was already on the stairs when, at the last moment, Kullych the clerk appeared at the top, holding in his hand a letter he had started, apparently wanting to ask K. for some instruction about it. K. tried to wave him off, but dull-witted as this big-headed blond fellow was, he misunderstood the gesture and raced after him in perilous leaps and bounds, waving the sheet of paper in his hand. K. was so exasperated by this that when Kullych caught up with him on the stairs he grabbed the letter from his hand and tore it to pieces. When, once in the cab, K. turned around, there stood Kullych, who probably still didn't understand what he'd done wrong, still in the same spot, gazing after the departing cab, while beside him the porter tugged his cap sharply. K. was still one of the highest officials in the bank; if he tried to deny it, the porter would refute him. And in spite of all his arguments to the contrary, his mother thought he was the president of the bank and had been for years now. He wouldn't fall in her opinion, no matter what damage his reputation had suffered otherwise. Perhaps it was a good sign that just before leaving, he had convinced himself he could still seize a letter from a clerk, even one who was connected with the court, and tear it to pieces without a word of apology. Of course what he would have liked to do best he couldn't: give Kullych two loud slaps on his pale round cheeks.

THE LIFE OF FRANZ KAFKA

1883   July 3: Franz Kafka is born in Prague, son of Hermann Kafka and Julie, née Löwy.

1889   Enters a German primary school. Birth of his sister Elli Kafka, his first surviving sibling.

1892   Birth of his sister Ottla Kafka.

1893   Enters the Old City German Secondary School in Prague.

1896   June 13: Bar mitzvah—described in family invitation as "Confirmation."

1897   Anti-Semitic riots in Prague; Hermann Kafka's dry goods store is spared.

1899–1903   Early writings (destroyed).

1901   Graduates from secondary school. Enters German University in Prague. Studies chemistry for two weeks, then law.

1902   Spring: Attends lectures on German literature and the humanities. Travels to Munich, planning to continue German studies there. Returns to Prague. October: First meeting with Max Brod.

1904   Begins writing "Description of a Struggle."

1905   Vacation in Zuckmantel, Silesia. First love affair.

1906   Clerk in uncle's law office. June: Doctor of Law degree.

1906–1907   Legal practice in the *Landesgericht* (provincial high court) and *Strafgericht* (criminal court).

1907–1908   Temporary position in the Prague branch of the private insurance company Assicurazioni Generali.

1908   March: Kafka's first publication: eight prose pieces appear in the review *Hyperion*. July 30: Enters the semi-state-owned Workers Accident Insurance Company for the Kingdom of Bohemia in Prague; works initially in the statistical and claims departments. Spends time in coffeehouses and cabarets.

1909   Begins keeping diaries. April: Kafka's department head lauds his "exceptional faculty for conceptualization." September: Travels with Max and Otto Brod to northern Italy, where they see airplanes for the first time. Writes article "The Aeroplanes in Brescia," which subsequently appears in the daily paper *Bohemia*. Frequent trips to inspect factory conditions in the provinces.

1910   May: Promoted to *Concipist* (junior legal advisor); sees Yiddish acting troupe. October: Vacations in Paris with Brod brothers.

1911   Travels with Max Brod to northern Italy and Paris; spends a week in a Swiss natural-health sanatorium. Becomes a silent partner in the asbestos factory owned by his brother-in-law. October 4: Sees Yiddish play *Der Meshumed* (The Apostate) at Café Savoy. Friendship with the Yiddish actor Yitzhak Löwy. Pursues interest in Judaism.

1912   February 18: Gives "little introductory lecture" on Yiddish language. August: Assembles his first book, *Meditation*; meets Felice Bauer. Writes the stories "The Judgment" and "The Transformation" (frequently entitled "The Metamorphosis" in English), begins the novel *The Man Who Disappeared* (first published in 1927 as *Amerika*, the title chosen by Brod). October: Distressed over having to take charge of the family's asbestos factory, considers suicide. December: Gives first public reading ("The Judgment").

1913   Extensive correspondence with Felice Bauer, whom he visits three times in Berlin. Promoted to company vice secretary. Takes up gardening. In Vienna attends international conference on accident prevention and observes Eleventh Zionist Congress; travels by way of Trieste, Venice, and Verona to Riva.

1914   June: Official engagement to Felice Bauer. July: Engagement is broken. Travels through Lübeck to the Danish resort of Marielyst. Diary entry, August 2: "Germany has declared war on Russia— swimming club in the afternoon." Works on *The Trial*; writes "In the Penal Colony."

1915   January: First meeting with Felice Bauer after breaking engagement. March: At the age of thirty-one moves for the first time into own quarters. November: "The Transformation" ("The Metamorphosis") appears; Kafka asks a friend: "What do you say about the terrible things that are happening in our house?"

1916   July: Ten days with Felice Bauer at Marienbad. November: In a small house on Alchemists' Lane in the Castle district of Prague begins to write the stories later collected in *A Country Doctor*.

1917   Second engagement to Felice Bauer. September: Diagnosis of tuberculosis. Moves back into his parents' apartment. Goes to stay with his favorite sister, Ottla, on a farm in the northern Bohemian town of Zürau. December: Second engagement to Felice Bauer is broken.

1918   In Zürau writes numerous aphorisms about "the last things." Reads Kierkegaard. May: Resumes work at insurance institute.

1919   Summer: To the chagrin of his father, announces engagement to Julie Wohryzek, daughter of a synagogue custodian. Takes Hebrew lessons from Friedrich Thieberger. November: Wedding to Julie Wohryzek is postponed. Writes "Letter to His Father."

1920   Promotion to institute secretary. April: Convalescence vacation in Merano, Italy; beginning of correspondence with Milena Jesenská. May: Publication of *A Country Doctor*, with a dedication to Hermann Kafka. July: Engagement to Julie Wohryzek broken. November: Anti-Semitic riots in Prague; Kafka writes to Milena: "Isn't the obvious course to leave a place where one is so hated?"

1921   Sanatorium at Matliary in the Tatra mountains (Slovakia). August: Returns to Prague. Hands all his diaries to Milena Jesenská.

1922   Diary entry, January 16: Writes about nervous breakdown. January 27: Travels to Spindlermühle, a resort on the Polish border, where begins to write *The Castle*. March 15: Reads beginning section of novel to Max Brod. November: After another breakdown, informs Brod that he can no longer "pick up the thread."

1923   Resumes Hebrew studies. Sees Hugo Bergmann, who invites him to Palestine. July: Meets nineteen-year-old Dora Diamant in Müritz on the Baltic Sea. They dream of opening a restaurant in Tel Aviv, with Dora as cook and Franz as waiter. September: Moves to inflation-ridden Berlin to live with Dora. Writes "The Burrow."

1924   Health deteriorates. March: Brod takes Kafka back to Prague. Kafka writes "Josephine the Singer." April 19: Accompanied by Dora Diamant, enters Dr. Hoffman's sanatorium at Kierling, near Vienna. Corrects the galleys for the collection of stories *A Hunger Artist*. June 3: Kafka dies at age forty. June 11: Burial in the Jewish Cemetery in Prague-Strašnice.

BIBLIOGRAPHY

Primary

While all of Kafka's works are interrelated, the following titles have a direct bearing on *The Trial*.

Kafka, Franz. *Letters to Felice.* Ed. Erich Heller and Jürgen Born. New York: Schocken Books, 1973.

———. *The Complete Stories.* Ed. Nahum N. Glatzer. New York: Schocken Books, 1983.

———. "Letter to His Father." In *The Sons,* trans. Arthur S. Wensinger. New York: Schocken Books, 1989.

Secondary

BIOGRAPHICAL

Brod, Max. *Franz Kafka: A Biography.* Trans. G. Humphreys Roberts and Richard Winston. New York: Schocken Books, 1960.

Citati, Pietro. *Kafka.* Trans. Raymond Rosenthal. New York: Alfred A. Knopf, 1990.

Janouch, Gustav. *Conversations with Kafka.* Trans. Goronwy Rees, rev. and enl. 2nd ed. New York: New Directions, 1971.

Karl, Frederick. *Representative Man: Prague, Germans, Jews, and the Crisis of Modernism.* New York: Ticknor & Fields, 1991.

Northey, Anthony. *Kafka's Relatives: Their Lives and His Writing.* New Haven, Conn.: Yale University Press, 1991.

Pawel, Ernst. *The Nightmare of Reason: A Life of Franz Kafka.* New York: Farrar, Straus & Giroux, 1985.

Wagenbach, Klaus. *Franz Kafka: Pictures of a Life.* Trans. Arthur S. Wensinger. New York: Pantheon Books, 1984.

THE TRIAL

Bloom, Harold, ed. *Franz Kafka's "The Trial."* New York: Chelsea House, 1987.

Canetti, Elias. *Kafka's Other Trial: The Letters to Felice.* Trans. Christopher Middleton. New York: Schocken Books, 1974.

Müller, Michael. "Kafka, Casanova, and *The Trial.*" In *Reading Kafka,* ed. Mark Anderson. New York: Schocken Books, 1989.

Pasley, Malcolm S. "Two Literary Sources of Kafka's *Der Prozess.*" *Forum for Modern Language Studies* 3 (1967): 17–29.

———, ed. "*Der Prozeß*: Die Handschrift redet." *Marbach* 52 (1990).

Rolleston, James, ed. *Twentieth Century Interpretations of "The Trial": A Collection of Critical Essays.* Englewood Cliffs, N.J.: Prentice-Hall, 1976.

Stach, Rainer. "Kafka's Egoless Woman: Otto Weininger's *Sex and Character.*" In *Reading Kafka,* ed. Mark Anderson. New York: Schocken Books, 1989.

GENERAL

Adorno, Theodor W. "Notes on Franz Kafka." In *Prisms,* trans. Samuel and Shierry Weber. London: Spearman, 1967.

Alter, Robert. *Necessary Angels: Kafka, Benjamin, Scholem.* Cambridge, Mass.: Harvard University Press, 1990.

Anders, Gunther. *Franz Kafka.* Trans. A. Sicer and A. K. Thorlby. London: Hillary, 1960.

Anderson, Mark, ed. *Reading Kafka.* New York: Schocken Books, 1989.

———. *Kafka's Clothes: Ornament and Aestheticism in the Habsburg "Fin de Siècle."* Oxford: Oxford University Press, 1992.

Arendt, Hannah. "Franz Kafka: A Revaluation." *Partisan Review* 11 (1944): 412–22. Reprinted in *Essays in Understanding, 1930–1945,* ed. Jerome Kohn. New York: Harcourt Brace & Co., 1994.

Beck, Evelyn Torton. *Kafka and the Yiddish Theater: Its Impact on His Work.* Madison: University of Wisconsin Press, 1971.

Benjamin, Walter. "Franz Kafka on the Tenth Anniversary of His Death." In *Illuminations,* ed. Hannah Arendt. New York: Schocken Books, 1969.

Bernheimer, Charles. *Flaubert and Kafka: Studies in Psychopoetic Structure.* New Haven, Conn.: Yale University Press, 1982.

Boa, Elizabeth. *Kafka: Gender, Class and Race in the Letters and Fictions.* Oxford: Oxford University Press, 1996.

Camus, Albert. *The Myth of Sisyphus and Other Essays.* Trans. Justin O'Brien. New York: Alfred A. Knopf, 1955.

Corngold, Stanley. *Franz Kafka: The Necessity of Form.* Ithaca, N.Y.: Cornell University Press, 1988.

Crick, Joyce. "Kafka and the Muirs." In *The World of Franz Kafka,* ed. J. P. Stern. New York: Holt, Rinehart & Winston, 1980.

Deleuze, Giles, and Félix Guattari. *Kafka: Toward a Minor Literature.* Trans. Dana Polan. Minneapolis: University of Minnesota Press, 1986.

Flores, Angel, ed. *The Kafka Debate: New Perspectives for Our Time*. New York: Gordian, 1977.

Gilman, Sander. *Franz Kafka, the Jewish Patient*. New York: Routledge, 1995.

Grözinger, Karl Erich. *Kafka and Kabbalah*. Trans. Susan H. Ray. New York: Continuum, 1994.

Kundera, Milan. *Testaments Betrayed: An Essay in Nine Parts*. Trans. Linda Asher. New York: HarperCollins, 1995.

Politzer, Heinz. *Franz Kafka: Parable and Paradox*. Ithaca, N.Y.: Cornell University Press, 1966.

Robert, Marthe. *As Lonely as Franz Kafka*. Trans. Ralph Manheim. New York: Harcourt Brace Jovanovich, 1982.

Robertson, Ritchie. *Kafka: Judaism, Politics, and Literature*. Oxford: Oxford University Press, 1985.

Rolleston, James. *Kafka's Narrative Theater*. University Park: Pennsylvania State University Press, 1974.

Sokel, Walter H. *Franz Kafka*. New York: Columbia University Press, 1966.

Udoff, Alan, ed. *Kafka and the Contemporary Critical Performance: Centenary Readings*. Bloomington: Indiana University Press, 1987.

FILMS

The Trial: A Film by Orson Welles. English translation and description by N. Fry. London, 1970 (Modern Film Scripts).

The Trial. Filmed by David Jones, script by Harold Pinter. Great Britain, 1992. (Script published as *The Trial*. Adapted from the novel by Franz Kafka. London, 1993.)